Paint the Sky

by

Kim Turner

Copyright Notice
This is a work of fiction. Names, characters, places, and incidents are either the product of the author's imagination or are used fictitiously, and any resemblance to actual persons living or dead, business establishments, events, or locales, is entirely coincidental.

Paint the Sky

Contact Information: info@thewildrosepress.com

Cover Art by *The Wild Rose Press, Inc.*

The Wild Rose Press, Inc.
PO Box 708
Adams Basin, NY 14410-0708
Visit us at www.thewildrosepress.com

Publishing History
First Edition, 2024
Trade Paperback ISBN 978-1-5092-5963-2
Digital ISBN 978-1-5092-5964-9

Published in the United States of America

Prologue

Northern Cheyenne Reservation, Southern Montana, 1882

The cry of a newborn echoed across the darkness, jolting Leaning Bear out of a disturbed slumber. His thoughts tangled as he opened his eyes, letting them adjust to the darkness of his lodge, the repeated squall of a cat echoing in the distant night. His totem, the mountain lion, had brought the babe's first breath to him. And Dawson McCade's child, a daughter, had been born. This he knew.

Nine moons had come and gone. Nine moons since he had seen the man he called brother. Nine moons of living on the reservation with a full pardon from the white president that had proven little by the way of true freedom. He touched the bear claw on the leather strap that hung around his neck alongside his medicine bag. A reminder of the many tribulations he and his white brother had endured together, bonding them for the entirety of their lives.

He sat up on the buffalo hide and stirred the embers of the dying fire back to life with a length of thick hickory. An orange glow danced across the canvas of the lodge as he chanted a whisper of prayers for the health of mother and child. The mountain lion had beckoned him many times in his life, but now as he tossed sprinkles of sage onto the flames, the quick answer of the spirits let him know all was well. The herbaceous scent cleansed his mind as he inhaled the truth of things. It was time. Yes, it had been much too long since a visit to his brother and today was as good as any.

He stepped outside his lodge, the crisp night bristling the skin of his forearms as he lifted the bow, tugging the quiver of arrows over his shoulder. The soldier's quarters remained quiet as he made his way behind the row of what few teepees remained and eased underneath the barbed fencing of the reservation. The white man's push for building cabins and wooden homes had done away with most of the lodges his people knew. He would not be stopped should he leave through the front gates, though he would be questioned about his intentions. His fate in having this freedom segregated him from his Cheyenne brothers, whose travels were limited outside the cage he would not call home. And it was with the white man's government on all things.

The night smelled of wet earth and smoke as he moved into the dense forest of green, his moccasins making little sound along the dew-covered path. He jumped the stream a mile from the reservation and made his way up a line of boulders to an overhang of a natural rock opening in the wall of the mountain. This camp in the trees offered him a solstice from all that was about his present life. Here was freedom for moments at a time when he chose them. No one knew of this place which peeked above the tops of the trees giving a view for miles.

He inhaled a depth of breath and faced the last of the night with its morning stars and drew up the knife from his moccasin. The sky held a bold saffron moon in the cradle of its night, as bright as he could remember. The mountain lion squalled again as he raised his arms to the heavens and closed his eyes chanting prayers to the spirits. The baby would be called *Yellow Moon*, for her child's name, though he understood Dawson would call her Asha. The Cheyenne meaning for hope. This was a good name. His brother would be content and that was well deserved.

Today he would leave the reservation with the purpose of seeing the child who would call him uncle, no matter the difference in the color of their skin. His absence would create little stir and his return would bring no punishment, though his Cheyenne brothers would scold at not having the same permissions. He inhaled the smell of earth and sky, the welcome of new life and ancestors long gone, mingling renewed.

He sat on a buffalo hide he kept inside the mouth of the cave beside the small fire pit he'd lined with rocks. He lifted a flint from his tunic pocket and added kindling to the pit. He struck it several times with effort and a flame sparked and then began to glow. White smoke filtered toward the heavens as he fed the flames moss, the night beginning to fade. And in the distance the howl of a wolf echoed his brother, Proud Wolf's reply.

Come.

Chapter One

Northern Cheyenne Reservation, Southern Montana, Spring 1883

The wind whipped through the trees, lifting the leaves on the white willow in a soft flurry around his sweating neck and shoulders. Leaning Bear dug his knife deep along the bark, cutting a solid square away from the base of the trunk. He brushed it clean of dust and tossed it into the canvas bag hanging at his side. The bitter part of the tree, boiled as tea, would offer relief to those who carried fever and sickness.

He used the knife bearing hard against another section of bark, above a previous patch of healing trunk. This tree he had taken from many times, its thickness showing its years of life. He tugged away the current wedge, turning at the shrill scream of a woman coming from the distant road that led to Lame Deer.

The sun bore through the trees as he scurried light-footed through the thick forest, his tunic flapping in the heated wind of his run. It wasn't that he needed trouble, but it found him often enough in coming to the aid of others. His access off the reservation was his own, though he carried the paper that explained his pardon inside his tunic most days. The promise of the white man's government he trusted as little as he did the small certificate stating his freedoms.

He settled in a thatch of reeds beside the stream and the picture before him explained itself. The three Baker brothers on horseback shouted and encircled a small buggy led by an old mare with a frightened white woman at the reins. This would not be good for either of them. The buggy weaved back and forth, spilling contents as the woman fought to keep it on the path before her.

The men ran the horse into the ditch opposite his camouflage, and he eased in for a closer view. The buggy tipped, dumping the woman and its contents but leaving the horse upright and straining at its harnesses. He ducked as the men circled their mounts and fired their weapons in their amusement. Trouble was about to find him, no matter he had not asked for it.

He stepped from the reeds, though he yielded no weapon. “Enough!”

It took a moment for the men to settle their horses closer to him. These were the sons of Roy Baker and their antics were of little surprise. The man owned the saloon and was a swindler of many in and around Lame Deer.

“This here ain’t none your’n business, Medicine Man,” Pete, the youngest of the brothers shouted, firing his pistol into the air, his horse rearing on its hind legs.

The woman scrambled up and trotted to her anxious horse and glanced back at them all, her clothing dust covered and disheveled. She was visibly shaking, her eyes wide in fear.

“That’s right, leave alone what ain’t yours to see about.” The eldest brother, Leroy, rode closer to him, holstering his weapon. “Seems you’re a little far from the reservation, might be that pass you carry worthless out this way.”

"An Indian might find himself in a mite bit of trouble." The middle brother, Don, sent his own threats, drawing his weapon and holding it high in the air.

The Baker sons were often up to this sort of harassment, dangerous and unpredictable. They seemed to think they were at liberty to make all the rules, which they did not follow themselves. This was not his only time to come up against the harassment of the brothers, nor was it his first in the protection of others.

"What is proven by harming a woman and old horse?" He stepped closer, placing himself in between the woman and the men harassing her.

"Watch yourself, Medicine Man. An injun'll find himself on the wrong end of a rope, how 'bout it?" Pete aimed his pistol up and down as his horse turned a full circle of protest.

The tomahawk held heavy at his side and the knife in his moccasin rested against his calf. He carried no gun as the law did not allow it for the Cheyenne or other tribes. It might be Pete would get him with a shot, but the eldest brother was no longer holding his weapon.

He'd not be fast enough with the bow in the challenge of three men, but he could take two quick enough with the toss of the tomahawk followed by the knife. But then, he would know that rope that was mentioned. He waited with no further comment, the woman easing to the other side of the small horse, likely anticipating a fight.

He did not suspect the men to make the small issue of this woman and an old horse to be worth their time. As predicted, the eldest brother held his gaze for a long moment and yielded his warning.

"Best you stay on the rez, not much of a pardon

gonna protect the likes of you here. Come on boys, we're late for poker." The man glanced back at his brothers and turned his horse. "Besides, she ain't got a horse worth takin'."

"I wasn't gonna hurt her, she'd be too pretty for that." Don gave a wide grin, glancing at the woman but then followed his brothers.

"She ain't gonna enjoy the likes of you anyway." Pete taunted his brother and fired into the air once more as he glanced back. "You're ugly."

"Yeah, well you're uglier." Don urged his horse to catch up to his brothers blasting his weapon once more as if for good measure.

The woman ducked against the side of her horse, holding its harnesses as it startled at the gunshot. With another shout of laughter, the Baker sons galloped out of site on the road toward town. That had been easier than expected. It was an interesting comment about the woman's old horse. He had long known of the Bakers stealing horses that they sold in other towns. Most often white lawmen hung those caught horse thieving, though with no law in Lame Deer, the men had never been held accountable for their actions.

He waited as the woman turned to face him. Her skirts were covered in trail dust, but the first thing that captured him was the depth of blue in her eyes, the color of the morning sky. This was a thought he should not hold.

"No good scoundrels." She grabbed several items from the ground and stepped farther back from him.

What purpose would white men have to harm a woman in sport of this kind? He began helping to gather items farthest from her. He lifted a brown case and a bundle of blankets but as he stood erect her concern was evident, her eyes wide and searching.

"Bring no harm. Only help." He brought the belongings he had collected toward the buggy, keeping his voice low and respectful.

Her hands shook as she brushed them along the horse's withers. "I thank you for stopping those men, it was very kind. You speak English so well."

Her assessment of him was no surprise. Many were astonished he spoke the white man's words with ease. "It is as you say."

"I hope she isn't hurt." She continued to keep an eye on him as he picked up another sack and moved at a slow pace toward the overturned buggy.

He glanced around them, but there was no one, though should she have screamed, this scene could be turned into far more. No matter his presence, he remained cautious around any white woman. Accusations came quick for any Cheyenne, even one with good intentions.

She picked up her bonnet and shook it, but did not place it back on her head. Her hair was light, like the white color around a morning sun and her skin was tanned.

He turned toward the horse to avoid her continued gaze. He had never much thought on the beauty of white women, but this one was very beautiful. And what white man would have allowed a woman this journey alone to Lame Deer.

He bent again to gather more of her belongings and placed them at her feet. He stepped to the horse, loosening the harnesses as the woman watched. His thoughts were not what they should be about her. She was tall, as near tall as he and she carried herself with strength in spite of the fear she had displayed.

"Horse is good. Buggy not so much." He bent and with a wholehearted gathering of strength, pushed the buggy to right it. It surprised him further when she added her own strength to help. It creaked and rocked as it landed back on its four wheels. The horse tried to pull ahead, but he grabbed the harness to hold the animal, speaking in Cheyenne to calm her.

He shook the carriage and straightened the horse's harnesses and pointed to the brake handle. "Broken. Must go slow. Not much rise in road to town. No need to use brake."

She leaned in to see the broken lever of iron beneath the front of the buggy for herself. "I have no idea why those men ran us aside. I'm Allison Crockett, from Chicago, well, by way of buggy for the last few hours, wagons prior to that and the train to Cheyenne out of Chicago weeks ago. I should thank you proper, but your name?"

He stepped back from her out of the sheer need to do so. English, he understood, but he had not expected the lengthy discussion from a white woman and much less the hand she held out to him with her greeting.

"I am called Leaning Bear." He didn't take her hand and she let it back down to her side. How free it was she chatted with him. Most in town were aware of his name and reasons for being there, trading herbs and accepting deliveries for the woman at the trading post called Maud. But it was rare any white woman found reason to speak with him in casual conversation.

"Leaning Bear, I do thank you for your assistance." She angled a glance at him and laid the things she had gathered into the back of the righted buggy. She folded several items of clothing with care and placed them as well.

He added a tied bundle of heavy books and placed more things beside those, a container of painting brushes and small jars of paint, some spilled within the tin that held them. He turned to scan across the road and ditches but no more of her belongings remained. He eased the brown case into the buggy, the heavy scent of flowers wafting around him at her approach.

Sun kissed hair curled around her face but it was the depth of blue in her eyes that pierced him again. This thought should not belong to him, and he pushed it away, as he had done moments ago.

"Oh, I'm sorry." She pulled a cloth from the outside pocket of her skirts and reached for his hand. It was covered in paint the color of leaves on the trees around them. "You've paint on your hand. You must forgive my initial shock, as I was warned of…well, of Indians before coming here. But it seems I should have been more afraid of the regular citizens."

Her comment was not the first time he had heard similar thoughts. His own experiences were of the same common ideas that white men and women held. That all Indians were bad and to be avoided. He rubbed the oily paint between his fingers admiring the depth of green and the tacky feel. "It is no bother."

He tugged his hand away from hers out of sheer need to do so, but she grabbed it once more.

"At least let me clean this up given you've helped me gather my belongings and came to my rescue." She began wiping his green palm and fingers with a tenderness that caused him to tense, it having been many moons since any woman's touch had found him.

"Poor Millie, I do hope she's all right. I purchased her and the buggy when the other wagons were coming no further, the last small town several hours back. It's nice to see a person, except not those men who gave me pause…" She shook her head and put a bit more effort to her scrubbing. "Riding alone was a bit unnerving but I'd been assured it wasn't far to Lame Deer when I left the wagon train. They were heading further north."

"Dangerous for woman with no escort." He opened his palm further noting the contrast of her white skin against his own. Where again, was the husband who had allowed this or was it she was on this journey alone?

"I suppose I knew things in this part of the country would be untamed. Dare I say I was fairly warned." She let go of his hand and lifted her gaze with a satisfied smile crossing her full pink lips. "There you are."

He hesitated to inhale another breath as if he were an awkward boy. She held much chatter, not allowing a break where his words would come.

She glanced up the road ahead, placing her hands to her slender hips. "Lame Deer shouldn't be much further if I'm correct. I had suspected to arrive long before now, but Millie is rather aged and moves slowly."

He pointed toward town, taking yet another step back from her. "Road makes two paths. Stay West."

She nodded in hesitation as if uncertain, giving a lift of her light brows. "West? Yes."

Women were not good with directions or packing for journeys. He used his hands, putting his palms together and separating them, moving his left hand. "At road fork. Go left. Keep stream on right of carriage."

"Yes, then." She gave a sure nod this time. "I should

make it fine. I'm the new teacher for the reservation, might I see you there when I begin?"

Now things made more sense. A new white teacher had been expected for the children of the reservation in the coming weeks, the last gone for more than a year. She was correct in that she would see him there. "It is as you say."

She stepped closer to her buggy taking up the reins as she climbed inside. "Well, that is good to know."

A white woman, alone and planning to teach the children of the village. It was a repeated scenario. The teachers never stayed long once they arrived. Most left with little notice, given the combination of fear, weather, lack of salary and accommodations. Some had been religious migrants arriving West and wanting the children to acclimate to the white man's God. Others seemed to be escaping their pasts for something more. He couldn't be certain of her reasons, but the thought did interest him.

"And the reservation is past town as I understand it?" She tucked her light hair into the bonnet again.

"Take other fork at burnt tree, follow smaller stream. Fencing begins reservation land." He raised his hands to explain once more. He supposed the Office of Indian Affairs had sent her like all the rest and how was it this woman would be any different?

"Burnt tree, got it." With a nod, she urged the old horse ahead, waving a hand in her departure. "I bid you good day, Leaning Bear. Onward, Millie."

Leaning Bear stepped back from the road and into the canvas of trees as her buggy faded out of sight toward Lame Deer. He turned to the trail that would lead him there as well. He was due to check on work with Maud at the Trading Post. But as he moved with ease through the woods, it was the teacher who played across his mind where she should not linger if he had good sense. Women were much trouble no matter White or Cheyenne and his thoughts betrayed him as he continued through the forest.

She did not fear him once he spoke her tongue. She also touched him without any hesitation when she took the paint from his skin. There were white women in town that made reason to cross the road at his presence in order to avoid him. The only woman who spoke to him with decency was Maud at the Trading Post, who relied on him for deliveries of lumber and supplies to homesteads outside of town.

But Allison Crockett was not to leave his mind for now. She had not treated him as an Indian, not as a Cheyenne, but as a man as if she had not seen the color of his skin and the feathers in the length of his hair. Some part of the mountain lion inside him stirred in caution at the ease at which his thoughts covered her. He began to run faster, his breath coursing loud as he pushed thoughts of her aside. Yes, that would be best.

Chapter Two

The afternoon sun shone through the trees, sprinkling a scattering of golden orange across the sandy road ahead. The creaking of the buggy sounded in a steady rhythm filling the quiet of the remaining distance to Lame Deer. Alli glanced behind her still in fear of the men who harassed her and Millie, worried they might show up once more, but there was no sign of them on her continued journey toward Lame Deer.

"That was not a fine howdy-do on arriving to our new town." She spoke to the old horse, who paid her no mind. She'd been unnerved with the ride alone, but she hadn't expected the attack, though she should have been more prepared for something of the sort. Her hands still shook but she hadn't come this far to turn tail and run back home.

The day was rather warm and sweat trickled down her neck and back, her travel clothing much too heavy for the spring weather.

"I should like to paint the lovely oranges of these colors to something. It almost appears as if it's glowing with life of its own as the leaf's shadows move on the road." She continued talking to the horse in order to keep her mind free from further worry.

With the brake broken, she was grateful for level ground and a well-worn path. Leastwise, the horse had settled down, the poor thing, though her own nerves remained a bit frayed in spite of her wish to keep her mind occupied. “Welcome to Lame Deer, your new home. I suppose we won’t have anyone to welcome us, Millie, but here we are.”

She mocked herself, but her first encounter with the citizens of Lame Deer handed her a few second thoughts on her trip. She’d had plenty of warning about the dangers of living in the untamed West. “Those men were being rowdy I suppose, but you and I will certainly avoid them from now on.” She gave a nod, though the animal continued on the trail ahead, her long thick tail dragging the ground and swaying back and forth with the rocking of the buggy.

The train only went as far as Cheyenne, and she’d had weeks of travel with two families that settled in northern Wyoming. The men from the wagon train had warned her of venturing farther all alone; but she had made the purchase of the old mare and the buggy because she was due in Lame Deer by week’s end. Millie had been the one horse for sale at a small livery in the last town she’d seen. Never mind the buggy that wasn’t in the best shape in the first place, though she didn’t think it would take much for the brake to be repaired.

She had signed up to teach on the reservation and now, here she was, in spite of the long tedious days of travel. Nothing thus far had been easy, but she was not turning back now. And to be honest she was very proud she’d made the trip on her own as if it were somehow liberating at having done so.

It was afternoon and she needed to get to the Trading Post for the information about the home that came with her teaching position. How the thought of home sounded good at this point in her long trip. A place of her own.

She was tired and disheveled and was due a nice hot bath. And she must look such a fright after her buggy was overturned. She tucked loose strands of her hair back inside her bonnet, hoping for the best on her appearance.

She thought of Leaning Bear, who had come to her aid, startling her at first. Everyone had warned her about the dangers of Indians, but to come face to face with one who was kind enough to help her had been a shock. She should've offered him a token of money for his assistance but as it was, she'd been unnerved by the entire happenings. "Straighten up, Allison, this is your new life." She scolded herself out loud. She hadn't arrived to a life out west thinking any part of it would be easy.

Thoughts of home invaded her mind. It had been weeks. And wouldn't her sister, Jaqueline, be scandalized by the very idea she'd carried on an English conversation with an Indian. A Cheyenne Medicine Man no doubt, based on the comments of the men on horseback.

Jacie had warned her about the *savages* found West, discouraging her from accepting the position as teacher for the reservation. But her sister, married with grown children, would never understand what it was like to bury a husband she'd adored and then fall victim to the people she'd thought were her friends.

Timothy's colleagues at the university had one by one dwindled from her life after his death, her own status not well to do enough to keep their company without him. That or the discovery of his infidelity where she'd been the last to know had left her lost for a time. Well, that was fine. She had no need for them any longer as her new life came into view before her.

Maybe she was due for a visit to the local sanitarium there in Chicago, but in spite of her sister's concerns, she'd made the decision to leave home for the teaching position on the reservation.

She used a handkerchief to blot the sweat trickling down the back of her neck. She'd spent the better half of the last year preparing for this trip and for teaching the children on the reservation. The ad about the job explained the true need for the Indians to learn in schools like other children and that it was a wonderful opportunity for a teacher. She'd been excited though a hint of sadness in leaving her sister behind edged close. "Oh, I can visit perhaps next fall. It isn't all that far." She wasn't sure if she were trying to convince Millie or herself. It was indeed a longer distance than she cared to travel again any time soon.

Millie slowed further as they entered the edge of town. Lame Deer was small by comparison to many places she'd passed along the way. There was one main road flowing through rows of buildings on each side. Some were two stories, but most were only one. Others were in varying levels of needed repairs. But there was a mercantile, barbershop, tobacco store, and a rather small boarding house.

She continued until she spotted the Trading Post ahead on the left, the sign painted maroon and brighter than most. She urged Millie closer and stopped her with the reins alone, the buggy settling in spite of the broken brake. People walked all over town, men, and even women with small children. She glanced back at the Trading Post, taking a deep breath. The correspondence from the Office of Indian Affairs had stated she'd find access to her home and supplies needed here.

There were several steps leading inside through a small door, while outside the building were tables lined in rows containing various commodities. Furs and hides, roping, fencing, and all sorts of wood. Lined along the tables were a couple of plows, hoes, picks, and shovels. Men and even women mingled around inside and outside of the establishment, no one paying her any attention. A line of more than ten wagons was along the road in a fashion of order, most led by oxen though a few had large draft horses. Homesteaders like the ones who welcomed her to part of their journey.

She glanced around, still a bit cautious about the men who had harassed her. A quick glance at the saloon blocks down showed her their horses and whereabouts. Maybe they were passing through town for their poker game and would move on. And with any luck she'd remain unnoticed by them, should they come back outside the establishment.

She pulled at her bonnet, and it fell down her back. She took a moment to smooth her hair and gathered her bag over her shoulder and stepped down from the buggy.

With another gulped breath of reassurance, she gave the old horse a quick pat. "Wish me luck, Millie, and you stay right here, mind you." Millie settled to munching on what little greenery was around the hitching post. Alli made her way up the steps and through the door of the Trading Post, nodding at two women who were heading back outside with armloads of items. She'd be searching for a woman named Maud. The paper in her bag didn't add a last name but stated to "check at the Trading Post."

Perhaps she would be a short time in gaining access to her new home and the staples she'd need. She pulled the oversized door behind her at the same time gunshots paraded the sky, echoing across town. She screamed and ducked to the side of the door as it slammed.

"Those no-good jackasses." A woman wearing men's britches trotted to the door pushing her aside to glance out the windowpane. "They cause more trouble than they're worth. And if'n I have to repair another glass on these front windows I'll take it from their hides, I will."

Alli stood again, the incident seeming to be over. She glanced out the window catching the tail end of the horse's leaving town. "I believe those were the same men who harassed me a bit earlier on the road into town. Overturned my buggy, leastwise my horse wasn't hurt and me either." She settled her bag back to her shoulder a bit unnerved yet again. "The brake on my buggy is now in need of repair, though I suppose it could have been much worse."

"They're gone for now. And I'm thinking you must be the new teacher, Mrs. Crockett." The woman was as round as she was tall, and she leaned and spat toward a spittoon in the corner beside the door, ringing it with ease.

"And you must be Maud…" Alli stopped, uncertain of the woman's status in last name or title preferred. "But please call me Alli."

"Ike Branson at the livery down the way ought to fix the brake for ya, mind he charges a fair price and not ask for a little more if you get my meaning." Maud slammed her hands to her hips, with a loud chuckle.

Some things never changed it seemed. Chicago offered much the same by way of swindlers and those keeping their eyes on any woman who was in the least bit pretty. And while she'd always thought herself of average beauty, she'd never understood how even as a married woman, men were always aware of her. It was the same with Jacie, both having the light curls and fair faces with upturned noses as many Irish women displayed.

"You received my list then, I had wondered of its arrival prior to me." Perhaps it was best not to ask anything more about the liveryman for now.

Maud pointed a dirty hand to the crates on the floor beside the counter at the back of the store. "All on the list from the telegram as well as a bit of lumber outside, the cabin is in need of repair. Mind you I don't own it, the government does, darn worthless cavalry won't be of much help though."

"Cabin?" Alli questioned, given a bit of hesitation. "My correspondence said the job on the reservation would allow me a small home, but a cabin? I was to ask for the key here."

Maud shrugged and spat again leading the way to the back of the Trading Post. "This is the northwest, Montana Territory, Mrs. Crockett, best you got in this job like everyone else is a run-down cabin in need of repairs. Won't need a key, front door doesn't lock anyway. Furnishings a little to nothin'. A bed, full of mites, a table, and a couple of chairs. But it'll keep the rain out, fireplace is a good one. And so's you won't freeze this winter, start piling up wood, branches and limbs as you find them. Build a hearty wood pile and plenty of kindlin'. Get the wood repairs done a'fore fall comes. And get to cannin' some foods from a garden or what you stock up in town. Smoke some meats to put away and that'll be a start."

Alli closed her mouth, her mind whirling. It wasn't

that she expected anything fancy, but her acceptance letter stated a “small furnished home.” And right now, she was tired enough to sleep on this filthy floor if she thought much about it. The idea of planning for winter was now weighing heavy at best. “I am sure I can make do and will heed your suggestions.”

But no lock, no key. Her words made her sound sure of herself, when in truth, she was worried it may be all too much for her in the long run. No, she wouldn’t think that now. She’d already seen how things might be, and she wasn’t running back home with her tail between her legs any time soon. Besides, she’d studied up on drying meat and preparing for hard winters by canning vegetables and stews. Canning was her specialty, though she’d have to purchase the jars, salt, and pickling spices needed for that process.

“Cabin’s a mile up the road, turn by the old burnt tree and you’ll see a trail, lead ya right there.” Maud leaned behind the counter to spit into the spittoon on the floor behind her and wiped a stained sleeve across her mouth. “Got a tab here for ya, I’d be paid monthly in full. I’ll have an Indian named Leaning Bear bring the wood to your place by afternoon. He’s never timely but he’s reliable.”

“Leaning Bear?” Alli questioned, the same Medicine Man she’d encountered earlier?

“That’s right.” Maud went behind the counter again. “He won’t bother ya’ none, though trusting the others comes one man at a time, a couple from that reservation lay around here drunk most often. Not a’kin to working. Lazy sons of bitches. Cavalry ain’t much different, only here to drink and womanize at the boarding house, which ain’t no boarding house if you catch my drift.” The woman cackled once more throwing her head back.

Alli lifted her brows, a bit shocked at the woman's language choice. Maud was the first woman she'd ever seen with a chaw of tobacco in her cheek and the words to match. And while she was a bit rough around the edges, she at least had all Alli's supplies ready. Such as it was. "So, will he, Leaning Bear, make the cabin repairs? I have no idea how to go about that. I believe he is the same man who helped me right my buggy after it was turned over a few miles outside of town."

Maud glanced at her for a long moment. "He might if'n ya pay him cash in golden eagles, he won't deal in paper money. I put a hammer and saw in with your purchases along with a bag of penny nails. Measure a lot, saw the wood to it, and nail it up. That cabin might even do well if you soak sod and mud into all the cracks a'fore winter too. Keep ya' warmer."

Alli nodded. The bottom of her bag held a small box of golden coins and it had weighed heavy her entire travels. She'd even slept with her bag inside her blankets to make sure nothing went missing. "I see."

Money was not the problem, but it would be a while before her funds were transferred into a local bank if that was safe.

"I run a clean business here, can order in what's needed, takes a few months on some things so order up a 'fore winter. Stage don't come this far much at all, 'bout twice a month." Maud ran a glance down the register and held a finger on her name.

"Yes, well, I've money to pay in full for my tab today." Alli reached into her bag for her purse and glanced at the ledger before Maud on the counter. She laid out the paper money, keeping the coins for now.

Maud snatched it all up and stuffed it into her ample bosom, glancing around at patrons inside the Trading Post.

Then the rotund woman whispered, “That’s a pretty purse of money Mrs. Crockett, mind you hide that well and not trust the bank here in town. I’ll help you get these crates to your buggy.”

Alli shoved the small purse back into her bag and pulled it over her shoulder. She lifted one of the crates while Maud picked up two, leading the way outside. So, no bank it would seem. Would the surprises ever cease? She shrugged and followed. The lumber set her back a little, but she had money. Her sister, Jacie, could manage her accounts and send what she required when she needed more. Though hiding what she had was now of vital importance, making her wonder why the men who had harassed her hadn’t asked about her having any money. That was odd, wasn’t it?

“You be careful out there Mrs. Crockett and make another list of items you need.” Maud chuckled, her belly bouncing as she heaved the crates into the buggy. “Last teacher on that reservation lasted about two months, high tailed it out of here with a preacher and his purse full of patron’s donations.” She spit to the ground. “Ain’t nothing out here much like you’ve seen a’fore.”

“I thank you, Maud and please, you must call me Alli.” She set her crate beside the others and offered a hand that Maud took with crushing strength. She took back her hand and wiped it along her skirt.

“Wait, you’ve a weapon of some kind, Alli?” She narrowed a hard glance at her.

“I’m afraid not, I suppose I thought as a teacher I wouldn’t need such a thing.” She shook her head. Did she need a gun? She supposed yes, but her sister and brother-in-law had insisted it was too dangerous to have a weapon as a woman. Well, if they understood what she did now, they would differ their opinion.

"Follow me. We got bears, fox, coyotes, wolves, cougars…" The heavy woman huffed her breaths as she entered the Trading Post once again, Alli on her heels. She walked to the back to unlock a cabinet with a key on a chain from around her neck. She held out a pistol that Alli took with hesitation. "And men who might find the likes of you very appealing, if ya don't mind me sayin' so. Keep this with you at all times."

"I hardly know much about shooting a gun." Alli glanced around them but no one was paying them any attention.

Maud took the weapon back. "This one's easy, open the side, load in the bullets, close it and fire. I'll add it to your tab next month. Mind ya be careful with it; they can fire if hit or dropped. Might want to do a little target practice."

Alli placed the weapon into her bag with care. Lord, but she hated such things. She'd thought of a gun for her trip but she understood little about them and she and Timothy never owned weapons of any kind. Well, if her nerves weren't frayed by now, perhaps she had arrived West.

"I thank you again, Maud. I suppose there's a lot for me to learn." Alli kept her hand to herself this time only offering a nod.

"Don't let Leaning Bear startle you, he's quiet for the most part." Maud added as she came back around the counter. "For heaven's sake don't shoot him."

"I shan't." Alli made it to her buggy not feeling the

least bit sure of anything. But she lifted her sights and postured in strength. She could do anything she set her mind to. Look how far she'd already come and the last couple of hours and she'd done it all on her own. She smiled in spite of it all, setting out with renewed confidence.

Chapter Three

The heat of the afternoon weighed as heavy as if it poured from a cauldron out of the sky. Alli inhaled a depth of breath, exhausted but content to have arrived in Lame Deer after weeks of traveling. Even if she'd not had the least of a welcome from anyone, other than Maud and the darn horsefly that had been buzzing around her for the last half a mile.

She'd thought the most difficult part of her travels to be the last few hours alone, but as it was that was the least since arriving to town. She hadn't expected the men who had overturned her buggy and she'd done well to keep free of the liveryman's advances when he'd fixed the brake. Ike Branson had indeed been a cheat and free with his ideas of how she might pay for the work. She'd scoffed his notions by placing cash in his dirty outstretched hand and hurrying to leave.

Now she faced the reality of her arrival, living alone and taking care of herself. And teaching children who would understand her little, while she taught them and learned their culture. But she loved teaching and it was that everything had fallen right into place for her to assume her new role. She'd taught in the slums of Chicago for a number of years but found her calling in working with those who were eager to learn. Much of her time and money had been spent to make things well for some of the children with the most needs.

And that was where she'd found her falling away from all Timothy's well to do university colleagues. None of them respected her work as a teacher for primary grades and were all consumed by money and possessions. Perhaps her husband's death had at least opened her eyes to the falseness of their ambitions and friendships. She'd been raised with money and somehow it wasn't everything to have wealth. Oh, yes, money mattered, but it shouldn't matter to the detriment of others, at least by her own thinking of things.

She shook her head as the horsefly dove toward her bonnet once and swooped at Millie before returning to her again.

"Oh, will you leave us." She batted again at the persistent creature that swarmed around her bonnet as if it mocked her further. "I expected little welcome anyway, but we are going to do this, Millie, we really are." Now that she'd convinced the horse it might be she could somehow explain it to herself. Having talked to the old horse on and off for the last several hours, it occurred to her the animal was becoming her new best friend.

She'd long passed the burnt tree, wondering about its fate as it was the only thing burned in the entire area. She should have thought to ask about it. The growth on the side of the road seemed to thicken as they rolled along with Millie pulling the buggy at a slower pace on a slight incline.

Alli swatted again at the horsefly and made contact, batting it away and startling Millie who trotted faster. "Ha, I got you, you little beast!"

Moments later, she slowed Millie with a slight tug at the reins and blinked at the bit of a covered trail to her right. No this couldn't be…her promised home? Her heart sank at the view of the cabin in the distance, small compared to her thoughts and in need of major repairs even from this distance. Maud had been right to go ahead and order the lumber, not that she had any idea how to begin repairs. At this point why should anything about her trip be a surprise? She urged the horse a bit closer to the place and stopped her once again.

Maud said she would see the cabin off in the woods with its simple barn. The "lovely home" that came with the most "prestigious of teaching jobs" according to the ad she'd answered, was nothing she might have expected. How on earth was this crumbling cabin to make her a home?

Tears threatened but she held them at bay. "Nope, I will not cry. Millie you and I have arrived home, or at least it will be. I can always sleep in the buggy until repairs are made, I suppose."

She sat back in the seat and studied the outside of the cabin. "Hello? Hello?" What if someone were inside?

At least Maud was sending Leaning Bear with lumber. Perhaps she could pay him to assist with making the cabin livable. Though the first glimpse of him had frightened her, she'd always been a decent judge of character and his dark eyes held a kindness she'd come to know in few. And to think of all the warnings she'd received about Indians long before now.

"Wait until I write home about this. Jacie will be all but worried over me speaking English with a Medicine Man no less." She stifled a giggle suspecting her sister would thrive on all she would send home in letters even though she'd been full of warnings.

She set the brake and climbed from the buggy, placing her hands to her hips as she assessed the cabin once more.

"Home." The roof of the cabin porch sagged in the middle and open boards let her see through the front door. She eased cautiously closer. What if someone were inside? Now she could understand why there was no key. The bush and grasses around the home had all but taken over, though the smaller barn appeared to be in better shape than the cabin.

She moved even closer to survey the scene before her. "Millie, I do declare this isn't livable by any standards. I suppose if your barn is dry, I'll be prepared to make my bed with you. But might as well I see how things are inside."

The horse began munching along the high green grass, not the least interested in where they were to be living. Alli shook her head and swatted at the horsefly yet again and stepped ahead. "Well, nothing like the present."

Her words gave her enough encouragement to take the two steps up to the porch and stand for a moment. She gathered her skirts and bounced along the various boards of the flooring. Sturdy enough. She glanced up at the roof caving down to a point above her and sidestepped from underneath, batting away cobwebs. At least the glass in the two front windows was intact though they would take a good washing to see through them.

"It'll be the home I make it. You'll see." Nothing here but an old cabin that hadn't been inhabited since the last teacher over two years prior from what she understood. With a deep breath she pushed the front door inward where it fell right off the hinges with a large crash, sending dust enough to make her cough. She fanned the air with her hands and yet again that darn horsefly flew toward her bonnet.

The afternoon sun gleamed inside the cabin, dust and cobwebs heavy across the ceiling and corners. She should cry now but she was too tired to bother. She could hang a drape over the doorway for the night or sleep in the barn inside her buggy for a few days. There was always a solution. Hadn't she taught her students that no matter what, things could always change for the better? Well, this was one of those times.

She stepped inside, letting her eyes adjust. The one room cabin held a small wooden table with two chairs and a large bed in the corner with a dry-rotting mattress. Not even a setee and much to her disappointment, no tub. Oh, how she wanted a real bath.

She yielded a soft sigh of defeat and stopped beside the old bed, the dust there at least an inch thick. She touched the top blanket and something growled beneath them making her drop the covers. The thing gave another louder version of its warning and she floundered back a few steps, where she promptly tripped over one of the wooden chairs, stifling a scream as she fell to the floor landing with a hard thud to her backside.

Her mouth dropped open as the creature emerged from the covers, across the room. A small racoon stood on its hind legs, scolding her in snarls, using its small paws as if reaching to snag her.

"And you were no pillow." She gathered herself up and tried to scare him away. "Go, shoo, get out of here." She waved her arms, but the creature didn't budge, making her wonder how long he'd claimed this cabin as home. From the smell of the urine coated mattress, she could only guess.

In the opposite corner stood a broom with frayed bristles. She eased that way and lifted it, intending to shove the critter out the front door.

"Shoo." She poked the broom toward the racoon. It gave her a grin baring its teeth. She wasn't going to hurt it but they could not coexist in this small place. Swatting, she nudged the animal. It gave her a snarl and disappeared under the bed. "Oh, darn it."

She bent and gave the broom a slide under the bed, scooting the critter out and sending him across the floor. He scampered out the front door, leaving her to glance around her for more critters.

The dust she'd stirred up made her cough again and the horsefly returned to nosedive at her bonnet. She tugged it off and laid it on the table as the flying bug dove at her again. She swung the remnant of the broom above her only to have the fragile reeds fall free around her like rain sticking in strands of her hair. She shook her head, a few falling free. "So, a mattress and bedding, a broom, and a tub large enough where I might bathe. Or is that all too much to ask?" Her voice broke. Tears? No, she'd not allow those, not after the journey she'd made to arrive here.

A screech from outside let her know the racoon wasn't yet defeated, but she turned to take a look at the cabinets and old wood stove. She hadn't noticed the stove at first. She placed a hand on the oven door and tugged but it was stuck. Giving it some effort, it opened and black soot powdered her like snow. She spat what landed in her mouth and gripped her fists in frustration. Her hair and clothing covered, she shook herself, but it was of no use. Was anything going to go well for her at this point? "Well, tarred and feathered then."

Near tears, she wiped a hand along the dust on the counter and reached to open the cabinet door with caution. It was bare inside but in good condition, well built. She opened the other and all she could do was scream and run. She climbed into the chair she had righted as hundreds of tiny mice fled from the cupboards, their straw nests falling to the floor. The creatures scattered all over the cabin, into the cracks of wooding and out the door. How could this many have been in one spot? No stranger to mice, she still didn't prefer so many at once.

She shuddered the complete length of her body about the same time the crack of splintering wood sounded. The chair gave way, spilling her to the floor onto her side. Pain scored through her hip and she heaved, the breath knocked from her lungs.

Another cloud of dust encompassed her as she sat up thinking nothing was broken though she gulped for air. Enough was enough. Tears came at the same time movement outside caught her attention. She wiped her soot-covered cheeks, her sleeves turning black in her efforts.

A horse moved into view outside the open doorway as she made her way to her feet. Before her, Leaning Bear sat on the painted horse, angling a curious gaze her way. Had he seen this entire charade? Tiny mice still scampered in every direction; the racoon long gone at least. She tiptoed to the porch, catching her breath as she noticed the slight grin that crossed his lips, though she was sure she appeared a fright in her condition.

"I suppose you find this more than amusing, given the day I have encountered." She fanned away the darn horsefly and side stepped more mice with a heavy shivering dance across the porch.

He dismounted, letting go of the slight smile and clucked his tongue for the animal to follow with its load of lumber on the small wagon it pulled. “Amused little. Put lumber on porch. Keep dry.”

Was that all he was going to say? “Maud said I should ask…that I might pay you for working to repair the cabin, so that it’s inhabitable.” She glanced around her feet for the varmints that still ran about.

He lifted several of the long boards and walked them to the porch laying them in order of size along the edge. “Work cost money.”

“Yes. I can pay a fair price of course?” She glanced at her buggy which held her bag and the gold coins in the box she would need to hide.

He walked back to the wagon and the horse nudged his shoulder as he lifted an armload of cut wood and lined it all up on the porch. He was a large man, tall and thick with muscles. His hair hung loose down his back, a single braid to the left side and a feather tied there with a strand of blue leather. She had noticed all these things about him a few hours ago, but at the time her shock hadn’t let her look too closely at him. His tunic and trousers were made of pale deerskin with fringe along his sleeves and the trousers. He wore moccasins, not boots though they were a darker brown and laced up to his knees.

“Will fix cabin.” He laid down the next armload of boards he held and turned to look at her. “One week.”

Alli swatted at the horsefly and tucked loose strands of her hair back in place behind her ears. She must look a disheveled fright, dirty and covered in soot. “One week? I’m afraid I’m ill equipped to know how to make repairs myself. The ad I answered had stated a home, not a cabin that's falling apart." She glanced back at the cabin and to him again. "What am I to do?"

He landed more lumber in a thud to the porch and dusted his hands and the hint of a grin emerged. "Teacher should think of this before travel so far."

She let her jaw fall open. How could he judge her for her choices, he didn't even know her? And that was enough of his finding any of this funny. "I am not asking for a lot, but I just fought to sweep a racoon out from under my bedding and fell, releasing a Sodom and Gomorrah of mice from where I should be able to keep my food. I have survived being run off the trail and an overturned buggy and this horsefly from Haiti has followed me all the way from town. A town where everyone shoots guns as if it is fireworks for amusement and I had to overpay that nasty liveryman extra to keep his hands off me. And I am tired and long overdue for a meal and a warm night's rest not to mention a very hot bath." She stopped as her voice let go to her emotions. She folded her arms and sat on the porch steps defeated, tears streaming her face.

Leaning Bear regarded her for a long moment as he mounted his unsaddled horse and urged it closer. He dug in the bag he wore over his shoulder drawing out various plants and tossed them to the porch beside her. They landed in a scattering across the boards.

Alli glanced at the heap of wilting greenery, using a sleeve to wipe her cheeks. "What's this?"

"Racoon no like garlic. Place in home. Small mouse no care for sage, put on fire. Fly will tire by nightfall." He gave her a solid nod and turned the horse and cart around heading back the way he'd come.

Alli shook her head in disbelief as she lifted the bundles together. Was that all he was offering to her in the middle of her nightmare? Herbs? Would he leave her like this to fend for herself with no shelter except a barn? She shook her head at the same time the horsefly dove at her face. "Shoo. Go away."

She refused to let the tears rimming her eyes fall. She wiped them away and got up, walking toward Millie. "I deserve this you know, Millie. I was so sure it would all be well and easy." She freed her harness keeping the reins in her hand to lead the animal toward the barn. She'd read it was necessary to keep horses or cows stalled and enclosed in a barn at night, with the threat of wolves or bears. Wouldn't that be her luck?

She glanced back where Leaning Bear had disappeared below the rise at the road. Somehow the life she'd left behind didn't seem too bad, given this day. But she wasn't going back there, ever. Not to people like that. She'd make it here if it was the last thing she ever did. Asserting her new confidence, she could hammer a nail and once she had Millie settled and a good night's sleep, that was what she would do.

She slung open the barn doors to lead Millie inside but out of nowhere an owl swooped down with talons bared flying past them both, then toward the cabin. She screamed and fought to hang onto Millie's reins, but the old horse pulled free, bolting back the way they'd come from town.

"Millie! Millie…Oh, no!" She took off after the animal on a run, holding her skirts high in both hands. If she lost the horse, she would have no way to town or her new job on the reservation. She ran as fast as she could, but Millie disappeared over the rise in the road, leaving her far behind.

Alli gave up the hard run, trotting and trying to keep going but she was out of breath. She topped the hill, stopped in her tracks, dust encircling her. Before her, Leaning Bear held Millie by the reins and came closer on his own horse still pulling the cart.

He stopped, considering her a moment and lifted his hand to hold out the reins. “Owl not happy you visit barn. Tie horse. Better idea.”

Alli grabbed the reins, not dismissing the warmth of his hand touching hers. “I am quite aware of that thank you kindly, but the owl startled us. Wait, how did you know about the owl?”

He gave a nod toward the burnt tree and there on the top remaining branch was the same owl, watching them both.

“Well, it’s my barn now, what herbs do I need to rid it of the owl?” She held his intense brown eyes. A bit of wind lifted the one feather in his hair. He studied her for a long moment and glanced back at the owl.

He grabbed his bag and shuffled things inside. He once again lifted green herbs with dirt hanging onto the roots, holding it out to her.

“Sage will rid the owl?” She recognized the plant and took it, looking up at him. “I thought it was for the mice.”

“Sage rid mice. Mice gone. Owl hungry. Owl, move elsewhere to eat.” He gave the hint of another grin for the second it took her to grab the herbs.

“Then I thank you.” She tugged Millie to follow without adding anything more. She didn’t look back as he’d made it clear he couldn’t help her with the cabin for a week. But then Maud had said he wasn’t timely but reliable. What would that mean?

Tears fell from her eyes almost without true emotion. And she let them. She held the sage and turned to walk the horse back to the barn. Well, she would cry today but after today she wouldn't cry anymore. She wouldn't no matter what. She was strong and capable, and she wasn't afraid of the racoon, mice, owl, or the blasted horsefly that followed her yet again.

She walked Millie into the small barn once they arrived, cautious as she entered, but the owl had not followed. The barn wasn't in bad shape, better than the cabin for now. She placed Millie in one of the two stalls and made sure of closing the gate. She then went back to the buggy, and heaving the last of her strength, pulled it inside the barn. Millie's oat sack was heavy, but she pulled it free and fed her.

As exhausted as she was, hunger beckoned. She moved things around the buggy until she'd made a semblance of a place she could stretch out and rest. And after lighting a lantern to a low flame, she hung it on a rusty nail on the post inside the barn. It gave a nice glow and with any luck would last until morning.

One night in the wagon wouldn't be the end of her and neither would more cold biscuits and jerky. She settled on top of the blankets and pulled the bundle of food to her lap and ate as she watched the light fade through the small cracks in the wood of the barn doors.

"Goodnight, Millie, best you not run off anymore. You and I must stick together. We'll have to make this our home even if it's not what we thought." She spoke though the horse only chewed her oats being loud about it. She dug through her bag and pulled out her journal. The one she'd kept since she'd departed Chicago in an effort to document her travels.

She fanned the pages, weeks of traveling by train, wagon, and buggy to get to this point. Her arrival to Lame Deer was somewhat bittersweet even though her tears were more about fatigue. She'd brought along several charcoal pencils thinking that ink was difficult to keep as were all the paint jars in various colors she had packed. Some of which had succumbed to the recent spilling of her buggy. She could order more paints. Gripping the pencil and angling the tablet where a bit of light lay across the page, she began to write about the day's happenings. She chewed pieces of the stale biscuit along with hard beef jerky and wrote her thoughts of this day, her arrival to her new home which had been rather defeating. Perhaps as it was, she'd one day laugh about the events that had found her on her first day in Lame Deer.

Chapter Four

Dusk had long passed, distant clouds echoing shades of orange and gray where the sky met the earth. Leaning Bear studied the movement of the wind, the night holding a chill the sunlit day had not hinted. He sipped water from a canteen that hung on a post outside his lodge.

He glanced toward the front of the reservation at the soldiers' quarters and Captain Bartley's office, a separate building smaller than the barracks sitting adjacent to them. The captain had sent a soldier to summons him an hour before and he had waited, not following orders on purpose. Captain Bartley was a good man and one he trusted, but there was still a part of him that rebelled against the men guarding the reservation. He resisted where he could for some sort of control.

He hung the canteen back on the post and pulled on his tunic, then walked the trail toward the captain's office. As he approached, the same soldier who had brought the request from the captain stepped forward, blocking his path. He stopped and met the man's gaze.

"Captain's been waitin' on you for more'n an hour." The soldier stared. "Captain don't much like to wait."

"Here now." Leaning Bear attempted to step around him, but the soldier moved in his way once more. He waited. It was the same each time from the soldiers, some who made their authority known and others who said little. To his count of the different men, fifteen were present from time to time on the reservation, today there were six. If he wished, he could make one move and take the cocky young soldier to his knees. Yes, and he could be placed in the jail behind the captain's quarters even if it was what the soldier deserved. But he had learned long ago to keep himself from trouble as was necessary for the tribe. The good of the many outweighed the good of the few as his friend Dawson often said.

The soldier spat tobacco to the ground near his moccasins. "Presidential Pardon, don't mean you are free to do as you please."

He had heard the same before. Many times. His pardon for crimes he had not committed was still the curse he thought it. It had sent him from the freedoms of the forest and prairies to this reservation where a pardon meant very little when measured by white men.

He wasn't as passive as Dancing Fox, the Cheyenne Chief, wanted to remind him. It was that not all things were worth the fight, for which reason he would not argue now even if the soldier wished it. The chief was quick to anger, but he had found with white men, it was best to be quiet when necessary.

He stepped forward. The soldier did not move but spat tobacco juice across his moccasins. "Watch yourself medicine man."

Leaning Bear gripped his fists tight, but this was no fight he wanted with a young soldier who had some growing to do. Instead, he angled a glance at the others and back. "Wonder sometimes not only me behind these fences. The truly caged, remain tied here for government paycheck. Mother must be proud." But of course, he could not leave well enough alone.

"Private, back to your post." Captain Bartley stepped to the door, glaring at the soldier until he moved back with the other men.

"Come on in, Leaning Bear." Captain Bartley held open the door that had a glass window in the top portion. "I'm sorry for their continued harassment but I can appreciate you not antagonizing further." The captain gestured to the chair before the desk.

Leaning Bear pulled the chair back from the desk and sat. Often these talks with the captain would go for lengths of time that he found too long. But that he sat, relaxed the man before him. "You request meeting."

"Yes, Leaning Bear…" The captain leaned back into his chair. "The soldiers continue to report your…being off the reservation mornings." The captain shrugged. "It's I suppose difficult for them to understand your ease to be gone without notice as the others are required."

The captain had helped Leaning Bear and Dawson when they were jailed and had faced a firing squad for crimes they had not committed. But the pardon received had sent him right to the reservation as his own reward. It was Captain Bartley that allowed him the freedom of his pardon here, but not many others did the same.

The captain continued. "I know you are out working in town and hunting medicines, but the men get a little more tense when things are at unrest in other areas of the country."

There were often reports of uprisings from various tribes farther south, which seemed to always stir the soldiers and his own brothers. He had thoughts on uprisings though news was scarce in detail most of the time, but it was rare he voiced his opinion of things. There was reason for his lack of words as he wished to remain unable to predict. Prediction caught a brave unprepared where white man and even braves of other tribes could be trusted. Even with the captain, he limited his words most of the time. Trusting white men most often backfired in some way and he had known that the whole of his life.

He dropped his gaze to an envelope lying on the desk to one side. *Mrs. Allison Crockett.* He let his mind stray for the moment at the idea *Mrs.* meant a married white woman. He had suspected as much about the white woman Allison Crockett, but where was this elusive husband with his wife alone in a broken cabin fending for herself so poorly?

"Leaning Bear, I don't want any trouble to come your way or to anyone else here on the reservation. I do what I can to keep my men in line, but they are gonna require you to report what you are up to, an explanation like all the rest in times when things are so uncertain. Whether you are working, hunting herbs, whatever your week will encompass written down." Captain Bartley shook his head. "All I'm asking is for you to at least let the men know you're heading to town or to hunt. Show them your pass and you can go and return, but through the front gate, not the back fencing."

The captain had never asked this of him before and he had come and gone as he pleased most of the time underneath the mentioned fencing. It seemed there he owed no explanation. Not to the soldiers and not to his Cheyenne brothers who were not allowed the same freedoms, nor to the captain.

He spoke his thoughts. "Plans change. Not the same each day. Will not be truth some days."

The captain nodded using his hands to explain.

"Yes, I realize that, you can even say you'll be in town all day. You'll be questioned less on your return either way. I can answer for your whereabouts when you aren't here. If your plans change, so be it. It's a formality of respect. If you know your plans for the week, jot them down and leave them here at the office. My first lieutenant will accept that."

The captain offered him a dipped quill and slid a piece of paper over. Written word on his upcoming week would not be predictable. He took the quill with his left hand as he stood and reached to turn the paper to the correct angle for his hand not to smear the ink. He added to that list the repairs to the teacher's porch roof, which he intended to begin soon. This would also keep those around him aware of why he would be at the white woman's cabin, though he would be there when he knew her to be teaching.

He signed his mark and slid the paper with wet ink toward the captain. "Soldiers prefer respect, but little know how to give the same."

The captain held his gaze. "I apologize where my soldiers are out of line and I'll speak to them."

Leaning Bear pushed the chair back before the desk and turned to go. "Not yours to apologize."

"Wait, I've a letter for you." The captain lifted an envelope from the drawer under his desk. "From Dawson. It arrived two days ago but I only got back in last night."

Leaning Bear eyed the sealed brown envelope and nodded as he took it. Letters from Dawson arrived at random, and he eased it into his tunic pocket as he left the office.

"Best you be watching your comings and goings

from now on, we'll be checking passes." The same young soldier stepped up to him once more.

"Best close britches as not to expose small things." He should have left well enough alone but the situation allowed him to mock the mouthy boy.

The soldier turned to button his trousers with a snarl, his ears turning red in his embarrassment. The other men's laughter sent the young soldier off to his own. A few of the elder soldiers did have respect for him and others in the reservation. It was their laughter he beckoned for keeping some peace.

Leaning Bear didn't glance back as he headed for his lodge for the night. The soldier would be angered but he had little to fear from the young man when it came down to it. That sort was never able to let things go and as it was, he should have kept his thoughts to himself.

He entered his teepee, closing the flap behind him and sitting beside the small fire. He took a stick and stoked the fire and pulled the letter from Dawson out of his tunic pocket. He used his knife to cut the side edge of the envelope away and paper bills of money fell to his hand. Dawson sent money with each correspondence for helping on the reservation. He grabbed the folded letter paper and tossed the envelope into the flames where it folded in on itself, turning to darkened ashes. The money he folded into his tunic pocket as he held the letter to the lighting of the fire to read:

A-Ho,

Hoping this finds you in good health. My family remains well and I am much better these days from my injuries. Haven wishes to thank you for the dried herbs that you mailed to her months back. She has put them to use as suggested. Yellow Moon is growing fast, no longer a small baby and very demanding in her attentions of all. I continue to speak to her in Cheyenne much to her mother's chagrin. Levi works on the ranch most days, having finished his studies, and James continues his schooling in town and makes high marks. My brothers and their families are well as is Dodge who asks about you often. It is my hope that I will visit in the early autumn, before the first snows for hunting alongside you. Until then, I leave you my best thoughts for much happiness and may the great spirits always protect you.

Your brother, Proud Wolf

He tossed the letter into the flames and lay back in the bedding, placing his hands behind his head. It had been months now since he had seen his brother, and it was good to know that Dawson continued to heal from the arrow to his side. The injury had been close to taking his life prior to and after their pardon. His last visit had been after the birth of Yellow Moon in which he had given her the Cheyenne name.

It was good Proud Wolf's family was well and hunting with his brother he would look forward to later in the year. He watched as the white smoke from the fire eased through the opening at the top of the lodge, hazing the evening sky. It was too early for sleep and his belly growled for food, but he remained still for a long while thinking of his brother, his placement at this reservation and of the work in the coming week of which he planned.

There was not much in each week he could predict. He had deliveries for Maud but those were few and she paid him in coins up front for each job she handed off to him. He saved a good bit of the money he earned, hidden in a depth of earth inside his camp in the trees. He kept little by the way of things. He pulled free the bear claw on a leather strap that rode around his neck beside his medicine bag, the weight of each always familiar.

He studied the claw from a grizzly his grandfather had killed, an heirloom of sorts and what had been given to him with his name. Over the years he traded the claw for a knife that Dawson now carried. It was an expected exchange each time they met one another. That first trade long ago when he had been a young man and Dawson a mere boy. The two surprised each other along a stream and in a quick moment of sizing each other up, made the trade of the knife for the claw. At the time, he hadn't known that would be the start of a lifelong friendship. Dawson was the one man he considered to be his true brother, though they did not share the same blood. He looked forward to the autumn when they would hunt for several weeks as each year they did.

He often examined the life he led where sometimes he did not feel he belonged to the Cheyenne, nor did he belong in his brother's white world. The people of the reservation always had need of him and his medicines and at times the whites, even the soldiers, were the same when they fell ill. But neither world held a place for him where he belonged. Same as his totem, always confused. The bear in him was often docile while the mountain lion who claimed him remained at unease. His fate sealed to a restless existence most days, like a pacing cat.

"And it is as my thoughts remind me." He rose to begin his evening meal. Lingering thoughts of Dawson would kindle his want to escape from the confines of the reservation for good. This had been on his mind since his return, but did he take the extended leave, one of two things would happen. He would either be hunted and returned, or no one would bother to find one lone brave who had been lost hunting his herbs. But here on the reservation his purpose as Medicine Man held him and for the meantime, his camp in the trees offered him some of the freedom he sought. But as it was, without the paper pass, a lone Cheyenne with no plan was often a dead one.

He mixed corn mash with a bit of water and patted it out to cook along a heated flat rock next to the fire. It sizzled and he let it crisp on one side prior to flipping it to the other. His belly growled once more as he added strips of deer meat to the rock beside the bread to let it cook, the redness of the meat turning brown, its juices soaking into the cornbread. He lifted the meat with the bread and took a bite.

This week he would do his errands for the woman in town, and he would begin the repairs to the porch for the teacher's cabin. He had not spoken of this to her, but she would begin with the children soon and while she was teaching, he would work on the repairs. It was best to get that done for her as she seemed to know little how to do things. She had been distressed when he hadn't opted to complete work for her right away. By his experience with women, no matter their skin color, impatience was common. His concern for now was that of her name. He had read the envelope on the captain's desk, and it had been written to a married woman. *Mrs. Allison Crockett.* She was married and his thoughts about her should stop there.

So why did she stay on his mind since last he saw her? He growled and shoved the last of his supper into his mouth, chewing and gulping to swallow. This was a thought he was not going to continue for this night. He would think of other things. Yes, that would be best.

Chapter Five

Alli pulled her buggy to a stop at the line of fencing outside the reservation. She had arrived early in order to spend time preparing. It was a bit intimidating as she looked on, soldiers about their duties as well as the Indian men and women at chores. Children played on the well-worn paths and the presence of real teepees filled her view. They were much larger than she thought and white smoke drifted from many. There were smaller cabin-like homes in rows as well. She hadn't expected that but some in the village lived in those as well as smaller homes near the reservation. Many of those planted gardens and herded sheep from what Maud had explained to her.

"Millie, I think we have arrived at the first day of school." She spoke to the horse now as if she were her one friend and in truth that might be how it was. "Now wish me luck."

She clucked her tongue and the old horse moved ahead, the buggy rocking to its start again. The reservation sat picturesque with the mountains behind it. She'd do well to sketch and paint this picture one of these days and made a mental note of it.

The sun, peeking above the rise adding filtered light across the prairie, highlighting the area in yellow hints of morning. She yawned. At least she'd slept last night in her own bed and not in the buggy in the barn. It had been over a week now since she'd arrived to the cabin, which was beginning to feel more like a home even if smaller than she'd anticipated.

She'd purchased a rolled mattress from Maud and burned the one the racoon had burrowed into, though she wasn't certain the racoon was gone for good. He'd returned, scratching to get inside, but she'd nailed wood to cover his entry and it seemed he'd finally given up.

Somehow, she was proud of that though she hadn't taken on the sagging roof of the porch. She'd propped two large pieces of lumber to hold it until Leaning Bear was able to make repairs. More than a week had passed since her asking but she'd seen no sign of him. Regardless, she was glad to have slept in the cabin itself, though the owl hooted through each night. The mice had not returned, thanks to the sage she'd placed into her now clean cabinets.

The trail ahead was well worn and the buggy bounced side to side as the gate came into view. Three soldiers waited at an open out building, two sitting at a small table under its protection from the early morning sun at a tense game of poker given their expressions.

"Mornin', Ma'am." The standing soldier approached her, and she stopped Millie with a gentle tug of the reins.

Her pulse raced in anticipation. "Good morning. I'm Allison Crockett, the new teacher for the reservation school."

One of the soldiers at the table chuckled and elbowed the other.

"Yes, Ma'am. The captain said we should be expecting you, Mrs. Crockett. You can go on in. School's held over there." He pointed to the open roof where benches were lined in rows appearing more like an outdoor church gathering sight. "Leave your horse and buggy on the closed side. We'll see to her when you've settled your things. I'll let the captain know you're here."

"Thank you, sir." She nodded, though her heart sank at the sight of the open school, having only a solid wall on one side. She'd been hoping for a real school room given the winters in this area. What on earth would she do come the winter? Maud and her sister had warned her of the harsh weather in the northwest but how would school be conducted when there was snow and freezing weather?

"Yes, Ma'am." He tipped his hat again to snickers from the seated men behind him.

Alli eyed the men but urged Millie to pull ahead. It seemed the young soldier was smitten with her that quick and his elder counterparts were funning him. Men. Why should they be any different here than back home?

Millie tugged the buggy up the slight incline toward children at play with some sort of stick and a leather ball. Their laughter was contagious, but they stopped their play to watch her. She lifted her hand in a wave, though they didn't return the gesture. A few older children worked in a large garden carrying baskets, most of them ill-clothed. The boys wore no shirts, with sewn material or buckskin britches, their chests bare, though they all wore beaded necklaces and feathers in their hair. She supposed this was normal for them given a quick glance of men moving about who wore nothing to cover their upper bodies as well. The women wore buckskin dresses or simple blouses in various colors and long skirts similar to her own. Each of them had beaded necklaces around their neck and on their clothing. Feathers adorned their hair and along their fringed handmade clothing. So many vibrant colors.

The women in the garden stopped their work to watch her. Even men at their duties were now looking. She tried to hold a smile as she stopped the buggy, unnerved by being such a spectacle, but she supposed it wasn't every day they saw a new teacher. She might have expected as much, but now arriving it was a bit strange to be the oddity. Maud had explained not many of the previous teachers had stayed, but she was hoping to be here for a long time. It had been hard to leave her sister and her family behind, but something was calling her here. She could feel it. Maybe this was a new beginning, offering adventures of which she'd almost settled at having enough excitement and would much rather this day go well so she could settle into the routine of her new life.

She straightened her skirts and reached into the back of her buggy, taking hold of the first crate of items for teaching. Books and chalk along with slates and paper, she'd also brought along painting supplies. If nothing else that might be a way of capturing the children's attention to begin with as she was uncertain how many would speak English.

"Allow me, Mrs. Crockett." A soldier tipped his hat. "I meant to be waiting here on your arrival. I'm Captain Carl Bartley, sorry for my delay."

She allowed him the crate and followed after he entered the open school. "Oh, I came early to make sure of time to set up things prior to the children's arrival. It's nice to meet you, Captain Bartley, at least after our several telegrams. I hope my last one arrived prior to me."

Alli added her pleasantries though she was still a bit nervous about her first day. After all the hardships of traveling west and settling into a semblance of a home she was grateful to meet this part head on. She might not know about living in the West, but she knew how to teach.

"Yes, Ma'am, I did receive it. I hope your travels were well." He groaned as he carried the crate and set it with care on the table. He was dressed like the other soldiers, in blue trousers and shirt with a yellow necktie, nothing at all fancy to tell her he was captain.

"It was quite a journey, as expected." That seemed the best response for now. Going into all the hardships behind her seemed futile at this point in her journey.

"And I know the school here needs some real walls, we'll add those prior to winter." He nodded to the openness before them.

"That would be wonderful. I am sure the winters here to be harsh." She glanced around the school, spotting an old stove near the closed section of wall.

He nodded toward the small stove in the corner. "Stove works, we'll get some walls up for you and things will stay warm. The previous teacher utilized one of the other buildings when the weather was bad, but we'll get to this, I assure you." He nodded toward the small stove in the corner.

"Thank you." Alli studied him as he spoke. He was a handsome man, younger than she might have anticipated.

"I'll get the other things from your buggy while you get situated." He went back twice more for the crates and bags, setting each on the one table at the front of the room. She supposed that would be her desk and there was a chair at least, though both were worn from time and use.

“I'll have the men see to your horse, hobble her nearby. She won’t come to any harm. And neither will you here on the reservation.” He held out a small key. “It'll open the closet there. A few supplies for the school and other items we keep inside.”

Alli nodded, taking the key and glancing at the closet behind her.

“I put wood in there a few weeks back to start in closing this in so once we get that done there will be more room inside.” He nodded, “Afraid I meant to have it all completed before your arrival, but behind on duties at times with less men placed here each month.”

She eased over to unlock the door and was met with a small cloud of dust.

“Not much there but some paper and ink. A few books and slates. I can request what you need but it takes weeks to arrive.” He folded his arms, waiting for her to step inside. “The Office of Indian Affairs sends a bit of money monthly for the school, how I paid for the lumber.”

“Thank you. And the bed?” She stepped back from the room facing him to ask about the bed in the corner of the tiny room that was stuffed full of wood, odds and ends.

He moved in behind her for a closer peek inside. “For the sick when needed, though we haven’t had any sickness in years now.”

She nodded. “And how many children should I expect to attend school this morning?”

“We got maybe eight or nine school aged children. It might be a few others will join if you…” he stopped with a shake of his head as if offering her a never mind.

Alli angled a hard glance at him. “If I…”

“If you stay for any length of time, Ma'am. Pardon my being presumptuous but most teachers leave in a short time for one reason or another.” He glanced out across the garden area and back to her.

“As a matter-of-fact, Captain Bartley, I do plan to stay for the length of my contract of two years or possibly longer.” She went to the desk and stacked a couple of books from the crate aside. So, her predecessors hadn’t lasted long at this job and it wasn’t the first time she had heard that. Well, she hadn’t come all this way to fail the first day. She reached for the remainder of the books, stacking them aside.

"I'll expect all of the children of school age here each morning by eight o’clock sharp. School will run until noon for a break of one hour and resume at one o’clock and I’ll ring the bell at precisely three to end the day’s course of learning.”

A slight grin covered the captain’s face, though he let it fade quickly. “There’s no school bell, Mrs. Crockett, but I'll have my soldiers round up the children. It’ll take a bit of time to get them adjusted to having school and a teacher once more. They hold little to timeliness.”

Alli lifted her brows and took up a hand bell from the crate. “I’m prepared for what it may take on my part and I thank you for all your assistance.”

“Yes, Ma'am.” He turned to go but glanced back, narrowing his brows. “I'll see what we can do to round them up, but you aren’t prepared to speak their language by any chance are you? Some speak English but others, not so much.”

"No. I do have an interpretation book for several of the tribal languages, but I'm afraid I know very little." She dug into one of the crates for a small booklet with a few torn pages and held it up. She'd spent months searching for such a book finding that not many choices existed.

"Two Doves will be of some help to you then and some of the older girls." He added. "They speak English well enough."

"Two Doves?" She lifted her brows. "A student?"

He shook his head. "Chief Dancing Fox's wife, he speaks English too, you'll need her help. The Cheyenne language is a bit difficult to learn, as you already know, and we got Sioux, Pawnee, and Arapaho on the reservation here too."

"Then I shall appreciate her assistance, thank you, Captain." She hadn't expected any help so that was a very nice surprise.

The captain gave her one last nod and left her to her day. She glanced at the full campus before her as he headed toward a group of soldiers lingering outside one of the buildings, perhaps his office. There were children about and it was her job to teach them what they needed to learn in order to assimilate into society, according to her guidelines from the Office of Indian Affairs. She'd spent hours poring over every word within the manual she'd been given. Her conclusion? The government was little interested in the children learning regular studies but more interested in their learning how to behave in a civilized manner.

She'd studied that word the longest, the one that made it sound as if these people were the savages that were talked about back East. But it couldn't be that all were savages just as not all soldiers were bad. Well, she wouldn't fall for what others stated and learn for herself about these people. What she'd seen thus far were families hard at work, though behind fencing which had never settled well with her in her years of reading about such things. But as it was, her sister's warnings of all those killed at the hands of different tribes weighed in her thoughts. She'd been careful this far, though most at home wouldn't think her a smart woman for this journey.

Though here she was, doing exactly what she'd set out to do. Wouldn't Timothy have been surprised at her taking up such as this. He was the reason she'd been so well read related to the plight of the different tribes. He'd been fascinated by what he'd read as well, though his condition of consumption had limited his ideas of travels, all except to some of the women faculty's bedrooms. She shook her head and tossed away further thoughts of her husband's infidelity. That was the past and she was determined to plan for her future with all that was new.

She eyed the furthest post behind all the benches. The first thing she'd do was order a bell so she could beckon the children to the start of school each morning. Meanwhile, the hand-held cowbell would have to do. She returned to the crates, jostling in the bottom of one and grabbing a graphite pencil. She lifted her tablet and jotted down *school bell*. As Maud had mentioned, it could be months for anything to arrive from back East, so ordering early would be best.

She laid the tablet aside and walked into the closet again, fanning away the dust. Besides the single bed, there were shelves lining one wall. There was a stack of slates and chalks. That would be of help in the beginning today. There were a few tablets of paper and ink in small bottles and a stack of feathers sharpened to points, though dust coated it all.

She dusted off the shelving with her hand and added some of the books she'd brought along, walking back and forth from the crates on the desk. And returning to another of the crates she placed a slate and portion of chalk to each along the benches. Two to each bench if around eight children arrived as expected. She took in a deep breath to vanish further nerves that wanted to creep in, reminding herself she was anxious to begin, not nervous about the task.

She placed two of the crates inside the closet and returned for the other, noting the chalking board on the wall right there on the outside of the closet. How had she not seen it except for the fact it was covered in dust?

"Well," she whispered to herself. "This will be nice." Though it did need a good washing. She grabbed a cloth and brushed the board from one side to the other, fanning away dust and cobwebs.

"That'll do for today." She laid aside the cloth and caught a quick glimpse of a boy hiding behind the edge of the closet on the outside of the school. He had no shirt, his long hair in disarray around his face. She lifted a paper from her crate and laid it on the desk, making sure he was watching.

He peeked around and she pretended to not see him as she took up a container of red paint and grabbed a brush. He lingered as she began to stroke across the paper, creating a whirl of red flower petals. She pushed the brush again and he moved closer. He was young, maybe five or six given his size. He wore buckskin trousers and a string of beads around his neck hanging to his navel.

When she met his gaze, he froze, big dark eyes wide as she held the brush toward him. "Would you like to paint?"

He shied at first, taking a step back but then trotted forward and grabbed the brush, sinking it into the jar of red paint all the way up to his fingers. Her first instinct was to scold that only the tip of the brush should go in, but this was progress, wasn't it?

He held the brush and let the red paint drip onto the paper but glanced at her instead of painting.

She smiled to encourage him. "Go on, paint."

"Paint." The boy spoke, surprising her as he moved the brush across the papers making more red streaks to create another flower. So, he had been paying attention.

She touched the jar. "Red. This is the color Red. Red paint."

"Red. Paint." The boy dipped the brush to its depths once more streaking it across the page with laughter as he swirled the brush in no particular design this time.

"He speaks English very well." A young Cheyenne woman walked closer, eyeing what was on the paper and then the boy. "White Crow, you should let the teacher know the truth of your understanding of her English words."

The boy ignored her and kept painting with a shrug and a giggle.

Alli faced her with a nod, assuming she was the woman the captain had mentioned.

"Good morning, I'm Mrs. Crockett, the new teacher." She began a bit uncertain. "But please call me Alli."

"I am Two Doves." The young woman turned back

to White Crow who had yet to answer her question. She wore a beautiful dress of light buckskin, adorned with tiny beads and gold color flecks of paint. Her hair hung in one long braid across her right shoulder and down across her largely rounded belly. Her bronze skin was smooth and her eyes a deep chocolate brown. Alli held her gaze long enough to be rude, caught up in her beauty.

"I am White Crow. I know white man's words." The boy interrupted, laying down the brush and taking a seat on one of the front benches.

"Well, it's very nice to meet you both." She glanced from White Crow to Two Doves once more. "The captain said you would assist as you speak English and I'm afraid I know only a few words in your language."

The young woman set about using a dampened cloth to clean the chalk board. "There has been no teacher here for the children in some time. More than one year. Almost two. Some of the children may have forgotten their English words."

"Yes. I was aware of that when I took this position." Alli lifted another cloth to clean the desk before her. She glanced at White Crow who used the chalk to draw a bird on his slate, having wiped the paint from his fingers onto his trousers. She bent before him, hoping to win him over in time. "What do you have there?"

He drew more feathers on the bird and added stick legs. "It is a crow, my totem."

"That's a lot of talent you have in painting and drawing. Do you know your numbers, counting?" She lifted her brows and waited for his response.

He looked up at her with a big toothless grin, his front teeth missing. "One, two, three, four, five, six, seven, eight, nine, ten." He counted as he held up each finger to match.

"And how about letters, the alphabet?" Alli glanced away as two girls walked in to take their seats, both around the age of eight. Behind them an older girl in her teens took the back row, lifting her slate and chalk. This was good; they were coming as she'd hoped. Now to make this day something they would like enough to return each day.

"A, B, C, D, E, F, G…" White crow belted out his letters and continued to the end, leaving the girls behind him to giggle as he got louder to the point of yelling. "H, I, J, K, L, M, N, O, P, Q, R, S, T, U, V, W, X, Y, and Z."

"Good morning girls. That's good, White Crow. Very good." Alli spoke to greet them as three boys of various ages came and sat behind White Crow, scrambling to fight for the seat on the inside isle and shoving each other until Two Doves cleared her voice. The boys stilled.

Before she could say anything more, a teenage girl came in holding the hand of a very young little girl. She nodded to Alli as she sat the little girl down on the front bench and returned outside to tug another girl from behind the wall. The girl didn't look up but took her seat, not lifting her slate as the older girl sat beside her.

So that was six girls and four boys. Ten. Alli cleared her voice and stood straight, scanning the quiet faces, so unlike her own and each very beautiful in their own differences. Here she was now, about to teach as she'd been planning for the better part of a year. She took a depth of breath and began. "Good morning, students."

Two Doves turned away from her cleaning and without a word, the look she gave the students produced an assorted mix of mingled "Good mornings" out of the children.

Alli went on, now understanding the presence of Two Doves, who remained quiet. “I’m Mrs. Crockett and I’ll be your teacher each weekday Monday through Friday. I think in order first is to have us each introduce ourselves and tell a bit about us, something we can share with each other. That will help me remember each of your names by knowing something about you. I’ll go first, while I am a teacher, I love art and painting, the mixing of colors and the brush to the canvas. I hope we can paint this afternoon to show you how much fun it can be to paint and learn about the making of colors. I have been a teacher in Chicago for many years. Now, who would like to go first?”

It remained quiet for a moment and Alli waited, not sure which children understood her or could even speak English. She half expected Two Doves to force one of the children, but the elder girl who’d brought in the little one raised her hand.

“Yes, please, begin.” She encouraged the girl, stepping a bit closer.

“My name is Elina. I am fourteen years old. I wish one day to attend the university I have seen in pictures. I would like to become a teacher too.”

“That’s very admirable and with hard work, anything can be accomplished.” Alli smiled. It was so exciting to think this young girl held the same dreams she once had.

Elina nodded to the teen girl, a bit younger beside her, the one who had hidden. “This is my sister, Waynoka, she is eleven and Toma is my youngest sister. She is six years of age.”

“My name is Waynoka and I’m eleven years old. I

will grow up to have babies and work like my mother." The girl dropped her gaze and sat again.

Alli nodded. "It's very nice to meet you."

"I'm Toma. I am six years old. I will be a hunter like my father." The smallest girl tossed out her chest with pride, showing her loss of teeth across the front. She then spoke in her native tongue to her eldest sister, the grin easing away from her tiny brown face.

"Well, you all must know, that as your teacher, I do wish for you to speak when you desire, as long as we remain on topic and complete our work." Alli offered. She'd been that kind of teacher back in Chicago, though the children there were often from neglected homes where education wasn't any more valued than it might be here. She'd allowed as free a classroom as could be tolerated, until at times the boys became too rowdy and they'd all be scolded by the headmaster. Well, there was no headmaster here and it was her will that these children find learning something to be excited about.

Another of the girls stood. "I'm thirteen. My name is Chelan." She sat back down as quickly as she'd stood.

"Chelan, what a pretty name, and what is something about you we could all learn?" Alli waited, coaxing with a nod.

The girl glanced around her. "I am good at sewing beads to moccasins and clothing in many patterns. I do this as my grandmother taught me."

The girl glanced down at the brightly adorned pair of matching moccasins she wore. And her hair was braided, carrying more beads but no feathers. She was a very pretty girl with her long dark hair, high cheek bones, and deep brown eyes.

"Well, the making of clothing is one thing but to

make it beautiful is a wonderful gift to have." Alli stepped to the middle of the benches. "And how about you two girls, what can you tell me of yourselves."

The two sat on the middle bench and glanced at each other in a standoff of who should go first, but then neither said anything.

Behind her, Two Doves spoke in Cheyenne and then followed in English. "Chameli is nine years, and her sister Darika is eight years. They do not understand English. They are not Cheyenne. They are Sioux."

Alli nodded in understanding. "I see. We will work on that very soon. Can you tell them so?"

Two Doves spoke to them and one of the little girls gave a nod, the other looking away. They each stood stating their names and sitting again to Alli's surprise.

"Chameli and Darika are such beautiful names." Alli turned to the other side of the benches to her left and eyed the boys. Never had she seen boys to remain still and quiet, all but White Crow who fidgeted, eyeing the paint again on her desk.

"And boys, might any of you tell us your name and about you?" She waited but they all remained quiet. Two Doves had entered the closet with some of the things from her baskets.

"How about you?" She touched a lad suited in buckskins who might have been around eight years given his size.

The boy's dark eyes met hers. To her surprise he stood and spoke with the hardship of stuttering. "I…am…am…am Little…Little Wolf. I like like…like to hunt."

The other boys giggled including White Crow who was now sitting on the floor playing with a stick pushing it through the flooring cracks. “Children, respect is proper in the classroom. White Crow, please sit on the bench once more.”

The little boy plopped back up on the bench. But another boy a bit larger than Little Wolf, stood. “He’s unable to speak right since he was born.” He glared at the other boys. “But he’s not dumb. He is my brother.” Alli had thought Little Wolf’s stuttering to be his nerves, but it was an affliction of speech she’d seen over the years in some children.

“And who might you be?” She confronted the boy.

“I am called Hawk. I am twelve years and I am a great hunter.” The boy folded his arms and puffed out his chest. “My father thinks this is much a waste of time to learn white man ways.”

Alli had expected this at one time or another. “Yes, well, first of all on respect. Of course, Little Wolf is not dumb. No one who comes to this school will be thought of as that word. We call what Little Wolf has stuttering and all it takes is a bit of time to slow down and think hard about what you are going to say. And we will not laugh here about anyone who has a tougher time of things. Everyone will be accepted to learn at their own pace.”

Hawk eyed her hard and sat again.

“And I will add to this to give you something more to think about. I realize it is difficult to learn a new culture and language, but what you learn here may be of help to you one day when you visit towns to buy goods and services. It will help you to understand the language and the money so as not to be cheated…” She’d intended on going further but in the distance, she spotted Leaning Bear and lost her thoughts and words for the moment.

He led his painted horse from the corral and when he glanced her direction she went back to the children. "As I was saying, if you know the language and how to count money, you will not be cheated at your efforts for instance. And no learning of any kind is a waste of anyone's time."

Hawk shook his head, folding his arms. "It is no matter; the Cheyenne are paid less anyway than the white man in most towns. Cheated even if it is counted correct."

Now what was she to do? She hadn't known that but then it seemed no surprise. It had been the same for the Negros back home, all freed but not assimilated into the world of white people like herself. But she had to try and help these children see things another way. "Then perhaps, by this learning, one day a young man such as yourself will see this be changed. Learning will add value to how things go in your future. And, besides that, I will need help from each of you to learn your language and your culture, which means, the way you live and do things. It is all very new to me and I would very much like to understand things in your lives you find important."

Two Doves held up her hand and the boy sat back down, but still shook his head. Alli wasn't sure what to make of the exchange.

One more boy needed introduction. "And our last introduction. Tell us of yourself." Alli touched the boy's shoulder, but he drew away, though he stood. He wore no shirt and had no moccasins. She would have to see about uniforms for the children when she could manage it.

"Takoda." He sat back down and didn't look at her.

"He is Pawnee. He speaks little English." Two Doves returned to stand beside the board.

"All right then, will you tell him he will learn a little each day." Alli asked as she went to the board to begin the day's lessons.

Two Doves spoke to the boy and lifted the broom, going back into the closet for sweeping. Alli grabbed the chalk and began with numbers, understanding the difference in the language that Two Doves had spoken in Cheyenne and then in Sioux and Pawnee. She wrote out one to ten and began with the day's lessons, knowing she would need to work hard to remember the children's names and abilities. It was going to be a long day of learning a lot of things for the children and herself included. But that was why she was here.

She'd come to leave behind her mundane world of which she'd never be accepted except when with her now deceased husband. And she'd finished the one year of mourning, deciding that she was a better person when her skills were used to help another, whether the elite of Chicago accepted her as one of them or not. In spite of them all she was a teacher, maybe not on the university level, but where she thought it counted even more, with children who needed her.

She turned back to face the classroom, and in the distance, Leaning Bear mounted his horse and trotted off outside the reservation. She blinked and all the children were staring at her. How long had she watched him, his hair and the fringe from his buckskins flapping in the summer wind as he appeared so comfortable on the beautiful animal?

"All right, who knows their numbers besides White Crow?" She grinned at the little boy who was now balancing on one leg beside his bench, his arms out wide. He sat with her glance but at the same time, knocked his slate off to the floor beside her.

Alli bent to pick it up and as she did, White Crow touched her hair and spoke in Cheyenne. She held his gaze, and he drew his hand back to the other children's giggles.

Alli smiled, though she wasn't surprised at the boy's interest in her lighter hair. "Why don't you tell me in English what you have said?"

White Crow turned to look at Two Doves and the other children who still giggled. "Much softer than sheep's wool."

"Well, then who can spell sheep?" She giggled along with them and so began the morning of teaching she had long awaited, even with the children's laughter. Now if her mind would sidestep thinking about Leaning Bear and where he might be heading. To town, perhaps to work for Maud once more, though she did hope he would get to more of her cabin fixes soon.

Chapter Six

Leaning Bear stepped back from Alli's home, inspecting his completed work on her porch roofing. He let his eyes travel along the eaves checking the precision of the work he had begun after she had left with her horse and buggy. It was her second day of teaching on the reservation, and it was better to do his work when he was alone.

He gave himself a nod. The porch now appeared in better condition than the roof, though he had climbed on top to repair a few places that would leave her leaks should a hard rain come. He glanced into the sky, the heat of the later afternoon scorching, and sweat running down his naked chest and back. He wiped his brow and lifted the leather water bag he had filled at the stream earlier, his third of the day. He drank in gulps once more until the bag was empty.

The owl, roosting in the eaves of the barn, hooted in warning and he turned as Allison Crockett arrived in her buggy, the old horse she called Millie, tugging her along. He had worked up until the time school would have ended for the day. He reminded himself to be more mindful of the time should he do further work for the teacher.

He should be gone by this time, but the work had taken longer than expected. He still needed to break up the rotten wood and add it to the fire pit, a circle of piled rocks that had been used for fires prior to now. He stepped that direction with his tomahawk and began working on separating the nailed pieces of rotting wood and rusted nails. He tossed each of the smaller pieces into the pile. The old horse took her time in ambling along closer and closer, the buggy creaking and bouncing with the teacher inside. It might be he should work on the buggy next. Better it would make more firewood.

The buggy came to a stop and the teacher climbed down, walking closer to inspect the porch, a smile crossing her features. The blue of her eyes was as clear at the sky above them. “I had no idea you’d be starting, and it looks as if you’ve finished all in the same day.”

“It is as you say. Roof will need more in days to come.” He turned back to his tomahawk, hitting wood pieces to avoid her continued gaze.

“Yes, well, I am truly indebted to you and will see to your pay for the work and any further lumber needed. I did manage the hinges of the door myself, though, it might be it isn’t quite level.” She pulled the bonnet from her head and her light hair fell down her back in a long single braid, though her hair was not straight and frays of it escaped its binding from the top of her head and lower. He went back to his work, the depth of her ice blue eyes penetrating enough to make him turn.

“Door is good.” He had inspected both doors and oiled the metal latches for better function. A woman alone would need the latches to lock, though he could not see that any lock would keep someone out who wanted in. It might elude predators from seeking entry at best.

She turned back to the porch and stepped to the front door, inspecting it as if she’d read his mind. “And you oiled the latch, that’s nice of you. This wouldn’t close all the way." She worked the latch testing it and turning back to move around the porch inspecting his work.

He was caught up for a moment in watching her but when she looked at him, he turned back to his work.

"Let me put Millie to her stall and I'll pay you. It's awful hot today, I do hope you drank plenty. I made sure of the children taking breaks today for water." She moved off to the horse not even waiting for him to answer that he had drunk enough water for the heat. She was quick to unharness the animal, which followed her right inside the barn, sending the owl across to the trees behind the cabin.

It amused him that she chattered to the horse the entire time and even inside the barn she did the same. He grabbed more of the planks of wood hitting the axe to it multiple times until the pieces parted, one board falling into the pile, and he followed by tossing the other. It might be she could burn some of the wood come winter, but most was so old it fell apart into the dust of age and weather.

Moments later she was standing beside him, and the scent of flowers found him. He stopped his work and faced her, once again studying the depth of her clear blue eyes and the almost white coloring of her hair.

"How much do I owe you? Maud said you'd prefer that you were paid in coins, not paper money." She waited but then her gaze found his chest, her light brows narrowing as she glanced back to her coin purse.

He supposed he should have put his tunic on in her presence, just as he did when he went to town for his work. It was clear she had studied the scars he carried on both sides of his upper chest.

"Three dollars." He worked for a fair price and

nothing more.

"That isn't enough for such work in my opinion." She rummaged through her coin purse and counted in a whisper to five, the coins clinking as she added each to her cupped fist. Her face still held a puzzled look as her gaze strayed to his chest once more.

"Were you injured?"

How did he answer her in choice words about his dance with the sun as a younger man? Most white people were quick to judge the things they did not understand about the Cheyenne and other tribes.

"I'm sorry, I've no right to ask so personal a question, nor do I have the right to allow my gaze to fall upon your scars." She placed her pouch of coins into her skirt pocket. "My mother always said I never knew the fine art of holding my tongue or my view of the world. I suppose she was right, always too curious about things."

He touched the scars along his chest on one side and spoke a simple explanation. "Dance with sun."

"The sun?" She narrowed her brows as if concerned.

He lifted the last two shards of rotted wood adding them to the pile. "Cheyenne is made a man with his dance with sun, skin is pierced and straps tied, leaving tethers from chest to tree post in ground." He explained maybe more than he should have, but it was that she had asked so he went on. "Must stay in sun until skin is broken and release happens." He did not add that many experienced visions that defined things for them.

She nodded, but at the same time found the frown once more. "Oh my, a painful rite of passage then?"

"Pain offers remember of importance. Scars are reminder of passage." He placed the tomahawk into his belt, sweat covering his upper body in the continued warmth of the day.

"I apologize that perhaps I shouldn't have asked but…the scars I thought appeared as bullets might." She shrugged, and folded her arms about herself though she cocked her chin up as if more curious.

How did this white woman speak to him with such ease as to ask further questions of the scars on his body which held many? Perhaps he would talk of more to see her reaction. He turned, pointing to the scar on his right shoulder. One where a bullet had caught him as a young man when he'd been chased by Pawnee into the woods. They'd blamed all Cheyenne for their loss of lands. "Bullet here if that makes no need for apology." She did not need to apologize for her inquisitions.

Her mouth fell open, but then a smile emerged. "Well…I will not…ask further of the reasons behind that, then."

She must have thought he made light of her and for the most part he was. She was easy to fluster and that added to his amusement of speaking with her so he continued. "And knife here." He turned back to face her showing her the small scar below his right ribcage. "Accident, boys playing with knife for skills. This," he bent to pull up his buckskin pants to show his left knee, placing two fingers to the dotted scars there. "Snakebite. Poison." He let a slight grin emerge, something he had not done in a long time.

"You are mocking me." She pouted but leaned closer to take a look. Her lips were pink and plump, and her nose was narrow, her cheek bones high under her sky-colored eyes.

"It is as you say." He struggled in the moment of silence and beckoned something to say. "Second day of school is good?"

She blinked hard and her face lit up. "Yes, very well, the children are incredibly smart and willing to learn. I suppose I knew they would be. Though I do think I'll see about ordering uniforms, school is better learned when comfortable and dressed properly for learning."

"This you think help learning?" He added his thoughts to the idea, though this brought the narrowing of her brows once more.

"Well, I mean the children come, the boys, like you with no shirt. At most schools a shirt with a collar is required as are trousers and boots with socks or stockings for boys. Skirts and blouses for the girls along with stockings and proper shoes." She was quick to defend her thoughts, her tone moving up an octave in her persuasion of him to her ideas.

Ah, he had long understood anything better than to argue with a woman who already had her mind set to things and so he gave a simple grunt.

"You don't approve?" She questioned him, keeping her arms folded.

"Not mine to decide." He wouldn't get into this argument and continued on toward his horse, Paytah, who grazed nearby.

She followed him, her arms still folded across her chest. "Captain Bartley let me know with a bout of laughter they'd tried uniforms before, but they hadn't been worn as they were supposed to. Then Two Doves frowned on my idea of dressing each student for class based on the fact that the children won't care much for English clothing as she called it. But I am certain that dressing for success is best."

He listened to her flurry of words and when she

stopped, he took her hand. There he placed two coins back into her palm. “Three is enough.”

He had expected her to insist, but she did not. He grabbed Paytah’s rope, and mounted the animal looking back at her, though it was best he said no more. The children would see no need in the clothing that white men and women wore.

She touched the horse along his large jaw. “What’s his name? He’s really a beautiful animal.”

“Paytah. Fire.” He responded with explanation though he was little to do so with anyone. What was it about this white woman that kept his thoughts coming right out of his mouth? He was not a young man anymore, nervous with a woman. But…now he needed to ride and not think the thoughts that were forming inside his head about her.

“Will you do more to the roof soon?” she asked as he took the horse farther away.

“It is as you say.” With that he urged the horse to a gallop, out of sheer need to do so.

“I bid you good afternoon and thank you again for your work,” she called behind him, but he didn’t turn back to say anything more.

Paytah's ears perked at her call, and it was the horse that glanced behind them. This should be as clear a sign as the owl bringing his messages of her arrival. Paytah little liked anyone and sometimes that included himself. The horse was strong-willed and cooperated when and if it was on his mind to do so.

He glanced into the sky and allowed the horse his measure in speed, heading back to the reservation.

He smiled in spite of his thoughts about the white woman, amused at her blush of viewing the scars to his skin. It had been too hot to wear the deerskin tunic given the work he had been completing, though he did wear the garment when in town. He should not have jested in showing her further scars, but she should not have inquired where she did not want the answer.

It was strange to him that Alli Crockett would approach and carry on a conversation with him and hold no alarm that he was Cheyenne. White women feared him and his brothers for many reasons most did not understand. The coins in his pocket weighed heavy and would be of worth in the purchase of medicine or food needed for families on the reservation.

He gripped his left hand into a fist. Her fingers had touched his palm as she gave the coins to him and again when he had held her hand to give her coins back. Her fingers were slender with well-kept nails. That should be his first sign a woman such as her had little business placing herself where she was. White teachers alone had no history of staying to teach the children. But a white woman alone in Lame Deer was not good. Was not good anywhere except back where she came from.

He remained perplexed at her having no husband, though he had seen the name that was spelled as if she were married. Perhaps a man would follow but then why would she need work on her cabin if a husband would arrive soon? This was a thought he should not be thinking. None of his thinking should be about her as it was. He would find work to do once back on the reservation. More work was for clearing his mind of thoughts of this white woman who had captured his attention. Yes. Harder work would be best.

Chapter Seven

Sweat rolled down Leaning Bear's naked back, soaking into the waist of his buckskin trousers. He bent at the stream and cupped his hands to drink several times. The cool water eased his craving, and he dipped his water bag into the depth of the stream to refill the pouch for later. He had slipped from the reservation before dawn, and against the captain's warnings, had not let the soldiers know of his departure. He would not live as an animal controlled by others, no matter the captain's request. He had written down his plans and left the paper with Captain Bartley.

He angled a glance at the edge of the water line in the sand, locating an empty tortoise shell. He pulled the white skeleton free and sifted it through the water to clear mud and leaves from its hollow center. The canvas bag across his shoulder hung at his side and was filled with herbs and mushrooms he had found on his morning walk through the forest. He placed the tortoise shell inside as the singing of a woman found him.

He was used to being alone in these woods, all but for the animals and birds. The voice came to him again, but the words eluded him due to distance.

He eased away from the water and made his way toward the voice. Greenery swayed across its banks, and water washed over small falls with various wildflowers along the edges.

The song came again, this time in words he understood. He moved closer and the voice lifted as he eased into the thatch of trees behind her. It was the white teacher, who sang her song loudly in a voice having much vibrato. He had not seen her since completing the roof to her porch, but he was all too aware that she taught each day on the reservation. He needed to keep himself busy as not to pay much attention to her.

She hummed with purpose as she sat in a fancy folding chair and stroked a brush across a white canvas on a wooden easel. The scene before her matched the landscape farther ahead of her. Her talents were many, though her abilities as a woman alone were questionable. He squatted as the hint of a breeze lifted the golden locks that lay across her shoulders. The edges of her curled strands were almost white as the rocks around her. She wore a less fancy dress, he suspected was for comfort on her days away from being a teacher. And though the song was foreign to him, the whispered words of her voice were calming.

She studied the scene for long moments and then dipped the brush into the paint and teased the canvas, etching in lighter blades of high grass beside the stream. The brush she used was fancy, made of wood and metal, the same as the ones he had picked up from the dusty road when her buggy had spilled its contents.

She hummed louder, her voice mingling with that of the trickling stream. The flow of her long slender fingers to the canvas matched her voice, intriguing him all the more as he stayed to watch her. Why was it white women made their way west in assumption they would find more than they had left behind? This he had thought about when he worked on her cabin.

She lifted her hair with one hand and then let it fall across her shoulders again as she continued to paint with the other. The blonde curls sprang up and settled again in swirls, the color of a pale-white sun. And why was it he continued to allow his mind this journey of thoughts about her? And why did some fate keep bringing them together? This, he would not think again.

The painting was very much a likeness to what the scene held before her. He was caught up in the individual colors of grasses and shrubs in the background of the trickling stream. But what she captured best were the yellow flowers along the creek bed on the far bank. Her canvas might have been a shrunken version of the scene before her. Much talent. He bent, leaning closer to take in her work. A twig snapped underneath his moccasin and he froze.

"You can come out now." She didn’t turn to look at him but continued her stroke across the canvas.

He swallowed hard. He had never been apt to use the curses he had learned from his friend Dawson, but it seemed fitting his thoughts said the silent word. *Shit!* It was a word to use when frustrated or not wanting to be caught as had just happened. He stood and stepped free of his hiding spot.

“It's a very beautiful day but a hot one already.” She painted another stroke to the canvas but still had not turned to face him.

“Heat is much.” He answered holding his stance several paces back from her.

She turned to look at him, scooting all the way around in her chair and crossing her boots at the ankles. “Frankly, I thought this painting would melt by now.”

He studied her canvas, which was missing the color

for the sky. "Soon to finish painting."

She turned back around to face her work. "Yes. Maybe. So, what do you think of it?"

Against his better judgement he stepped closer. The painting was as clear a copy as he could imagine of the scene before them. "Much likeness. Sky missing color."

She sighed with a shrug of her shoulders, a slight frown crossing her features. "Yes, well, I never seem to get the blues of any sky as they should be. I was told once by an art professor to paint the sky first and then blend in the trees and scenery. But that has never worked for me either."

"You paint many things?" It was a question. She must have done this for a lot of years given her use of technique and colors.

"Oh, mostly outdoor scenes and sometimes people. As a hobby, though I did sell a large canvas of the sea once in New York." She beamed with pride and a quick glance at him showed the blush of her cheeks.

He didn't share that one of his own drawings had gone to the same state but was not purchased due to his being Cheyenne. Dawson McCade had taken many of his drawings for review by those who taught art in colleges and art museums. He had not known this at the time. But his brother had returned disappointed there was no money for what a Cheyenne man created. It had bothered his brother more than it concerned him.

She glanced at him again, the depth of her blue eyes darker as the shade of the trees covered her face. "You didn't know I saw you, did you?"

He had not.

"I look hard at a scene; I saw the edge of your shoulder as you crossed over the falls into the wooding there." She pointed to the falls and then touched her painting. "Here."

"Should be more careful." He always prided himself on his ability to stay hidden when he wanted. He had let his guard down and that he must not do.

"I should tell you I am enjoying the porch being covered and the latching of my front door. And I do think the racoon is long gone as are the mice I encountered my first day in the cabin. But the owl and I are in a standoff on who owns the rights to the barn." She laughed and a part of him wanted to join her.

"So, you can smile." She lifted her light brows with her observation.

"Owl has reason for stay." He offered though most white people little believed in the spirit of animals. The owl would be a visitor of someone lost, or long gone from her.

She laid down her brush and held his gaze, the blue of her eyes, as deep as the crystal waters of pools farther north. And now he was a fool. He stepped back. Too close for his own comfort in the casual conversation.

"Well, the horse is no longer frightened of the owl. But I hear her hoots in the night no matter her reasons for remaining." It was a moment more before she spoke again. "I am also enjoying the children very much."

"This I know." He explained further. "I hear the laughter and songs of the children."

"It's difficult that some speak English while others are still learning. Two Doves has been a great help to me. She is very kind to help me understand the Cheyenne words as well as speaking to the children who are Sioux and Pawnee." She stopped the stroke of her brush and turned to him.

“Two Doves speaks many languages.” He added, but figured the chief placed his wife there in order to understand what Allison Crockett would be teaching to the children each day. The chief was not happy with any idea of the children learning the white man’s ways, but the government made their insistences. This he would not tell her.

“I suppose things are very different than I had thought they might be. The children are coming on time and over the few weeks are enjoying class as you said. Though only Elina and Waynoka do their homework.” She shrugged and faced him again. “It’s funny, the boys here or the boys back home in Chicago are not much different in their dislike of sitting still to learn, and there is nothing they like about homework.”

“School work for school. Not for home.” He added his thoughts. Why it was necessary for children to have papers at home did not make sense to him. Perhaps a book as he often read one when he had the chance, though he handed them off when done.

“Work at home helps a child retain information and the skills they learn better.” She stood, folding her arms and taking a step closer. “So, what did you mean about the owl?”

He took yet another step back and she stayed where she was. He should have been on his horse and not made this intrusion. He scanned the full view of her and dropped his gaze to the stream. She was tall and slender with narrow shoulders and…and she was very beautiful. Something he had not taken liberty to think of any woman in a long time. Yes, he was a fool because love for her would never be allowed by anyone around them or elsewhere. And his thought should stop at once.

But he answered her question. “Owl wise, brings spirits of the lost.”

She considered that for a long moment and whispered. “Timothy.”

“Someone you have lost?” It occurred to him he had no right to ask.

“My husband died of consumption; it’s been two years now.” She turned back to her painting. Perhaps she had continued sadness and now he understood the reason her name he had read was stated as a married woman.

“Tell me more of the owl.” She waited, tilting her head at an angle where the sun stroked through the strands of her light hair.

“The Cheyenne believe owl brings news from camp of the dead, brings thoughts from a person who is there or other place after gone.” He struggled to explain the concept he was sure she did not understand.

“Heaven, perhaps.” She turned back to her canvas.

His thoughts on heaven held no more than his ideas on the camp of the dead. One day each would know. Now was not that time.

“Oh, I do wish I could get the colors of the sky right this time. It’s such a nice portrayal.” She shaded her eyes with her outstretched fingers and above the trees before her. “I have three more like paintings from back home that were beautiful until I added the wrong color of blue for the sky. Oh well, I’ve lost the way the sun was hitting the leaves anyway.” She dipped her brush into a tin of water and closed her case with its many colors of paint, turning back to him.

How easily her mind jumped back to her painting. And his own to her beauty.

“Tomorrow I will paint again since it’s Sunday,

probably in the early afternoon." She stood and set the canvas against the rocks and folded her chair and the easel.

This woman always had too many things but stacked them with care to be able to carry them all. Had she told him about her plans for him to know this?

"Tomorrow, you paint the sky." He waited as she turned back to look at him once more.

"If only…I'll make no promises I can't keep." Her laughter echoed back to him as she continued in the direction of her cabin, which wasn't far. "And of you, more fixes to my roof will happen soon?" She turned to hold his gaze.

He glanced into the sky and back to her. "No. Rain coming, but soon."

And with a lift of her brows, she continued toward her home.

He waited until she was no longer in sight, though she was loud in beginning to sing and hum once more as she moved farther away. And yes, he was a man who was a fool, in the thoughts of her that lingered with the knowledge the two of them would never be accepted together. If he spent too much time with her…this would not end well for either of them and putting her in danger he would not do.

****

The steam from the tea kettle on the old stove whistled. Alli grabbed a cloth and gripped the handle carefully as she poured the boiling water over the tea leaves, the last of the Earl Grey she'd brought from home. That would be one more of the items she'd need to add to her list for Jacie in her next letter, hoping her sister would send things as soon as she was able.

Thinking of her sister made a bit of regret flow through her. She missed her family, but she was here now, teaching the children on the reservation as she had planned. This was her home now.

"Even if it's only been a few weeks." Sometimes lonesome invaded, but too often she was tired enough to go right to bed after her evening meal and after one more check on Millie.

And several weeks had worn her to a frazzle when she thought hard about it. The boys became rowdy any time Two Doves wasn't there to call them out. And none of the children completed homework as she assigned it. While there were ten children, they were all on different levels of learning making it difficult to give each the time they needed. But she was still making progress and the older girls read so well that she shared her books with them each week, allowing Two Doves to make a small library in the closet on the shelves.

She set the kettle back on the stove away from heat and carried the teacup with her after dropping a sprinkle of sugar and stirring. No cubes were to be found in Lame Deer, but the loose crystals worked fine. She made her way to the table, noting she might have Maud order her a small desk. Something about having a desk made things feel more like she was a teacher.

She sat and thumbed through the stack of papers she'd gathered from the children. All had accomplished writing and speaking the sounds of the letters though she beckoned this and numbers they had learned from a previous teacher and most only needed reminding. But if they understood she really wanted to do a good job, make their lives one day become more than it would be on the reservation alone.

She took up the paper Elina had written about her hopes for her future. She'd now read this one several times. Elina was smart and wanted to learn more and more. She wanted to study at one of the universities when she was of age. What was to stop her from going to the university, save her parents hadn't the money and the color of her skin? She sighed. But she had money and lots of it. Perhaps when the time came, she could support Elina in her endeavors. Yes, if the girl’s parents would allow, she could see this fully happening and she’d gladly pay for all that was required.

But perhaps she was dreaming, as always, of a perfect world that would allow a Cheyenne girl to go to a white university to become a teacher like herself. While she’d never see anything at all wrong with that idea, the rest of the world would never accept it.

Had she not desired her own dreams of teaching children and worked hard for it she wouldn't be here now. Her pay for this job was low, but money wasn’t the reason she loved teaching. Her family had come from money though Timothy alone had left her rather wealthy. And yes, when the time came, she would help Elina if there were a way.

She sighed and laid the paper down and dipped her quill into the ink and opened her tablet to write another letter to her sister, though the single candle she’d lit wasn’t giving her enough light. She needed to buy another couple of lamps when she was in town.

She struck a match and raised the glass on the lamp and let the flame catch the wick. The cabin came aglow, and she dipped the quill once more into the ink and placed it to the paper.

My dearest Jacie,

I find myself at the first evening after finally settling into my new home where I have actual time to write a real letter. I realize weeks may have passed since my last letter that I left in some small town with the post after we left Cheyenne. So, I believe my letters are arriving to you out of order as I have already received a shipment of my things you sent.

The night is drawing to a close and I've lit a candle on my small table in the home I have been given. You must know this home is no prize. It's a cabin that upon arrival needed more than simple repairs. It was falling apart in shambles of barely four walls of which I have had to make repairs on my own except where a Cheyenne Man called Leaning Bear fixed my sagging porch and leaky roof. A very kind man who charged a fair price. While I was warned of the dangers of Indians, I have found those on the reservation to be a very kind people, staying most often to themselves. Leaning Bear is a medicine man, often caring for the Cheyenne and other tribes as well as the soldiers who fall ill.

So far, I have run off the racoon who was living in the mattress that remained here from the last teacher. I had to burn it out back as it was putrid with urine the creature had left behind. I have a new mattress that I purchased from the Trading Post and while it isn't any luxury it will do for a while. The mice are all but gone, though an owl who had taken up residence in the barn remains, I suppose causing little harm. I will certainly have to tell you the story of my arrival to my cabin on that first day, it must go down as the day of all days, and I realize I will laugh of that when I am an old woman.

I assumed an old mare called Millie, prior to arriving in Lame Deer. She pulls the buggy that is my only form of transportation to town and the reservation. She hasn't much of a personality, but she follows direction well and always enjoys her oats.

Lame Deer is anything but a formal town. It's streets of mud and most often men at their errands, is also full of men who fire their weapons at will harassing many in town. I have a mind to go to town when necessary and not on a scheduled basis. It seems the local saloon has more visitors than the bank or Mercantile, but Maud at the Trading Post seems to look out for me when I am there.

I know you worry, warning me of the dangers of this endeavor but besides one major buggy overturn, I am doing very well all things considered. The soldiers have been nice in caring for Millie. Captain Bartley has borrowed books for his wife to teach his two little girls and he is often by to see that I have what I need. A very kind man.

And now, several weeks into my teaching the children it is very apparent they are in need of many things. These children have so very little, yet they are happy. Some speak English very well, while I am teaching others the simple words first. One older girl even has her heart set on a university, such a smart girl, and eager to learn. Her name is Elina and she'd like to become a teacher. Perhaps you could check on this for me to see if acceptance might happen at one of the women's colleges. She is very bright, helping me to teach the other children and would be a very good teacher one day.

Two Doves is the name of the chief's wife, and she has been a great help to me in learning the Cheyenne Language while at the same time the children are learning English. I find this travel and settling in very much what I needed to find work that has some meaning. I still cannot explain why I needed to leave. There simply has to be more to this journey in life than living melancholy in Chicago alone. Here I have the beautiful scenery and enjoy the children though I do have to insist weekly that some return to school.

I have enclosed a list of the children's sizes and would like to purchase full school uniforms for each of the ten children, girls and boys. The standard uniform with stockings and boots for the boys and the girls' dresses with stockings and boots. I've been allowed no budget as of yet for this but will simply allow you to utilize from the funds I've keep there in the banks for the full purchase. Of course, I know this will take time, but I do think the children will benefit from being dressed properly for learning.

When you've the liberty, I would ask that you send my trunk of clothing and perhaps wait on the furniture I had set aside. As it is I suppose furniture would never make it this far. The stage runs through Lame Deer a few times a month and the nearest train is back in Cheyenne, and I cannot make such a journey any time soon. And there is no Law in Lame Deer to speak of, though there is an apothecary and a mercantile that has things the Trading Post doesn't.

And please know I miss you to no end. It seems long since we said our goodbyes at the train depot. And please give Easton and the children my love. I do promise to send a weekly letter as I can, but certainly once monthly if things become busier.

All the best and much love to you, Jacie. Please know I am well and indeed have made the right decisions.

Your loving sister, Alli

She laid her quill aside and laid the letter to dry. It wasn't a long letter but enough to keep her sister happy that she was well. The journey had been hard and the last days of making her home livable and working with the children had been hard but rewarding. She sipped the sweetened tea and glanced out the window, darkness complete. Tomorrow she'd make another trip into town for a few things.

Perhaps she hadn't told her sister everything, but she'd not have her worry any more than she probably already did. It was now in the lonesome of night that some of the ghosts of her past wanted to creep in. And why she let these things play again in her mind she wasn't sure. Timothy was gone, his illness taking him from the world and leaving her in the aftermath of his infidelity, of which she hadn't known.

"The wife is always last to know," she whispered. It was true she hadn't known, though all her husband's colleagues and the women she'd thought her friends had. Her life had been about money and things and people of prestige. "Friends indeed."

She shook her head. The last two years of getting over that and Timothy's death had been difficult but had also enlightened her to the idea of this journey. What other woman would have done this alone? What other woman had her own determination? And here she was. She'd make a life here or give it her best attempt. All back home, including her sister, probably thought she'd lost her ever-loving mind.

Maybe they were right, but again, she was proving nothing to any of them, save herself and look how far she'd come. Her long-gone father had once told her she'd go far in life, and look at her now. She smiled to herself and dimmed the lamp, taking her thoughts to her new bedding and dimming the lamp there. It sometimes took sleep a while to find her but tonight wouldn't be the case as she'd been yawning all evening. She turned to her side and pulled the blanket high, offering her prayers for the coming day, and closed her eyes.

Chapter Eight

Alli stepped into the Trading Post, her first visit in almost a month. She thought this hour was a better choice of time to avoid any more mishaps with the Baker brothers. Town was busy with wagons and men on horseback, but arriving early did seem best. Inside, several men and women lingered at their shopping. She closed the door, spotting Maud in the back speaking to two women as she eased closer. One woman wore a bonnet and fine dress of taffeta in pink, the other wore a similar dress in lavender, adding colors Alli hadn't seen in a long while.

While she had packed along two of her finer gowns, she'd not seen purpose to wear either of them. But she had brought a number of skirts and blouses of various colors from the finer shops back home. She glanced down at her clothing and touched the copper buttons of her long-sleeved white blouse that buttoned down the front. She hadn't met any other women from town save Maud who, well, was hardly classified under the title of lady. A bit of nerves fluttered through her middle as she approached, reminded quickly of the lady professors from back home who had more than betrayed their friendships.

Maud spat tobacco behind her into a tin on the floor and lifted her gaze. "Oh, Mrs. Crockett, I'd like for you to meet Mrs. Elizabeth Landers and Mrs. Arlene Rogers.

Ladies, Mrs. Crockett has arrived for a teachin' on the reservation. Been expecting a new teacher for some time now. She's arrived in from Chicago, and I hear she's doin' a fine job o' things."

As soon as Maud explained, the ladies eyed each other, smiles fading. Alli eased her hand back to the bag that hung over her shoulder giving Maud a quick glance of uncertainty.

"I can hardly imagine why any upstanding woman of society would arrive here for such work." Mrs. Landers looked her up and down, her bushy eyebrows wrinkling.

"I agree, the savagery of the parent passes right into those filthy children." Mrs. Rogers used her folded fan for a moment and closed it again. "Barbaric."

"I assure you nothing I've seen has been barbaric. Several of the older girls are very smart, reading at high levels and consuming the books I've brought along. Even the boys are very good at arithmetic and reading. Each of them has been eager to learn." How could these women think the children savages? She'd expected less prejudices here in the west than the ones that had lingered back home and this caught her somewhat off guard.

"Well, it won't do them any good, learning to read as if they will ever go any further than their current situation of belonging on the reservation." Mrs. Landers added, scoffing at the few dresses hanging on a nearby rack.

Alli gritted her teeth. How dare these women judge things they clearly didn't understand? Why was it she thought anything would be different here as compared to Chicago? Even her sister hadn't understood her reasons for wanting to teach the children who possibly needed her most. “I assure you I am teaching as proper as the classroom I maintained back home in Chicago with far more eager students on the reservation. I disagree that any child belongs behind fences placed by government authority.”

“Ladies…” Maud interrupted, clearing her voice. “I think we can all see that the children on the reservation deserve to get a right good education as much as any.”

Mrs. Rogers sneered. “I hope, Mrs. Crockett, you'll join us at services one of these Sabbaths, as well as Maud, who hasn’t been to services in some time.”

Maud shook her head. “I’ve a hankering for the lord, I can pray right here where I mind my business isn’t robbed when not looking, Ma’am.”

The ladies eyed each other, and Alli shook the feeling she was right back in Chicago once more. “Perhaps, once I’ve gotten better settled. There has been much for me to take care of since arriving.”

The women excused themselves but not before a last rude assessment of Alli.

“Best you stay clear of those two, as thick as vipers in a den of churchin’ thieves that’ll expect more and more money as you attend.” Maud warned her with a roll of her brown eyes, the chaw thick in her cheek. “I’ve your order in the sacks there. The sugar, flour, and dried beef.”

“Thank you, and could I have you mail this letter to my sister?” Alli asked, taking heed of Maud’s words about the women. “It’s probably going to need a bit of extra postage.” She’d sent Jacie a complete list of each child and their needs where clothing and boots were concerned. The costs would set her back, but she was sure it was best to have the children wear proper clothing to school so that they did view their learning as something important. “I’m having her order uniforms and send them here when she’s acquired them. Boots too, for the boys and girls.”

Maud took the letter, weighed it and placed a stamp and then another on it. “That’ll set you back two cents.”

Alli dug in her change purse and laid down the pennies. “Here you are.”

Maud placed the letter in the basket behind her. “Chief Dancing Fox won’t be a’kin to that idea I’ll be a bettin’. Seems another teacher tried the same with real clothes, but the families didn’t have no money for the purchase.”

Alli waited until the rotund woman turned back around. “I suppose I never asked the Chief, but I am paying for this myself. I won’t have the families pay for any of it. It's my schoolhouse and some of the children wear very little. Part of schooling can be proper dress, you know.”

“A might ornery chief Dancing Fox is.” Maud added with a shake of her head and a hit to the spittoon on the floor behind her.

“Well, then we shall see.” Alli’s pulse raced. She hadn’t thought uniforms to be an issue, in fact wouldn’t the chief be happy the children had brand new proper clothing? And she’d be sparing no expense in her purchases. She’d never even had a conversation yet with Chief Dancing Fox whom she had seen very few times.

“Come on and I’ll help ya’ load up.” Maud led the way outside and placed one of the two sacks inside her buggy and she added the one she carried beside it.

“Thank you, Maud. And I should also thank you for

having Leaning Bear work on my porch roof at the cabin. It makes the cabin have a much better appearance and no rain leaks to the roof so far, though he may do a few more repairs coming up soon."

Gunfire erupted down the road at the saloon causing Alli to duck behind the buggy and try to hang on to Millie who startled.

"Those blasted Baker boys." Maud ducked beside her. "Always up to no good, need a real sheriff here to lock them up for disturbing the peace on a regular basis. That and horse thieving, though no one dares to cross them."

"The same ones again who overturned my buggy when I first arrived?" Alli ducked farther as more gun blasts sounded and the whooping cowboys mounted their horses down the way at the saloon. "Horse thieves, but that's punishable by hanging in most states."

"Ain't no law here to enforce such. The one in the black hat is Leroy, the eldest, the other in the red shirt is Donald, and Pete is the youngest there in the white shirt." Maud explained, pointing a finger and spitting tobacco juice to the ground. "Best you stay away from the likes of them or their father Roy, biggest cheat to all in town running the saloon, like I told you, hide that money of yorn, don't use the bank here or you'll lose it all."

"I shant." Alli peeked over the buggy again, eyeing the men who were coming their way. Around them shopkeepers closed doors and the town cleared of people rather quickly.

Leroy blasted his gun and dismounted as Alli caught sight of Leaning Bear who was crossing the street. Where had he come from? She let her mouth drop open. She hadn't seen him in several days, not even when she was teaching.

"Lookie what we got here boys. It's Leaning Bear, the famous medicine man with his pardon paper from the official government." Leroy holstered his gun and stood before Leaning Bear, narrowing his gaze.

Pete laughed and gave Leaning Bear a kick as he sat his mount, pushing him back a step, though he held his ground. "You got papers to be off the reservation injun?"

"Maud they can't…" Alli wasn't sure what was happening in the harassment to Leaning Bear.

"Got any money on ya, you wanna run around town you gotta pay your way like all the rest." Donald stopped his horse, blocking Leaning Bear when he tried to step around them.

"Shhh, they won't hurt him, they're afraid of him on account of his pardon, right from the president. Long as he doesn't fight back, he'll be fine. They mostly leave him alone on account of it." Maud whispered grabbing her elbow to keep her behind the buggy. "Keep down."

Alli continued to watch, upset at the display. "Pardon?"

Maud nodded and spoke in a continued quick whisper. "Couple of years ago, Leaning Bear and a man he knows named Dawson McCade got accused of turning Dog Soldiers onto the cavalry killing some soldiers, only they didn't do it. Nearly faced a firing squad until a last-minute pardon came from President James Garfield himself. Leaning Bear got sent back here to the reservation, but word has it he can do as he pleases, don't have to have no permission like the others to be off the reservation."

Alli tried to take in the full story, but the harassment of Leaning Bear continued, her heart racing the same.

"No money. Let me guess." Leroy said in a shout as if wanting all who were watching to hear him. "He's in town all the time to work and never has any money, well, we're gonna have to charge you interest Leaning Bear. I don't know, some say you've a nice horse. You gotta horse, Injun?"

Leaning Bear didn't answer, keeping his eyes fixed on the man.

"Cat got your tongue medicine man?" Pete shoved once again with a kick though Leaning Bear didn't budge, glaring at the man.

Donald butted in. "Ahh, let him go boys, but you beware, we're watching, Injun and wherever you hide that money of yours, we'll find it sooner or later."

"Yeah," said Pete, egging things on further. "And I'll be sniffing out that horse real soon."

"Watch yourself, medicine man…come on, boys." Leroy mounted his horse once more and laughed as all three of them circled Leaning Bear leaving him covered in dust before they rode away from town.

Alli stood again, straining to meet Leaning Bear's gaze through the haze of dust.

"Jackasses." Maud commented. Spitting yet again. "Best you head back home before they return."

"Yes." Alli climbed into her buggy at the same time she met glances with Leaning Bear. But he turned toward the livery, making her wonder at the quick exchange between them. Was he embarrassed or angry? Wouldn't most men have fought back, but then he was Cheyenne, and it might be that fighting wasn't a good idea.

She glanced at Maud once more. "Why didn't he fight back?"

Maud stood erect again. "No use, Leaning Bear's

smart about things, if you don't play into their antics, the Bakers tire easily. Why he never rides that horse of his into town. They'd take it. And if he raised a hand to defend himself, they'd string him right up or beat him within an inch of his life 'cause he's Cheyenne. The Indians don't get much respect out this way, Ma'am."

"But isn't horse thieving a crime? Why can't the Federal Marshalls be called in?" Alli asked, knowing men were hanged for as much.

"It is unless your last name is Baker." Maud shook her head. "Why you hide things well at your cabin. I do the same. Roy Baker lets them sons of his run amuck causing all kinds of hardship on us all. I pay to be able to keep my store from being ransacked by them, no other option with no law. Only they want things and not my actual money mostly."

"Well, it's not right." Alli shook her head, holding the reins. "I'll see you soon, Maud. Please watch out for yourself as well."

"Yes'm." Maud hopped back up the stairs to the Trading Post.

Alli clucked her tongue, urging Millie toward home, thankful the Bakers had headed the other direction, though she worried about Leaning Bear. In town they were more aggressive, though when her buggy had been overturned, they had seemed to stop their antics quicker when Leaning Bear showed up. Maybe Maud was right that if the Bakers were ignored, they went on to other things.

She could imagine that it took great restraint for Leaning Bear not to fight, though she supposed he had little choice. And the story Maud told her about Leaning Bear's pardon made perfect sense. She'd seen him leave the reservation without stopping to check in with the soldiers like the others in the tribe were required to do. She supposed his life was full of surprises much like the various scars he'd decided to share in funning her a bit. Well, she had deserved that given her asking such personal questions of him.

But as it was, she was new here and many things were handled differently in the town of Lame Deer without any formal law. Millie pulled the buggy off the road and toward the barn, long used to arriving home where she'd be fed and was happiest in her stall. Alli glanced behind her once more, feeling as though she were being watched, given the scare with the Bakers, but they had turned the opposite direction. She climbed down from the buggy and made a full circle, unable to shake the feeling as she unhitched Millie and led her toward the barn.

And once again as she opened the barn doors, the owl swooped down at her and then out into the air toward the cabin.

"It was probably only you watching me anyway." She scolded the owl yet again. "Come along Millie. I have a bit of light yet to paint from the porch if I get you fed first."

****

Alli glanced at the darkening sky. Rain was sure, which ruined her plans to paint in the afternoon by the stream. The clouds were thick and dark, almost alarming in what would be a coming storm.

She lifted the basket of clothing she'd placed on the porch and dumped the items into the metal wash bucket of lye soap suds. Her morning had been spent collecting water from the stream, heating it on the hearth and adding it to the larger wash bucket she'd purchased from Maud. The same metal bucket she used for bathing each evening, which she relished. It was large enough for her to sit and soak but hardly the luxury of a real bathtub where she could stretch out in the warmth of water and soak for a while.

Thunder rumbled in the distance as she lifted the washing board and began with the bar of lye soap to wash several skirts, blouses, underclothing, and her teaching frock. She glanced at the owl who never failed to watch her at her duties around the cabin. She was getting used to it, as was Millie, who no longer startled at her warning swoops when they entered the barn.

"I see you watching me." She eyed the fowl as she dunked to rinse the blouse she'd just washed and scrubbed. "Might be if you are going to stick around, I should give you a proper name."

She soaped another shirt speaking to the creature that eyed her, unblinking. "And since I think you are a female, I shall call you…Annabelle. Because despite my annoyance, you are graceful and beautiful in flight."

The owl paid her no mind as she wrung the blouse she'd rinsed and turned back to grab another, scrubbing it across the board with effort. The clothes would dry by afternoon, and she could spend her evening ironing inside as the rains came, the iron already on the hearth to heat right near the pot of dumplings she'd started earlier.

"Oh no!" She'd forgotten the dumplings. She ran inside, grabbed a rag, and lifted the cast iron lid from the steaming pot. She stirred the contents, thankful they hadn't stuck, her belly giving a growl at the hearty aroma. She replaced the lid and touched the basket of morning biscuits still on the old stove to keep warm.

She'd have time for more wash, and then could enjoy her meal.

She turned back for the door but took a moment to admire her small cabin. It looked like a real home now. She'd washed the floorboards by hand, and it had taken almost a complete day, as had the walls. Soot had covered the fireplace and hearth and she'd spent several hours cleaning those to reveal gray rocks once again. She'd sewn curtains for the windows with material she'd gotten from the mercantile and the table cloth matched. Fresh flowers filled a vase any time she could find them.

She had gained the small desk from a family who needed to lighten their load of things going farther west. She could understand that, and she'd paid them more than its worth. And her bedding now included new blankets that Jacie had sent from home. Inside much of what was sent by her sister, cash and coins had been hidden and her sister had let her know the uniforms would be sent to her soon.

With a nod of satisfaction, she headed back out to the wash as thunder rumbled closer. She glanced at the barn where Millie was happy to stay for her days off from pulling the buggy to the reservation. Her habit of talking to herself had now come to having full conversations even with the old horse, but if she wanted to admit the truth, she'd always talked to herself. At times it had been her downfall and often enough it had been Timothy who shushed her out of necessity while he tried to read or study. Oh, he'd meant well enough most times, but how she missed having conversations with real people.

She grabbed another blouse and dunked it with the bar of lye and began scrubbing as Annabelle decided to hoot and fly from her roost as if startled.

Alli turned, catching the owl's flight over coming riders on horseback. Four to be exact and she instantly recognized Roy Baker and his sons. Yes. All four. She grabbed a cloth and dried her hands. The pistol was inside her bag in the cabin but there was little time.

She laid down the cloth and stepped up to the porch as the owl swooped back to the perch in the barn rafters. She'd not seen the brothers since her last trip to town but their arrival here was concerning.

She glanced at the shovel she'd leaned against the post at the porch steps. That might come in handy but…

"Morning, Ma'am." Roy Baker stopped his horse before her as his sons caught up one by one, almost right to her cabin.

She thought it best to add no hesitation or fear. "Morning."

"Mrs. Crockett. I'm Roy Baker and these are my sons." He glanced behind him where the men had stopped their horses and the one called Don held back with three riderless horses on a lead behind his own. And how did this man know her name as he'd spoken it, though talk in town was cheap she supposed.

"Got a couple of horses for sale Ma'am, and you being new to town thought you might be in need of a good animal. We'll make you a decent price. My understanding your horse is a bit old for its duties." He glanced her up and down and nodded toward her barn where Millie was in plain sight in her stall.

"I know who you are. I met your sons my first day arriving to town when they overturned my buggy with me in it. Thankfully, neither I nor my horse were harmed." She answered before thinking hard on if she should have said it or not given Leroy's frown.

"Awe, we were just' a funning' a bit, Ma'am." Leroy made an effort to explain, though it was his father he spoke to.

"I have a horse and won't be in need of another for the time being." She ignored the elder brother's ploy, looking back at their father.

Roy Baker turned to his sons, Pete's horse right beside his own. "You boys do what she said? Overturned her buggy?"

None of them answered.

"I asked a question!" He shouted so loud she gave a start and their own horses startled.

"Yeah." Don in the back spoke up.

Roy Baker scowled at each of them. "Apologize to the lady. Now!"

Leroy spoke, looking at her for a moment. "Sorry, Ma'am."

Don echoed the same, dropping his gaze.

When Pete said nothing, his father smacked the back of his head, his hat flying to the ground. "I said apologize to the lady."

Pete looked at her. "Sorry."

"You'll have to forgive my sons' manners, Mrs. Crockett." Baker moved his horse closer. "I raised 'em without a mama and they're plum hardheaded. And they do get into mischief now and again, but they don't mean no harm as you can see." The man made his excuses for what they had done that easy.

Alli folded her arms and took a step closer to the stairs, nearer to the shovel. "I appreciate your consideration of a horse, but I have no need. Apologies accepted if indeed sincere." She was all but unnerved by this entire exchange, her hands shaking, but she was not in need of a horse, and she would not back down from them like a coward.

“Like I said Ma’am they're boys, funnin’, when they should be working.” He eyed her cabin. “Who repaired your porch? Thought that was gonna fall in any time. Ya, know we do work as such too.”

“That'd be Leaning Bear, Pa. Seen him here couple times in passing.” Leroy spat tobacco to the ground and wiped his chin.

Mr. Baker glared her way again as rain began in hard drops. “That right, Ma'am? You paying that crazy injun to help you?”

Alli waited a moment. “Yes, he has completed the porch and repairs to the roof. And yes, he was paid for his work if it is any of your concern.” Without a doubt she should not have been so bold, but she would not be pushed around.

He leaned on the saddle horn, and she thought he might laugh but he focused hard on her, narrowing his brows as water ran off the rim of his hat. “Mrs. Crockett, it'd be very wise not to pay him for further work. Most don't abide much about Indians like Leaning Bear showing in town. Best to keep them Indians on the reservations where they belong or in no time, we’ll have them all over if we don't already have too many. Run off a couple this morning. Nothing but drunks, most of them.”

“As I've said I have no need of another horse at this point. And I have wash to do. Good day to you.” She had dealt with their same kind back in Chicago. Maud had filled her in on Roy Baker and his sons and to her best figuring, standing up to them would keep them away.

“You’ll wanna heed my advice, Ma’am. Good day

to ya." He nodded, turned his horse and his sons followed, Pete giving her a smirk his father didn't see.

Alli waited until she could no longer see them before she took a deep breath and tried to calm her nerves. Others hired Leaning Bear as he stayed busy through Maud's sales of lumber, and he sold his herbs to the lady at the apothecary each week. She'd not heed such advice. And she would not purchase a stolen horse from these men.

She turned back to her wash as the rain picked up, her hands still shaking. She'd stood up to the Bakers but wasn't sure that was a good idea after all. She didn't sell in town. She taught the children on the reservation. It's a good thing she'd hidden her money where she thought no one would look, a suggestion from her brother-in-law, Easton. He'd offered her all sorts of hints about her existence out west before her travels. She'd taken great steaks to hide a tin of her money inside the outhouse on a small ledge she had nailed under the seating to the left, where no one would wish to even look.

She soaped and scrubbed her brown skirt and worked it on the board. Trying to calm herself, she rinsed it several times and then hung it to dry along with others. But glancing around again, she had the feeling of still being watched.

Surely, with the rain becoming heavier the Bakers wouldn't return, would they? And now she had a mind to keep the pistol with her when working outside her home or when she went to paint at the stream. Not that she understood much about how to use it. Maybe practice was in order, and she'd see to that soon.

A stronger feeling of being watched made her stand erect away from the wash. She searched the landscape from one side of the porch to the other, settling that she had let the Bakers upset her and nothing more. Yes, that was it. She began the rest of the wash, not allowing it another thought. This was her home now and she would have to be brave about it all.

Chapter Nine

Leaning Bear shivered as he sat on Paytah in the depth of the forest outside the teacher's home. He had been waiting and watching since Roy Baker and his sons had come into view while he was hunting. They had not seen him but when they did not turn for town, he suspected they were headed to Allison Crockett's cabin. Their harassment would end up with each new person arriving in Lame Deer if they stayed for any time, and it was clear that they had not forgotten her.

He left his hunt to follow the men without their knowing. And it would be that some things never changed, like his recent skirmish with them in town. It was not the first and it would not be the last, given there was no law in Lame Deer. The cavalry had no claim to the law of those in town and were of little help. Fighting with the men would only prove to harm the tribe in the long run but the men were not interested in what little money he made. They were most interested in Paytah, as the painted horse would bring them a nice price.

The harassment from the Bakers for most was accepted, money paid for merchants to sell their products. Those that did not pay were beaten or the Bakers took their merchandise, leaving them no way to make their living. Many times, he found ways to avoid them, but his work in town did not always allow that. More than once, he wanted to raise a fist, but that would not be the answer. He owned guns, well hidden, but the use of them was forbidden for the tribes. An Indian carrying a pistol or revolver was a dead man. He did not fancy swinging by a rope around his neck. Having come close to facing a firing squad had changed his thoughts on his wanting to live his life.

But on this day, he followed to keep Alli Crocket safe and nothing more. One son carried the leads to three horses that did not belong to any of them. The men had been at the art of taking horses and selling them elsewhere for profit and no white law had done anything about it. Even now and again, horses went missing from the soldiers on the reservation, but nothing had been proven. He suspected the captain did not want to deal with Roy Baker by making accusations. It was why he often paid Hawk to watch Paytah when left in the reservation pastures. The boy enjoyed having a bit of money for the work of feeding and caring for the horse in his absence as work took him away.

But now as the teacher went back to her wash, he continued to watch her. It was not a day for school, and she hummed along with her actions, her voice coming to him in spite of the sound of rain along the leaves and grass before him. She was graceful in her movements. Tall and slender. He should have done the repairs to her roof prior to the rain. He grumbled to himself. This should not be his thoughts of seeing her again or his worry of how many days. No…he should urge Paytah away for good. Not to look back.

She had taken a stance against Roy Baker, but not making the purchase of a horse angered the man more. At best she had stirred a viper's den. Crossing Baker was not wise for any. He should think of some way for the white teacher's protection, though he could not always know what the Bakers were up to. He was sure that the white teacher had money, a lot of money given her fine clothing, but what was obvious to him had mostly likely been obvious to the Bakers.

A dog. Yes. She would have benefit of warning and protection with such an animal. He would find her a pup. One that could be trained and trusted. He nodded to himself, as thunder rumbled closer. He turned the horse without a sound and let the animal have his own pace. He made a wide berth around Alli's cabin and toward his camp in the trees. Today was rain. No work would be done. And in his thoughts the white teacher held her space in his mind…a place he should not allow her to stay.

****

The morning sun had welcomed Alli to her Saturday of painting beside the stream. She sat at her canvas with another week of school complete. She was free to paint, all but the darn blue sky it seemed. She scoffed at herself and removed the ribbon from her hair allowing it to fall free across her shoulders.

Funny, her mother would scold her for allowing the sun to her ivory skin, but she relished the freedom of the warmth anyway. Later she'd also removed her boots and let her feet soak in the cool of the river while she painted. Well, if she continued this painting of which the sky might never receive any color. The neigh of a horse turned her.

"A-ho." Leaning Bear dismounted Paytah and in the crook of his arms was a puppy. At first glance a wolf pup, shepherd appearing with grays and browns.

She hadn't seen him in a number of days, and he still

needed to see to her roof as with the recent rains she'd kept pots and pans all over her cabin to catch the water drips.

"A-ho." She used her new knowledge of the Cheyenne language Two Doves was teaching her. "What on earth do you have there?" She put her brush down and stood, walking toward him.

He met her gaze for a long moment, almost as if something was wrong but then placed the puppy on the ground at his feet. It whimpered and sat on its hind legs.

She eased a little closer and bent, waiting.

"This for you." Leaning Bear nudged the pup who scampered up and began sniffing the grass and wandering toward her.

"I hardly need a dog…in fact or a wolf." She protested, though she did like animals, as proof Millie becoming her new best friend.

"Part wolf, yes." Leaning Bear folded his arms. "For protect teacher."

"It's a puppy, more that I would be protecting it for now." She bent and the pup licked her palm.

"Pup grows fed by your hand. Will protect in short time." He wore no shirt, a beaded necklace, and pouch hanging around his neck and resting on his chest. She'd more than become used to half-dressed men of the reservation but she dropped her gaze for the moment. And as much as she shouldn't think it, he was very handsome. His features strong, his hair banded in one braid behind him, accenting his face. He had high cheek bones and a strong jawline, and his skin was bronze and as smooth as the sand at the edge of the creek.

She shook her head. "Why would you think I need a dog for protection…wait a minute. You saw the Bakers come by here, didn't you?" She wasn't sure how she knew that but her sixth sense had let her know even after the Bakers were gone someone had been watching her.

"It is as you say."

His honesty didn't surprise her but how would he have known otherwise? The idea he was looking out for her warmed something inside her that had long been vacant, and her pulse raced at the idea. How had he known the Bakers were coming? Had he watched her all those times she'd known someone was near?

"But why would you do that? For me?" She waited though somehow the heart in her chest shifted a size larger as his dark eyes told the truth of it.

"I see Baker and sons come this way."

For a long moment her emotions held, and she fought tears. He had been her protector and she'd known the full time of his presence in doing so. But while her pulse had raced at the Baker's arrival, she was not going to allow them to scare her. "I'm not afraid of them. I won't let them force me to pay or purchase from them."

It was rare he showed emotion, but his brows narrowed. "No fear, not wise."

Alli shook her head, giving it some thought. "I saw when they harassed you in town. Why doesn't anyone do something or contact the law or federal marshals or for goodness' sake we have the cavalry right here?" The pup rolled at her skirts, chewing at the laces of her boots as she sat again.

He glanced away and then back to her. "If I fight, might hang by rope or die by gun. This not good for tribe. Less medicine and food in winter. My anger I must control for now until it is not time to be in control. That day will come too."

"Maud said they won't hurt you on account of your pardon." The moment she mentioned it, she thought perhaps she shouldn't have, because his gaze narrowed hard on her.

He moved away, walked to the edge of the water, and after a moment turned back to her. "You have no understanding of this." His tone didn't change and his words were stronger.

"No, but enlighten me. Why is this allowed for these men to cause such havoc for everyone in town and no one is at liberty to stop it?" She lifted a brush and set it aside again and stood once more. "I want to understand."

It was another long moment before he spoke as a lot of the time he seemed to think hard about his word choices. "My world is much different from yours."

She waited, not saying anything more.

"Pardon is good and pardon is bad." He frowned and gave a slight shrug. "Pardon was to free me from firing squad. Now I must carry paper to say I have freedom. Pardon sent me here to this reservation with my brothers who have not the same freedom. Pardon separates me from white men. Pardon separates me from men of tribe. Pardon is my fencing."

She took a step closer thinking she understood. "A blessing and a curse, then."

"It is as you say." His tone softened as did his gaze.

Now she understood more. Somehow, he was caught in the middle of two worlds, neither one of which she could understand. He had a pardon, but he was still confined to the reservation for the most part except for his work, and yet he had freedoms his own people didn't have. She shouldn't have asked so personal a question once again. "I'm sorry, but I'm glad you could share that with me."

"No apology needed." He walked back to his horse, who nudged his shoulder.

"It's been years since I've had a dog." It was but a whisper lest he know of the tears she was trying to avoid. She bent and the pup came to her again chewing at her boot laces, then rolling to her back.

"A female." She glanced at him.

"Makes better companion. Male will wander." He folded his arms and if she wasn't mistaken, almost smiled. How quick his mood and voice could change.

"But where did you get her?" she asked, having no idea if this was a good thing or not in thinking about having a dog. She had a lot in keeping up her cabin and Millie along with her teaching, but a dog would be a lot of company she supposed.

"Sioux woman raises pups each season. Litter three moons. Pup will eat food you provide now. She should eat after you have eaten and when given permission to eat. She should sleep by your bed. Once she grows, she will protect. She must go where you go." He explained as he moved a bit closer, dropping the rope to Paytah who stayed in place.

Alli allowed a deep breath as he sat on the rocks near where she painted. So, he must be planning on staying for a moment. She walked back to her canvas and sat in her folding chair. The pup followed, still interested in her laces. She lifted her brush, still thinking on their conversation and the words that were not spoken. Could he have feelings for her as she seemed to for him, where her thoughts at night would always wander to him?

She dipped the brush as the pup trotted to the stream and drank laps of the cool water. "She was thirsty." She stroked yellows into the leaves of a tree at the far edge of her painting, while at the same time watching the puppy chase a butterfly.

"Did you name her? She'll need a name," she asked though she didn't look at him and focused on the canvas.

"No name." He answered as he used a small knife from his burlap bag, to clean his nails.

"Well, I shall think of something fitting. Or should you help me with a Cheyenne name? Do the Cheyenne name their pets? Your horse is named," she asked as she added more paint to the brush.

He nodded, sticking the knife back into the bag. "It is as you say."

"What name then?" She asked the question to herself.

The puppy walked over and lay in the middle of the ferns beside her, chewing at the swatches of long stems of small green leaves. "She seems to like the ferns well enough so how about Fern?" She leaned to rub the pup's head and the animal rolled over once more causing Alli to giggle. Maybe she did need a puppy, as it had been a while since she'd heard the sound of her own laughter. Except for when she was with the children.

"Is good name." He stood and reached for Paytah's reins once more.

"I'll see if I thank you later if she sleeps at night." Alli lifted the pup into her lap. "And doesn't chew my cabin apart."

"Keep pup busy day time. Pup sleep at night." He tugged the horse crossing the stream and the pup whined and tried to wiggle from her, though she took a good grip.

"Leaning Bear?" She waited until he glanced at her.

"I thank you for caring enough to watch out for me and even to bring me the pup to make sure."

He shrugged and changed the subject and this time he did show a slight curl to his upper lip. "You still not paint the sky." The echo of his continued laughter lingered behind as he disappeared over the rise, likely amused at making light of her once more.

The pup whined again but settled in her lap with Leaning Bear gone. "Don't worry, I have the strong feeling we'll see him again very soon."

She stroked the brush again letting her mind wander. No, she hadn't painted the darn blue sky, but she would. And while she hadn't planned on a puppy, Fern would be a bit of company for her evenings and when she painted. She supposed he was right that the pup would protect her by at least warning her of someone's presence.

But she couldn't stop thinking that it had been he who had watched her. He was Cheyenne and she was a white woman and their worlds clashed in uneasiness around them. Any thoughts she had of him wouldn't be allowed, would they? But the exchange between them had happened and now what was she to do, knowing a bit of truth in her heart about him, allowed or not. Of all things she smiled and placed the brush dipped in blue to the canvas. "Yes, Fern, I do believe we'll see him again very soon."

Chapter Ten

Leaning Bear glanced into the sky and back to the trail before him. It was early and not a day for school as the children had been playing loudly, waking him early. He paced along the stream, leaving his camp in the trees, where he had slept the night before in order to escape the remarks of Dancing Fox. His chief and cousin had noted his fondness for watching the teacher at her work. Yet here he was, headed right for the place he was sure she would be found.

He stepped across the narrow part of the stream and already the sound of her humming filled the air. And then as it would happen, the pup gave a barking growl, warning her of his presence. Now is when he was aware he should have had that conversation with his own mind of not seeking out the teacher since she would not be teaching.

"She's learning." Alli smiled and continued her painting and his breath held for the slightest moment at her beauty.

He bent as Fern raced to him and rolled to her back. He gave the pup a good rubbing glad to let go of his current thoughts. "Good she already warns of stranger."

"You are not a stranger, to her or I." She stroked the brush across the canvas as he stepped closer, followed by the pup who lay down again at her feet. That was a good thing, this dog already taking to her.

He took his usual place at the nearby rocks, which also allowed him a view of her work on the canvas. But sitting there were a tablet and chalks she must have placed.

He remained quiet watching how her hand moved across the canvas with a simple stroke of ease.

“You knew we’d be here?” She focused on her work.

“It is as you say.” He inhaled a deep breath and studied the light color of the braid falling down her back. It was as if the white morning sun had touched it to make the colors swirl with the darker strands of yellow. And this was not what he should allow of his mind, nor should he wish to touch as he did.

She glanced around them as she brushed a stroke of green grass to the corner of the canvas. "You were right, Fern has been a lot of company for me, and the children adore her. I brought those for you, the tablet and chalk, as you said you liked to draw.”

The length of her skirt covered her ankles though her bare feet touched the edge of the stream, her toes wiggling. She was unique, he supposed in that she had no fear of things most women would hold, himself included.

He lifted the tablet, thumbing through it. The best he’d ever drawn on was a single piece of paper and ink or a pencil. “Much appreciate.”

Real paper and his memory triggered a thought he’d never shared with anyone else. “Gift of paper tablet from Dawson long ago, many drawings inside.”

“I’d love to see if you could share it one day.” She smiled at him and went back to her canvas. Her ease at this pushed a warmth through his center. A comfort in being near her was what he had come to expect. And yes, he was indeed a fool.

"It was lost to soldiers when I was jailed. Not returned." He confessed, the loss of it not as painful as many things lost in his life.

She stopped painting and a frown covered her face, her voice soft. "I'm sorry."

"It is the way of things." He had thought of the tablet little over the years.

"That doesn't mean it's right." She continued to paint. The puppy whimpered at her side, and she reached into one of her bags and held up a piece of jerky. The dog sat, her tail thumping the ground. "Good, Fern, very good."

The puppy wandered off with its morsel and Alli spoke again. "If I may ask, what happened about your pardon, I mean, how did a pardon come to both you and Dawson? What really happened. I've told you I never stop talking or asking questions I probably shouldn't."

He gave a moment of thought for his best answer. "Medicine Man and Dawson meet for treaty negotiations. Always lies from government but important to be there. Listen what Cheyenne and all nations hear from government that can be given to tribes. Promises written on paper many times are not given in truth. Dawson makes sure of this."

"So, he translated?" She asked as she picked up her brush again.

He drew his knife and began to sharpen one of the chalks, the scrape across sounding of metal with each stroke and a reminder of the scars left by their brutal treatment. "Dawson speak Cheyenne. Knows language I taught him as young man. Smart. Very smart to negotiate more than would be promised. Fights hard for little."

He pressed a thumb to test the point and continued. "Dog soldiers not with tribe since many years, but band attacked soldiers and captain points finger to Medicine Man and Dawson. He said we planned this attack which was not true. Only choice to flee. Dawson injured with arrow of Dog Soldiers, not of tribe fighting alongside cavalry. Not good even long after pardon. Sickness in the wound almost take his life."

She painted a few strokes but then looked at him and searched for the pup that came ambling back toward the stream.

"Better now. Dawson and Medicine Man beaten by soldiers many times. Then government says trial for prove innocents." He shook his head. "No government trial proves this. Not for Cheyenne, not for white men who help all tribes. Dawson's family wealthy. Fight with lawyer from New York. End of trial both to face soldiers firing squad anyway, no matter money." Talking of this time increased the beating of his heart. He had never spoken of it to anyone except Dawson until now. As it was, he could hear the crowds and the drums as he and his brother had walked to their fate. "We walk to firing squad in chains. But Haven brings injured General and pardon is granted and truth is told."

"Dawson's wife?" She asked.

"Yes." He shook his head. "But not wife yet. Medicine Man escorted by cavalry here, not given choice."

"But the soldiers here, they let you come and go as you please like you said." She painted another few strokes and glanced at him.

"Still have to carry paper of pardon to be allowed

this. You see reservation. It is fenced. Braves are not free to hunt and provide for families. Little promised rations come." He took a deep breath and let it out. "Sometimes freedom does not mean free. My brothers are not free. The children you teach are not free. I am not free."

She held his gaze for a long moment as if she were choosing her words with care. "That is why I teach them. So maybe something they have learned from me will make their lives easier where they are accepted and can trade in the towns and can lead lives on the local farms as some do without being harassed. I have always found my teaching for a cause was of much more value than not. If one child finds his or her way to a better life, I'd like to think what I have taught has helped that happen."

Her voice broke and he suspected she might have fought tears as women would do. Her words were true for her but he had doubts much would change for the tribes any time soon. He did not need to tell her that now. Her passion for the children was good for them day to day. And he would not change her thoughts on that.

He blew the chafe from the chalk and opened the tablet and began sketching the pup as Alli continued to paint. The quiet surrounded them and when he was finished, he closed the tablet as she lost herself in her work. But he didn't look at the art she created. He watched her slender fingers. And the movement of her hand and arm and the way her face changed depending on the way she stroked and how she angled her head to see the colors better.

His time here should be done. His day of work should have already begun. He stood and the pup ran to him, jumping for attention. He bent and pushed the dog's rump until it sat. He spoke to her in Cheyenne and her ears perked. She returned to Alli.

"What did you tell her?" Alli stopped painting. "She came right over."

He stood upright again and lifted the tablet and placed it and the charcoal tin into his bag with herbs he'd picked on the way. "Remind her to protect teacher."

"Me?" She patted the dog's head. "She understands your language then."

He turned to go, looking back at her. "She understands hand that feeds her."

****

Leaning Bear had not returned to the reservation the night before, but instead had slept at his camp in the trees. It was easy for him to know why, as his thoughts seldom left Allison Crockett. Time talking with her stayed with him, long after their conversations. The comfort of her was something he had never held in his life.

He had left his camp behind at dawn and watched the reservation. He could return with ease, right through the front gates but then he'd be questioned and released a short time later. This he didn't wish. Too much of his time was already wasted on the requirements of the soldiers and government.

The captain had made the request he submit a written plan for each week. He wrote the same one each week and never followed that plan, though little in questioning had come. Why write the notes if they were not being reviewed for him to be questioned? It was as if the captain was seeking his help in appeasing his own soldiers to allow the freedoms of his pardon without scrutiny. He preferred his days of work as he decided and liked the idea of changing plans when he wanted.

Some inward part of himself, his very totem, the mountain lion, had been wise enough to remain silent at his transgressions of living on the reservation, but there were times he paced like a caged cat. He was not free. He studied the soldiers in the distance and made his way to the Eastern fencing, quiet as he navigated the dense wooding. He lifted the fence post, stepped through, and replanted the post, not having taken his horse the night before.

The day had already begun for the reservation. The children were in school as their laughter was audible and the women were in the gardens with their tools and baskets. Men tanned hides and worked to continue building more housing that his people did not want to live inside. But the soldiers pushed for this each day. Orders from white officials who had never been West.

He walked past Dancing Fox, who was bent at an elk hide he'd taken weeks before. It lay stretched over the ground, tacked in place and his brother was adding salt once more to dry out the hide.

The Chief spoke as his shadow passed. "You delay more each day on your return."

Leaning Bear ignored the remark and continued to his small camp in the shade of two large trees. Stepping near his lodge he lifted the cloth bag from across his shoulder, reaching in to extract the contents. He laid out several pieces of willow bark he had taken from a grove of trees along the river, south of the reservation. It was at the river he collected watercress and several horsemint growths. He laid each section across a drying cloth in the sun.

Giggles and laughter from the children turned him from his work. The teacher stood before them, holding up pictures of various animals and she was speaking the name in English and the children were teaching her the Cheyenne words. She had found a way to capture their attention with her many school supplies. She handed each of the children paper and a brush and explained they should paint one of the animals of their choice.

He glanced back at the herbs, focusing to press the leaves apart for better drying, though he watched her again as she spoke to the children about the details of their painting. She was animated explaining the use of mixing colors. Her hair was pulled high on her head, and she wore a smock to cover her clothing in protection of the brilliant colors the children used to paint. Her voice echoed across the camp and had caught the interest of the families too. Each time the children laughed, the mothers and some fathers glanced that direction. This was much different than usual teachers. He supposed laughter was good for all.

The last teacher had been one who wished to push her religion onto the children with corporal punishment. *Spare the rod, spoil the child* had not been accepted as popular and even the soldiers gave up on getting the children to class. That the teacher had moved along had also seemed of relief to Captain Bartley, who was tired of being caught in between the tribe and the causes of spreading a religion they did not understand.

He folded his arms, his bag now emptied of herbs. Allison Crockett was smart to find the children's interest and the adult's respect, even if for her first efforts. There had been no white teacher in the pavilion for many moons and her arrival would be of interest for a time. Acclimating the children to the White man’s ways gave the government hope for more power over the tribes. It was the reason teachers were paid to teach the children on reservations.

Maybe he understood the need for this more than most of his Cheyenne brothers due to his time spent with Dawson McCade and his family. It was inevitable that all the tribes acclimate into a white world or nothing would change inside these fenced borders for generations. But it did seem the white government was determined to make he and his Cheyenne brother's farmers, and saw little that they were hunters and gatherers.

He hung his canvas bag on the nail in one of the trees, but the children laughed again and when he glanced back, he met Alli's gaze. It was her smile that turned him away. It would not be good that they were thought of knowing each other except for his work on her cabin, of which he had a bit more to do.

"Painting on paper, a white man's waste of schooling time." Dancing Fox's voice turned him.

He glanced at the children again and back to his cousin, six years younger than himself but raised as his brother. "Laughter for any child is good."

"Maybe your time away has gone to your head, agreeing once again with the whites." He angled his jaw in challenge.

He turned to face his brother. It would come. The fight between the two that had yet to surface since his return after his pardon. It was always the same. Dancing Fox was made chief by their grandfather even though he was younger. Leaning Bear had accepted that long ago, but it seemed his brother still tried to prove his worth on the point over and over.

"Perhaps it is as you say." He turned back to his

work but not without another glance at the woman teacher who again laughed with the children.

His own totem was conflicted. His grandfather had known this and pushed him toward learning with the old Medicine Man. He shook his head. The chief would never understand it happened as it should have. He would always be competing in trying to prove this to himself.

He lifted an elk antler he had been shaving with a blade to make a knife handle.

"Your eyes stray often to the white teacher." The chief had not walked away as he should have.

He glanced away from the school with a calm ease. "My eyes stray to many things within these fences." They spoke in their native tongue and his brother gave a grunt of denial.

Dancing Fox stepped closer glancing at the school. "This teacher brings the same as all. A promise to teach our children how to become white and with that wear white clothing which I have halted."

He had expected as much. His brother would not care for any decision Allison Crockett made.

The chief glared at him. "And what good comes of this as always before every teacher finds her way back East. No white teacher finds this place any better than do we."

"Maybe in time, the children will be able to do more than stay on the reservation." He added his thoughts though he did not think any of this would happen soon or even in their lifetimes.

"Now you speak like Dawson McCade." The chief's tone held resentment. That he carried a depth of respect he would never admit for Dawson, but at the same time resented that Leaning Bear called the white man brother.

"I would take that as an honor. The fight is done. More will only bring bloodshed as it still does many places. Give a little. Take a little of the white man's ways. The generation of children now will face greater hardships than the ancestors before us as Dawson has often reminded us." Leaning Bear spoke in support of the one man he could call brother.

The chief glanced at the school again with the laughter of the children and the teacher along with them. "Maybe you have forgotten the cries of the dead, those who fought to keep our land and way of life. Weren't you close enough to death in the hands of our white government?"

Leaning Bear's pulse raced. He had no fear of Dancing Fox. But the mention of his capture…moons behind him, drew him back for a moment to his fate. He had almost faced death, and that changed a man. Something the chief was little to understand.

"A white woman is only trouble for you. And the soldiers watch you too. They watch her closely also. Tread with care, older brother." Dancing Fox walked back to his work.

Leaning Bear shaved at the antler once more. If he had been a younger man, he would have raised a fist to his brother as he had on a number of occasions, in their youth. There was no fight left for him inside this cage. But that was what made him see the hope for the children of the tribes in acclimating little by little to the white man's world. If they didn't then this was all there was—wire fencing and gates, nothing more to offer hope.

But his brother had not taken long to figure his ideas about the teacher. And this was not good. She was the reason he stayed outside the reservation the night before. He followed her to make sure she arrived at her cabin after leaving the reservation later than usual. Then he waited until she completed her chores and went inside before he gave in to heading to his camp in the trees.

He did this because she was not protected except by the pup, he did this because it was some part of his duty, and he did this because he had become helpless not to. He continued with the antler but the children laughed again and he was caught up once more in watching her teach. Yes, he was showing himself again that he was all but a fool. The chief had figured that too, but no matter, he could not keep his thoughts from Allison Crockett no matter how hard he tried.

Chapter Eleven

Leaning Bear sat on the rocks in the shade as Alli stroked across the canvas, her toes in the water at the stream and the sunlight across her features. It was early afternoon, and the sun was intense except where a soft breeze lifted the heat from the sweat of his skin. Beside her, Fern lay in a patch of sunlight sleeping with her muzzle on her paws. Already the pup had figured Alli to be her master.

"And what of your family?" Alli sat in her folding chair and continued painting with her multiple questions for him. He suspected her becoming accustomed to allowing him thoughts prior to speaking, even though she could talk faster than any woman he had ever conversed with.

Why did she wish to talk of so many things? Yet some part of him wanted the conversations she led him to, even if to hear her voice, a lower pitch for a woman, a tone that was pleasant. He continued to use the small knife to sift through the dried petals of flowers keeping the seeds in his hand and tossing the crackled dry leaves to the ground.

It occurred to him he had never shared many things of his past with anyone except for Dawson on occasion. He sprinkled the seeds into his bag and held the small knife tighter as he thought of his brother and the hunt that would come when the weather hinted at winter.

"Have not much memory of mother. Was young when sickness takes her." He had in fact been at the small age of what he thought was two or three years. He could not be sure. "I remember warmth of embrace. I remember softness and music she would hum as she held me still finds me sometimes. Songs the women still sing when they are to their work."

"Oh…Leaning Bear, that's sad, but the music must be nice when it finds you as you say." She whispered, stopping her painting and glancing at him. "And your father?"

"Father wounded in fight with soldiers when I was ten years. Died two days." The memory of his father was at times painful, but most often held admiration. His father had been much like the grandfather who had raised him, and both had been men to admire.

She glanced away but not before he saw the tears collecting in her blue-eyed gaze. It was strange how such a strong-willed woman could succumb to tears, though she brushed them away as if she wanted him not to see.

"No need for sadness. Was raised by grandfather and women of tribe all share children." He never dwelt long on the losses in his life. There was little point in doing so. "Father had good life. Good death."

She dabbed at her eyes with her fingers and smiled. "I am still sorry that you had them no longer. Your grandfather raised you and him together. Two Doves mentioned this to me."

He took a depth of breath. Two Doves was young. But she would know from her husband things of the past, where his uncle, Dancing Fox's father, had also died during the wars with white men. "It is as you say."

"And Dancing Fox is chief but not you, and you're

older she said." She settled her hand back to the canvas stroking in tiny swipes of high grasses.

"He becomes chief because of grandfather, Stalking Eagle." It was the best he could offer to her on how the placement for chief was made. "Not done by age, done by what is best for tribe."

"So, your people didn't want you to be chief?" Her light brows furrowed, and he caught himself in the depth of her blue eyes. Like a crystal lake as if he could swim in the ocean he had only seen once. Like the sky she had not painted on her canvas, her eyes held the truest of blue.

"Grandfather does this for reason I understand. He knew my interest in plants and medicine. That I cared little to lead, but more wanted to roam free of tribe's dependence. It is as it should be. Dancing Fox will see this more as he grows in age. His anger is short lived most days."

"But you were not like that at all? Carrying anger? I suppose it would be fair if you had because of your losses." She stopped painting and returned to it again.

How did she see the things he had not spoken in full? And how did he explain what had caused him turmoil all his life? "Father gives my child the name of the mountain lion that brought the squalls of a cougar to our lodge when I was born. This cat still comes in spirit to me. *Nanose'hame.*"

"*Nanose'hame*?" She fluffed her skirt and leaned back to view him better, trying her best to say the Cheyenne word.

"I would wake when small. Want to run outside. When older, almost a man, I took my dance with the sun. It was the bear who fought the big cat to claim my totem as his own. I was then called Leaning Bear. But the spirits brought a storm, and I remained ill for many weeks and the mountain lion still holds me." He suspected it to be confusing for her. Most times he stayed tangled in his own mind of it.

Alli stroked the brush across the canvas streaking the stream a deeper green. She was aware Leaning Bear watched as he often did when he sat on the rocks near her. He'd gone quiet as maybe she'd asked too many questions or things he was not comfortable with sharing. "I think I've the colors right for the stream."

"Color rich. Like water." He moved closer though he continued to scrape a piece of willow bark into a small pouch using a very large knife.

She turned to look at him, but he studied her canvas closer.

"Every tree in place. Every rock in place. Why not sky have color of today?" He moved beside her on the closer boulder, pushing her box of paints aside. He touched the canvas where it remained as when she'd purchased it, white.

She stroked at the river again. "I never seem to get the sky as it should be. The colors can be vivid sometimes that I mix the blues too dark or too light."

He shrugged. "Easy. Paint sky color of eyes."

Pink shaded her cheeks as she held his gaze for a long moment. The color of her eyes? Had he offered her that? Her breath held short as he didn't glance away but seemed to study what her eyes held as he leaned ever closer. Was he going to kiss her? Did she somehow long that he did?

He jerked up his arm holding the knife's blade as a mirror before her face, and she held still in spite of the startle. "Find color of eyes. Paint the sky."

She lifted a tentative hand and touched the metal, but he drew the weapon back from her as if she were a child.

"Very sharp." The depth of his warning vibrated through her as he stayed so close to her.

Fern, who had been sleeping at her feet, yapped at him for the quick movement but stayed where she was.

He reached for the linen tissue from her lap and tossed it into the air and turned the knife blade up before her. The tissue fell across the blade and shredded a clean cut, two pieces falling to the earth by the pup. Alli's breath held as the moment stilled between them. Had he wanted her to know how sharp the blade was, or did he want to be this close to her, to see the depth of her eyes himself?

"Oh my…" She let the whisper escape her as he moved ever closer to her. He was going to kiss her. She closed her eyes for the impact that never came. She blinked as he bent past her and lifted the pieces of the tissue and placed them into her palm.

Oh, men were so fickle. Why didn't he do it? Kiss her with some kind of reckless passion that without a doubt she would accept, regardless of their differences. She sucked in a breath she'd forgotten to take. And before she could take another breath he was gone, disappearing into the woods that always brought him on a soft wind. She glanced around wondering how he could be so elusive…light-footed and quiet as to shrink from all existence in a single breath of seconds. The trees behind him never even moved, the wind still.

She touched a finger to lips that still tingled in anticipation of his touch. And yet she understood it was forbidden that he should ever touch her as she longed. Like it or not he was an Indian and she was a white woman. They both knew better. And what of Timothy? How did he always surface even though he was gone and her memories of him tarnished by his infidelity?

But she was certain, based on the way Leaning Bear had looked at her, that he held the same feelings and thoughts. And wouldn't the town folk or soldiers find even their meeting at the river inappropriate? Yet, did they neither care what others might think in their continued time together?

She glanced at the landscape she'd been painting and to her canvas. And was it wrong of her to think of Leaning Bear as maybe the one real friend she'd had since arriving and what about possibly more? Was she wrong to think of the idea?

"Fern, I am going to attempt again to paint this sky." She glanced at her easel, mixing the latest concoction of blue with whiter colors as the pup's ears perked curious. And for the first time since her arrival to Lame Deer, she began to paint the sky the very color of her own eyes.

****

A drizzle of steady rain cascaded around the open school as Alli stood before the children to end the day. It had been a full session of learning and with the rain, they had studied the weather and clouds. And all of the children, even Hawk had come on time and participated as they were expected. Well, if the rain meant all of the children would arrive on time and remain all day then she'd be grateful for gray skies, and it did seem she was getting through to Hawk little by little.

He was smart and quick to learn but he held little trust for her and talked as she imagined the Cheyenne men did. It seemed his words of not trusting the white ways were from what he may have heard from the men in his camp. Perhaps his father. Strange she had figured out a few of the children's mothers but not many of the fathers, but for Hawk and his brother she hadn't been sure. Though he did seem to hold a high respect for Two Doves when she was at the school. More so, than the other boys. She made a mental note to start placing together the children with the parents they belonged to as she discovered their connections.

"All right children. I have a special surprise for each of you this afternoon. And while it's been gloomy today it does appear the rain is stopping so…" Alli opened one of the boxes she'd placed on her desk and turned back to the class, as Two Doves stepped from the closet where she'd been sweeping.

"Because you are such excellent students, I have taken the liberty to order each of you clothing appropriate for school, including boots and stockings. You've all studied hard and are learning so much it is well deserved." She held up one of the boy's shirts and a jacket.

Mixed variations of Cheyenne and Sioux language filled the classroom, and it sounded as if they were happy. The commotion caused Fern to exit her basket in the corner and she pranced around as if understanding something was exciting. It hadn't taken the pup long to gather a routine of the school day, and with the rain, she'd napped in the basket with the children still at their studies.

"This is why I measured each of you and your feet a few weeks ago." She motioned the children closer. "Come up…we'll find each of your fitted sizes. The girls have skirts, blouses, and smocks with stockings and the boots with heels."

The children were quick to join her, and Two Doves grinned as well. And everything became a rapid succession of shirts, jackets, trousers, knickers, boots, skirts, blouses, and stockings. In utter chaos the children began dressing with the younger boys dropping their buckskin britches naked before all.

"Oh…no wait. Girls into the closet. Boys…keep…yes, get dressed." Alli turned away at the boys' lack of modesty and the girls scrambled for their clothing in giggles and excitement inside the closet. Two Doves joined the girls, leaving her to the naked boys. She shrugged and handed off the clothing as she read the sizes on the various items.

In a short time, Two Doves sent out one dressed girl at a time with Elina helping her with the younger girls. Smiles and chattering filled the school room as Alli began with the smaller boys. Little Wolf and Takoda both fitting their trousers backwards.

"Oops, wrong way, turn them around; the buttons go in the front." The other boys were pulling on shirts and jackets and putting on their knickers and stockings with the same enthusiasm as the girls. Alli took in the sight of what she'd thought she might never see, but the uniforms had arrived in a few weeks with a letter from an excited Jacie.

"Little Wolf the boots go on after the socks…stockings first." She ruffled the boy's shaggy head, and laughter erupted as the boy pulled his boots off of the wrong feet and tugged on his stockings. Alli bent and rearranged his shoes to make sure he got them on the right feet. "Like this."

"Boys the boots are specific to right or left foot. Remember we discussed shoes a few days ago." She tried to raise her voice above the commotion as the children giggled and praised each other. Fern barked making circles in all the excitement.

She glanced up as several women from the gardens were looking their direction. She had supposed this to make a stir. But weren't the children happy scrambling into their new clothing? It reminded her of her and Jacie on Christmas with their many gifts from family. Her heart warmed by the spectacle.

"Oh, Chameli don't you look so pretty." Alli admired the little girl, who twirled a bit in her dress and walked as if her new shoes were made of glass. It occurred to her none of these children had ever worn anything but moccasins or went bare footed. They each walked around looking at their boots more than the clothing.

"All right, once you are dressed let's line up. You'll wear these to school each day and please keep them clean. No working or playing in the mud in your new clothes." The boys made a semblance of a line after Two Doves directed in Cheyenne.

Outside the school a few men including soldiers had collected to look at the scene.

"Hawk, don't you look as handsome as ever." The edge of his lip curled in a hint of a smile.

"Now boys, the buttons match up. See Takoda has missed one so let's fix that." She undid three sets of buttons and realigned to connect them for the smaller boy.

"And the knickers cover to the knees with the stockings high." She pulled up Little Wolf's sagging socks.

"And for the girls the blouse is buttoned the same in line." Elina was helping her smallest sister with making the buttons line up. "The boots must be tied, and we may need to practice that with the smaller children."

Elina lined up her sister and her own smile was one of real happiness and maybe the first Alli had seen. "Elina, you already look the part of a teacher."

Two Doves moved around the room assisting the students and inspecting each.

"My you all look very nice. Now remember you must wear this to school but you also must not play or work in this clothing. Even the soldiers are interested in how nice you all appear. We are a real school now." Alli beamed at them all having noticed the soldier's interest. "So, class dismissed."

The children scrambled to gather their discarded clothing. She scooped up Little Wolf's buckskins, handing them to him, and he scampered away. Fern followed the little boy out onto the grounds but returned a short time later to her basket.

"I hadn't known they would enjoy the clothing this much." Alli turned back to Two Doves.

"It must be much money." Two Doves grabbed the broom and began sweeping as she did each day.

"Yes, but it makes me happy to see them rewarded for their hard work." She had suspected it to make things feel like a real school would.

The woman touched her belly and glanced up. "My baby is restless. Perhaps he would like English clothing too."

Alli walked closer. "That feeling must be very special."

“Yes.” Two Doves rested a hand to her middle again. “You had no children with your husband you have told me about? You would make a very kind mother.”

Alli shook her head. It always a subject she wished to avoid. “No. I'm afraid when I was very young, I had an illness, and the doctors removed those parts that…” she blushed. “The inside of me that was made to carry a child, is no longer there.”

“This must sadden you.” Two Doves picked up the broom to sweep once more. “And your husband was unhappy of this too. Maybe he was disappointed.”

Alli shrugged. Timothy had wanted children, but he’d known of her condition when they married and never dwelt on it. All too busy at his own endeavors of other pleasures she supposed but she answered. “My husband knew of my condition and was never terribly concerned as he was much older than I by twenty years or so.” It sounded good at least for now.

“Come…feel.” Two Doves set the broom aside once more and grabbed her hand, placing it on her low belly.

Alli had touched Jacie’s pregnancies many times and it was something amazing to feel a baby kick. She waited and several small nudges came making her smile. “So strong.”

The expecting mother sat then for a moment, holding her belly. “My time will come soon. I will take to my lodge for the weeks of healing.”

“Of course. This is your first, you must be frightened?” Alli asked as she’d often thought she would be had she ever carried a pregnancy.

Two Doves shook her head. “Yes, worry at times of pain but good pain. Dancing Fox would like a son. This would make him very happy.”

"Well, I shall hope that a boy it is." Alli let her eyes stray to where Leaning Bear walked toward camp. She glanced back not wanting to give herself away, but it was the first time she'd seen him in days.

Two Doves smiled, glancing to him and back. "I see you watch Leaning Bear many times. I see that he too watches you."

Alli shook her head. "He was very kind when I first arrived in town and my buggy was overturned and in making repairs to my cabin." She made excuses and went on. "He seems to work very hard most days."

Two Doves lifted her brows and gave a hint of a knowing smile. "I am young, but a woman knows and I see this look in the Medicine Man's eyes. He cares for you."

Alli's cheeks heated. "He's been very kind is all."

The young woman glanced again as Leaning Bear moved outside to the wood buildings where cooking happened. "He is very handsome, no?"

Alli's face heated further and she had no idea if she should answer but she did. "Yes."

"Leaning Bear and Dancing Fox are much at bickering, but my husband is happy his brother is back home as he spent many years away from the Cheyenne." Two Doves offered the explanation, still holding her belly.

"He has spoken of the negotiations with his friend Dawson." She added the bit she was aware of. "I suppose the pardon placed him back here."

She nodded. "He spent many years working with Dawson McCade for making better treaties. My husband still thinks this did little for our people."

Alli wasn't sure how to answer anything more. "I

suppose that he tried to help was a good thing."

"Yes, but your secret is safe with me. And the children have asked me to speak to you about the upcoming dance for rain. Our culture to share. They would like very much for you to attend with us when it happens. To dance with us by the big fire." The chief's young wife's eyes widened with her grin.

"I did hear the girls speaking about it." Alli commented. "But we've had rain."

"Yes, the dance is much like when the white town has a festival. It is a renewing and a time of celebration of hope for our people." Two Doves explained as she collected the children's slates from the bench she was sitting on. "The children have accepted you to be part of our people as have I."

"Yes, I'd love to attend if it is all right." Alli sat beside her, relishing in the conversation. Real sharing with her new friend.

"He will be there." She smiled. "Leaning Bear. The men dance first and most often we women laugh about them. But Leaning Bear is a very good dancer as is my husband."

Two Doves got up. "When my day comes, you'll come and see me and my child? I will ask the woman to allow this as you are my new friend."

"Yes of course, I would love to see you and the baby." Alli hugged her and was surprised she was embraced back. A true friend in the midst of her long and sometimes lonely journey made her weep once Two Doves turned to head home for the evening.

It was nice to have another woman to talk to. Someone to share with but she feared she'd offered too much about Leaning Bear, though Two Doves had already figured them. Perhaps she'd been too obvious with the continued glances when Leaning Bear did appear. But the truth of her heart was she did watch him, and her pulse raced a bit faster anytime he was near. And she wasn't even sure why. She hadn't expected her feelings, especially for a Cheyenne medicine man, and what would the world think about that anyway? Oh, how was she even thinking of this. He was a Cheyenne man, and she was a white woman and them together would never be accepted by anyone around them.

Chapter Twelve

The schoolhouse was empty and quiet. Alli finished up the sweeping, glancing across the reservation where today, an elderly man, Walks With Moon, was dying. It was Elina, who had let her know that it was a very sad day for all. And as was due, Alli told the children school would pause out of respect. She had not been sure of the proper thing to do, but she'd noted the children's sadness.

Canceling school wasn't a good thing as the children were wearing their uniforms and working on activities at a rapid pace of learning. But, how could she hold school when incense floated in the air along with a flute song and the soft echo of light drumming that had continued since before her arrival that morning. She had not met Walks With Moon but somehow, she allowed tears she quickly brushed away.

And now, as she glanced the direction of the old man's tent, Leaning Bear stepped from the lodge where men and women had kept a vigil for hours. It wasn't her place to intrude or ask any more than she could see but her heart held heavy. Leaning Bear wore his full tunic, something that was rare, and he carried a tray he set aside at a small table crafted of pine. And it was the first time in a long while that the length of his hair was bound and hanging down his back.

Two Doves had not come to school to help. She was

needed with her husband the chief. And it had surprised her that Dancing Fox had gone into the old man's tent and not returned the entire day. She found herself curious, not about death among the Cheyenne but of the rituals that were common.

She went back to her work, gathering the slates to put them away but then Fern jumped up, her tail wagging though she gave a small growl. Alli turned to Leaning Bear stepping inside the school room.

"It is well with you?" He approached but stopped past the students' benches and gave Fern a good rubbing. "The children tell me you have had tears." He angled a glance at her, the smell of incense on his skin and clothing strong. Fern scampered off from the school as she often did, leaving them alone.

Alli nodded as heat flushed her cheeks. "I'm afraid I don't know Walks With Moon, but I found myself reacting to his long life and the children's sadness."

She hadn't cried but her eyes had rimmed with tears and her heart melted when Elina explained to her the way the tribe and all the children had adored the elder man, all calling him Grandfather. But her thoughts led her back to Leaning Bear showing up to check on her once again. Had he cared enough to come and see to her well-being?

"Elina was upset in explaining to me what was happening. I suppose it isn't that anyone should ever cry alone if I am present." She shook her head, blinking away more tears she supposed due to his kindness.

"Sadness find many as Walks With Moon has died." He took a deep breath and let it out in a puff. A reaction of his own stress or relief she supposed.

For a moment she fought her emotions trying to

keep them in check, but a tear escaped down her cheek and she turned away from him. Lands, she didn't know Walks With Moon, but wasn't it sad for all? She used the back of her hand to wipe the tear away but at the same time, Leaning Bear touched her back, moving in behind her.

"Was best. Very ill for long time." His voice was soft and as she turned, he let his hand drop to hers. "I will follow you to your home, now. Will be dark soon."

"You don't have to do that." She sniffled but offered a smile, and relished in the touch he offered in taking her hand.

He held her gaze and tilted his head, stepping closer. "Want to do this. Not safe for you alone at this time."

"I should post a note, let the children know school will not be in session…but how long will things take?" She asked and he let go of her hand. "I want to be respectful."

"Take three days, but mourning takes much longer. Maybe school Monday one week." He glanced behind him and then back to her. "I will tell children and families."

"All right. Fern?" She pulled her bag over her shoulder, calling the dog who returned and sat waiting "I'll go to my buggy."

"Paytah waits too." He nodded where his painted horse stood outside the corral alongside her buggy. He had planned this, to assist her home as well?

In a matter of moments, she was urging Millie to pull her in the buggy off the reservation and toward home with Leaning Bear riding behind her by several yards, no questions asked of him as they left the reservation. Once the reservation was behind them, he rode Paytah alongside her, though he remained quiet. He was handsome against the graying skies, only a hint of light remaining.

"I should have said I am sorry to you for the loss of Walks With Moon, instead of your trying to support me," she offered, her hand on the reins as Fern jumped to sit on the seat beside her.

It was a moment of riding before he responded. "Was a good death. Easy, when spirit gives up. Some not have last moments easy with family near."

"I agree," she answered. "The children told me he was Grandfather to all of them. I find it beautiful that the Cheyenne share in raising of all the children. They admire you too. Little Wolf told me you would make sure that Walks With Moon would be in no pain with your herbs."

"Little Wolf shows interest in herbs and animals, things of mother earth." He perked with a bit of pride, but he went on. "He is smart, and he is learning plants and seeds."

"Oh, I didn't know that, so he may one day be a Medicine Man like you?" she asked, that thought never occurring to her.

"Hard to say. Might choose other." He shrugged, though he looked at her for a long moment.

"Well, he is teaching me Cheyenne words and seems to enjoy making fun of my pronunciation, but it's a fine way to learn." She'd enjoyed that Little Wolf was teaching her and not realizing at the same time he was learning more English.

"You wish to learn Cheyenne language?" He angled a puzzled glance at her, Paytah bucking a step and then settling with his native words to calm the animal.

“I think in order to teach the children, I should learn all I can about the Cheyenne language and your way of life,” she explained. “I’ve already learned things from you and a good bit more from Two Doves. I find it fascinating to have the opportunity.”

It was a long time before he spoke again. “Will teach you more. First must have Cheyenne name.”

She smiled as he studied her to the point, she focused on the trail ahead and then back to him.

“Call you *Paint The Sky*.” His expression remained unchanged, and he gave a solid nod.

She’d thought he might be kidding, but that wasn’t the case. “Paint The Sky? Well, I’ve little managed to do that, but I did mix a blue I think might work.”

“Then must paint it to celebrate Cheyenne name.” He shrugged, glancing behind him and then ahead again.

“I suppose it’s been so long that I’ve not painted the blue skies that I have a fear it won’t be right regardless.” She shrugged, but maybe she liked her new Cheyenne name for no other reason than he gave it to her. “Paint The Sky. Do I write that as three words or am I Paint for short or is Sky my last name in Cheyenne.”

The look on his face was serious. “No first name. No last name. Just name. Paint The Sky. Good name.”

“Well, I suppose since it is from you, I will accept that name as my very own.” She urged Millie off the trail, and he followed on Paytah toward her cabin. Wouldn’t Jacie be beside herself that she now had an official Cheyenne name and was being escorted home by a Cheyenne Medicine Man?

He didn’t dismount as she climbed from her buggy, but he did urge the horse closer to the barn, eyeing the owl who stayed on her perch in the barn.

"Yes, she is still here, I've named her Annabelle." She glanced at Millie who was already munching the grass and walked closer.

"Owl must be angry, reason for staying." He glanced at her and back to the creature, his face serious.

She didn't understand his comment. "She's angry at me? Why on earth?"

"She is a boy named Annabelle. Not happy of this." He looked back at her and clucked his tongue for Paytah to turn again the way they'd come.

Alli glanced at the Owl. "How was I to know that he was a boy anyway?"

Leaning Bear's laugh found her as his horse disappeared over the rise. Once again, he mocked her with his laughter, though his tender touch earlier was still not forgotten. She allowed her thumb to trace over her fingers.

"Well, at least he can laugh." She turned back to her buggy. "Millie, our owl is not a woman, and I have a new name. Paint The Sky."

She turned again to look back toward the way he'd gone. It wasn't surprising he'd insisted on following her home, but his giving her a Cheyenne name was as much a personal gift as she'd ever received. She'd have to send a letter to Jacie to tell her she had gained the name and that the uniforms had been wonderful for the children.

She unharnessed Millie and led her toward the barn but stopped to glance up at the owl. "I beg your pardon, Mr. Owl, but at this point I think a new name is in order. How about Andy instead of Annabelle?"

****

Alli gathered the last of the slates and made her way to the closet to store them in the basket Two Doves had placed there. It had been several days since her new friend had come to school due to not feeling well in the end stages of her pregnancy. She missed her assistance, but the children had been improving in all their marks and were enthusiastic each day. If she highlighted the main studies in the mornings and a bit after their noon meal, they seemed to look forward to painting about the sciences she taught them in the afternoons.

Today each child had brought a leaf to class in order to learn about it by painting it and making impressions on paper. Some of the older girls had created beautiful copies of their leaves but it was Hawk who had gained the most attention. He'd used a combination of blues, browns and greens and he'd painted with a small brush to make the leaf appear as a fish complete with eye and fins and a fanning tail.

She'd praised him for his abilities in art but also mathematics where he had scored higher than all except Elina. He’d actually smiled and boasted a full chest of pride at his abilities and her praise.

She turned back to her desk intending to straighten things but gave a start. Chief Dancing Fox and Hawk stood just inside the open school. She hadn’t even heard them.

“Good afternoon, Chief Dancing Fox.” How was she to address him? She'd seen him watching from across the camp several times as he waited for Two Doves return in the afternoons, but they’d never formally spoken.

She waited for a response though his face never changed expression. It unnerved her that he said nothing for such a long pause. “Welcome to our school, please sit if you like.”

"My son will come to this white school because he is required. But he will not wear English clothing." He tossed down the bundle of folded clothing onto one of the benches adding the boots. Hawk was wearing the clothes a short time ago, but he'd called the boy his son. Now she was confused. Two Doves had never said as much, but now wasn't the time for clarification.

Alli glanced at the boy who dropped his gaze. He was bold in class, why would he not look at her now? But she answered the chief, lowering her tone. "With all due respect, these are proper attire for any child attending school."

Dancing Fox's dark eyes pierced her. "This is not proper attire for Cheyenne boy."

He spoke very good English and yet he didn't raise his voice, it was more as a comment.

"Children learn when dressed for the success of schooling. This is the requirement for our time of studying in this school and all of the children are doing very well in their studies, Hawk especially." She tried to keep her voice even and steady the same.

"White man studies taught by a woman to Cheyenne children who wear English clothing." His tone still changed little. "Is required by government who confines us to the borders of this reservation. Some dignity of our culture will be preserved, and my son will come to school but not in this clothing."

Alli let her mouth drop open. How dare he? "I can respect the collision of our different ways of living. But in my classroom, I will be in charge of how the students dress and what they learn. And with all due respect should I be outside these school boundaries I will follow with what would be expected of myself within the

Cheyenne ways. I have spared no expense in making sure each student has the full dress and that it would not cost their families anything." She folded her arms and stood her ground. He might be chief, but this was her classroom.

Dancing Fox never blinked. "Cost of clothing unimportant. Wearing English Clothing unimportant. Losing way of the Cheyenne of very much importance." He gave Hawk a shove and the boy turned to leave, and he followed. What did that mean? Would Hawk no longer come to school?

"Have you any idea, Chief Dancing Fox, how smart your son is while in our classroom?" If he didn't want to see her side of things, perhaps he would respect that his own son was exceptionally gifted in his learning abilities.

The Chief stopped, turning to face her again and folded his arms before him as he glanced at Hawk and back to her. She had indeed caught his attention because he lifted his brows waiting.

"He is very bright, reads and writes and ciphers arithmetic as well as does Elina the eldest well studied girl in the classroom. She must study, but it comes easily for Hawk which is a gift to have such abilities. Please don't deny him that related to the dress required." She lowered her tone further with the last sentence and he eased his rigid stance.

Hawk stepped closer once more and spoke in Cheyenne to his father but Alli only understood his wish to wear the clothing. Or at least that is what she thought he was saying. The two exchanged more words of which she couldn't decipher.

"My son will come to school." Dancing Fox scoffed

and turned away once more following Hawk, who grabbed his clothing and boots giving her a quick smile. Had it been that easy? Was he allowed to wear the clothing and attend class?

She sighed to herself and turned, not having seen that Leaning Bear was standing nearby. He held a hammer and long saw as well as a smirk that faded from his face as she placed her hands to her hips.

“And you find this amusing, I suppose?” She continued cleaning, annoyed at the idea he’d find her situation the least bit humorous.

He shrugged as he laid the tools on one of the benches. “Dancing Fox sees little in children learning white language and ways.”

“Well, what about you? Both you and Dancing Fox speak English very well. Why would you not want that for the children? I don't understand the fact he cannot appreciate the importance of learning no matter the language or culture.” She still wasn’t sure if it meant Hawk would wear the clothing if he did come to school.

He turned away from her and touched the top of the ceiling with his hands, seemingly to size up what he was to be working on.

She continued to explain when he didn’t add to her comments. “The uniforms remind the children they are in school and that is where they must behave and follow the rules so they can learn. It was no different all my years of teaching back in Chicago. The children were most successful when dressed for their learning and respect was obtained for the teacher as well.”

He went past her into the closet and returned with an armload of the stored lumber and he shrugged yet a second time.

"That's all, a shrug? You must have a thought about this one way or the other." Alli boasted, wanting to hear what he might add to Dancing Fox's thoughts. "And if Dancing Fox didn't want Hawk to wear the clothing, he said nothing about it of Little Wolf or the other children? I am also confused as to why Hawk took the clothing back with him. Is he coming to school, and will he wear what is required?"

He tossed the lumber in a pile on the school floor. He lifted one board and pulled a handful of nails from his bag. "Clothing now belong to Hawk, he keeps. Perhaps chief will appreciate his own gift of clothing."

Alli shook her head, not understanding that thought at all. "What?"

He measured the length of board and laid it across the bench to saw away a piece of it for fitting. Dust covered his hand that held the lumber and the scrap fell to the flooring with a thud.

"You mean I should buy Dancing Fox his own English clothing?" She folded her arms and walked closer. Why on earth would the chief want the same clothing as she required the children for school.

He held the board in place near the ceiling and hammered in several nails to keep it there. "That is what I say. Chief can never turn down gift from another. Required to accept the gift. Will wear it, my guess but also will make a gift to you in trade."

"But he hates it for the children, why would he wear the clothing himself?" Alli shook her head. "And Hawk is very smart with all his studies, why would his father keep him from the ability to have more knowledge and learning because of what he must wear? And besides that, I never understood Hawk to be his son. Two Doves has never shared that either."

Leaning Bear angled another board and batted it into place, running a hand across it. The depth of his brown eyes met hers again. "Gift for Chief. Trade will happen. Hawk is not son in sense you would see it."

"I don't understand…" What did he mean by that? She'd spent a lot of time with Two Doves and the children, and it had never been mentioned that Hawk was the son of Dancing Fox. She did know that Two Doves was young and this was her first pregnancy.

"Hawk and Little Wolf are son of tribe. Father and mother die of sickness several years now. Dancing Fox becomes father." Leaning Bear interrupted her and began with the cross boards on the wall he was completing.

"I've spent time with Two Doves who has never told me that, nor have the children or Hawk himself." She took a deep breath trying to understand how unfortunate for Hawk and his younger brother, Little Wolf.

She leaned against her desk giving his idea thought. "And what if I do purchase a gift of clothing for the chief, will he accept the gift and let Hawk come to school? And Hawk calls Little Wolf his brother but the chief didn't worry about the uniforms for him. I frankly don't understand."

He stood again and dipped to grab more wood lining it up and sawing. "It is as you say. Hawk is age of young man; Little Wolf is still child. Dancing Fox does not worry of child as much as Hawk who is learning to become a man."

"Oh, it's so confusing, I only want the best for all the children, can't he see that? What are you doing anyway?" She walked closer as he bent and tapped the nails in place.

"There is lumber enough for walls to school room. Will have walls by winter for keep warm when teaching. Fire in stove help. Will add sod when done to keep out wind. Make nice winter schoolhouse so winters you can still teach." He held her gaze for a long moment but as she held his gaze he turned back to his work.

She glanced at the small stove sat in the back corner. "That'll be nice, but why now when not for the last teachers?"

He scoffed in a slight growl. "Ask many questions. Other teacher not stay."

Was she to think his quick irritation meant he had at least a little concern for her?

He placed two boards on the table and took up the saw in his left hand. She added her hand to hold the end of the board steady. He glanced at her hands but didn't look up as he began to saw.

She'd often helped Timothy with such things. But it was odd Leaning Bear was closing in the school, but he hadn't asked her about it. "Did the soldiers or the captain have you do this for me?"

He grabbed the board, turning his back to hammer it into place. "No."

"I see." So, as she suspected this was his doing for her and something about that made her pulse race of its own accord. Why would he do that, lest he did care about her well-being?

"You will paint by stream tomorrow?" He changed the subject as he continued to work.

So, he was interested in her endeavors at painting…or perhaps her. She angled a glance at him with a lift of her brows. "What reason would you ask?"

He stopped hammering. "No reason."

Men…were all the same. Oh, so be it. “Yes, I will paint if the afternoon gives me the sun.”

He bent again to place more wood. “No clouds will come. Sun will be strong.”

She had wanted to head back to her cabin once school was done since it was Friday but as it was, talking with him was far more interesting. “Does that mean you will be there?”

The grunt came again. “Too many questions.”

“Then I will see you tomorrow afternoon.” She grabbed her bonnet and turned to leave the school, Fern following and running ahead toward the buggy. He'd be there. She had no doubts and she didn’t look back.

Chapter Thirteen

Leaning Bear strode through the dense forest, leaving his camp in the trees behind. It was midday with the scorch of the sun, and he wore no shirt, sweat already collecting along his back and neck. He paused, before him an elk stood in a thicket yards away. He lifted an arrow from the quiver across his back and with practiced ease, placed it along the bow to take precise aim. He drew back and held a breath, but before he released for the kill, the elk fell.

He pulled the arrow free of the bow, spotting Hawk to his far left. He gave a nod and stepped forward, meeting the boy at the unmoving animal. A clean shot to the chest was no surprise as Hawk had spent a lot of time hunting with Dancing Fox.

"A-ho." He greeted as the boy jumped from the last part of the rise he'd been standing on.

Hawk bent and touched the Elk, speaking in Cheyenne. "It is my kill."

"You are a good hunter." Leaning Bear gave the praise due to the boy.

Hawk met his gaze, his dark eyes searching. "I did not see you."

"We did not see each other. Dancing Fox will be proud." Leaning Bear bent to the Elk. It would be much too large for the boy to carry back to the reservation alone.

“Yes, I am a fine hunter, and he will know this.” Hawks tone held much pride as he laid a hand on the animal’s middle.

Leaning Bear nodded. “I will help you with preparations and tonight the tribe will eat of your game.”

Hawk pulled his knife and bent once more to the unmoving animal. “I think, yes, the tribe will feast, but I will give you the hind quarter to share with the teacher. You were heading there, to her cabin?”

He narrowed a gaze on Hawk. How was it the boy thought of this or understood his intentions? It was a question he was not going to answer. “The teacher will enjoy the meat.”

“I will keep the hide for Two Doves’ baby.” Hawk pulled his knife and began gutting the animal. “I will tan it until it is soft.”

Leaning Bear pulled his own knife and in no time, working together in the quiet, they managed the hide of which Hawk laid open fur side down. Then they put the carcass on the fur all but one hind quarter of one leg.

Hawk glanced at him as he continued his work. “You are fond of the white teacher.”

He did not look up as he had hoped the conversation related to Alli was done. But the truth was best. He nodded but offered no words.

“My father does not like the teacher.” Hawk explained as he wrapped the carcass in its own fur with help. “The teacher tells him I am very smart, but he does not like the clothing we are to wear. He told the teacher I will not wear it. I would like to wear it and I told my father this.”

None of this was something he did not know. “Father has many reasons for not wanting the tribe to lose more of the old ways. You are old enough to decide on your clothing."

"I am old enough to anger my father." Hawk spoke as he continued working on the Elk. "I think Father would fight for us to have our lands over and over. The freedom he speaks of still gaining. Sometimes I think he is wise and we should have these things. Sometimes I think I would like to learn what the teacher shows me." Hawk settled more of the animal meat to the hide.

"Father is smart, wants tribe to be free, but even as we are here today, in other places across the land, many tribes still fight and are killed as are the white soldiers." He used his knife to take apart more of the animal. "I think the tradeoff of living much better than that of dying."

"Even if no land or freedom?" Hawk looked at him waiting on an answer.

"My work in town is for medicine for tribe." Leaning Bear dug his knife into the mud to clean it. "I do not wish this work. I do this for the Cheyenne and others. Your father does his work for tribe. For you. For family and people. He is angry about the past. Right to be so. But he is wise to know it is best to keep tribe alive even on the reservation."

"But you are a medicine man and even the whites allow you to care for them. My Father said when I am older and take my dance with the sun, my visions will show me the way of our people and the way of my own life to choose." Hawk's chest jutted forward with pride; the right of passage would still be a few years off for him.

"Father's anger will fade." Leaning Bear stood again, taking the arrow from the animal he'd laid aside and handed it to Hawk. Dancing Fox had told the boy he may well find his own path. It was wise advice. "Elk is large, this you can manage?"

The boy pulled together the hide as a sack. "I am strong. Can drag it when I tire. You will say this is my elk to the teacher?"

Leaning Bear lifted the hind quarter and waited until Hawk had the pack across his shoulders and back. "This I will say."

Hawk grunted through the first few steps of heading back to the reservation. Leaning Bear looked on and followed, but the boy was able as he had said, and would find much praise on his return to camp with such a large kill.

Leaning Bear turned back toward the woods with the hindquarter over his shoulder. Alli would appreciate the meat and she would praise the young hunter too. But he still wondered about the boy having guessed his plans to visit her. He'd have to be more careful and hope that Hawk did not share his knowledge as Dancing Fox was already aware of too many things where his thoughts of the teacher were concerned.

As he approached the stream, Alli was there in her usual spot, stroking the brush across the canvas. He watched her though it was only for that moment before Fern perked her ears giving him away. He stepped forward and Alli set her brush aside facing him, her expression widening.

"Oh, my you've been hunting." She dunked her brush into the tin of water shaking it and then laying it aside.

"It is Hawk who gained the kill and sends you meat." He laid the hind quarter on the rocks above Fern's reach. "Your painting is done?"

"Yes, for today as the sun is changing again." She stood and walked closer. "Hawk sent this for me, really?"

He nodded. "Good hunter."

"He wished to share…sometimes I'm not certain he cares for me as a teacher, though he does come and has worn his uniform, in spite of his father's demands."

"He is a boy in school, but a man before tribe, will decide for himself his path." He added, knowing she would not understand the things she knew little about.

"I suppose. Then I should be happy he comes in his clothing and continues with high marks." She glanced at him, but her gaze followed Fern, who scampered after a squirrel. "I must thank him. It'll be nice to have real meat, given I've lived on dried beef for a time now. I'm afraid I know little about how to smoke meat to keep it, though I have read about it." She began picking up her paints and rinsing the remaining brushed in the tin of water.

"Come, will teach teacher." He waited on her to pack her paints and along with the hindquarter, he took her chair, Fern trotted ahead of them as she led them back to her cabin.

"I do thank you, perhaps I could make a stew for us to share while the meat is fresh." She caught up to him, keeping beside him on the trail.

"Smoke the meat, will save for all winter into spring if needed. Winter sometimes hard, food needed." He spoke, the smell of honeysuckle reaching his senses as was usual with her near to him. And why had he volunteered this time to share with her once more? He wanted to shake his head and use those swear words Dawson had taught him once more, but thought better of it.

"Yes, Maud has given me a list of items to accomplish but there is so much it seems." She shrugged and trotted to keep up. "And it must be if Hawk sent meat, that he does like me a little."

"Hawk fond of learning." He studied her painting, the colors as vibrant as if real.

"I suppose he doesn't want Dancing Fox to know how much he does enjoy learning." She adjusted the wet canvas to keep it from touching her clothing, holding it away from her body.

A wisp of her light hair fanned across his shoulder, making him all too aware of her proximity as they arrived at her cabin. He stepped away from her and laid the hindquarter on the porch. Fern made her way up the steps and to the meat and he pushed her away scolding her in Cheyenne.

"I suppose she's not seen raw meat, only the dried beef I share with her and the biscuits I have each morning." She didn't look at him as she spoke, hopping the stairs and setting a large bucket of water to the porch. "I keep the stream water here each morning for drinking and washing."

He turned to the fire pit where he had burned the rotten wood of the porch and bent, taking up his flint and working to ignite kindling that remained. He leaned to blow on the flame as Fern came to inspect, though she didn't continue her attempts at getting to the meat.

"What do we need first and I'll get a pot for beginning a stew?" She placed her paint bucket and canvas inside her cabin door and rummaged inside still talking what he could now not hear. Always with so many words, so much chatter though he did wish to hear her voice. She returned with a small black kettle.

"Will start fire, no need for more. Just kettle for stew. Meat to cook by smoke slowly." Leaning Bear stood again as she settled the kettle into the ash. A soft breeze blew her hair and the trees offered shading to her face. Her skin was flawless, deeper in color than when she'd first arrived and the depth of blue in her eyes always captivated him. He turned back to the fire, avoiding her further gaze. Yes, it was that he should know better than to allow his time spent with her.

She stepped from the porch, and he caught himself watching her again as she joined in the work, not leaving it to him alone. He placed more wood into the fire until it was burning well. "Important, smoke to cook the meat, not fire."

He lifted his tomahawk from his belt and began splitting pieces of long wood. From his bag he pulled free strips of leather and tied the pieces of wood together to set high above the fire in a frame similar to the roof of her cabin. He went to the hindquarter and cut long strips of the red meat. Fern whimpered, eyeing the strips but it was best she learned she could eat when she was fed and by Alli and not him. He laid the strips of meat across the wood brace which was not close enough to burn from the fire, but which would allow the meat to take on the smoke to cook it. Fern followed him back and forth giving Alli a reason to giggle.

"At least Fern is interested. This is all, and for how long does the meat smoke?" She walked back to him looking at what he did.

"This is thin meat, but long, maybe several hours. Once it is smoked, hang for more days to dry, then place in jars or between papers. Best each piece does not touch the other." He explained. "Will last one season in glass jar sealed tight."

"All right, but I've read about adding salt to preserve the meat." She explained though her brows lifted in question.

"If salt meat, cooking not needed. But salt much cost." He handed her his knife. "Cut thin strips, drape here. This you learn."

She nodded and went to work, shooing Fern once again away from the hindquarter. He stepped closer to watch her, but she did a fine job of cutting the strips as he had shown her. In about an hour the meat was all draped across the fire, smoking with his continued adding of dried grasses and more kindling for the fire to smoke.

They worked in silence and for him comfort of sorts he was sure he shouldn't allow. How did she have such ease of being near him as no other white woman? How did he accept the feelings settling something inside him long restless? He wanted to shake his head. The world would not accept his thoughts of her and likely neither would she.

Suddenly, Fern snatched a bone he had pulled from the hindquarter and made off with it faster than he could grab her. This took his mind from thoughts of Alli as he pursued the pup and took the bone from her. He turned to Alli. "Must come from you, not be taken, not be given by me."

"Fern, come." She bent and called the dog to her. "You must wait until it is time to get your meal, now stay."

She handed the meaty bone back to her. Fern took it and ran to hide on the opposite side of the porch, chewing at her morsel with greed and eyeing him as if he might take it away from her again. She must learn food was only from Alli in order to protect her.

"Leaning Bear…" Alli beckoned his attention with the alarm in her voice.

He followed her gaze. Riding up the trail to her cabin were two of the Baker Brothers, Pete and Leroy, both with horses tied to their own. More theft no doubt. He lifted strips of the meat and spoke to Alli in a calm voice. "Begin your stew. Keep fire between you and men."

Alli added the contents of the water and flour mixture and stirred the aroma causing his belly to growl as he eyed the men who continued closer. She had taken his cue on continuing what they were doing as not to appear alarmed.

Fern scrambled before them yapping at the men as they stopped their anxious horses,

Leaning Bear hung two more strips of flesh, the tomahawk still in his left hand, his knife with Alli as she had been using it to cut the meat. He turned back to the men who stayed on their mounts.

"Well, well, well, lookie here what we got." Pete rode a bit closer than Leroy did. "Ain't it a thing where you're here quite a bit, Medicine Man, seems now you're cooking and keeping house."

"A white squaw to rut with how 'bout it." Leroy spoke first laughing at his own comment.

"You are out of line, Sir!" Alli held her fists tight, the knife still in her grip. "I've paid Leaning Bear for work on my cabin and to teach me how to smoke meat for winter."

Leaning Bear stepped ahead of the fire closer to the

men, to block her in hopes of quieting her. Fern moved in beside him, her barking ceaseless. These men were not worth arguing, but he could not protect Alli if she was willing to argue and stir the fight as kindling. And he had long learned she was not a woman of few words.

"That right, Medicine Man, she paying you outright?" Leroy kicked at Fern who was now nipping at his boot each time she jumped. "The way we're hearing seems a lot of things been purchased in town, including new clothes for all those children on the reservation. I hear there's lot of money for the asking from someone back East, Ms. Crockett. That dog bites me I'll shoot it."

"Fern. Come." Alli stayed where she was, calling for the pup.

The dog snarled another growl and went to sit beside her and Alli held her neck roping. "Stay."

Pete laughed. "Must be more going on here than the eye meets, don't you say brother?"

Leroy nodded. "Tell ya what, we'll not be giving either of you away on this sharing of home duties, but I'll be riding back by in a few weeks to collect on payment for it."

"I will pay you nothing." Alli kept her voice calm to his surprise. "The items I've purchased have been paid by the Office of Indian Affairs and again are of no concern to either of you."

Leaning Bear did not take his gaze away from the men. He still held the tomahawk. These men would know his abilities in using it.

"No need to posture there, Medicine Man, your secret's is safe with us." Pete laughed again. "Long as the little lady makes her payments on time. That or, we take our payments another way."

Alli stepped around the fire and Leaning Bear grabbed her. Pete dismounted, Leroy behind him, both reaching for their weapons.

"I'm not afraid of either of you." Alli's body was shaking visibly but she tried to pull away from his grip. "And it is not what you are saying. I pay Leaning Bear for his work and that is all, as does Maud and a few others in town. You both well know this."

"Come now, sweetheart, we ain't gonna hurt ya…just gonna look around a bit. Might be that painted horse is found here." Pete stepped closer and when he did Leaning Bear shoved Alli behind him, keeping himself in between her and both men.

"Horse not here." He spoke the truth of it and as the men moved closer, he lifted a piece of wood from the fire with his right hand, the tomahawk still in his left.

Pete's horse reared and the animal tied to it pulled away and took off into the woods, Leroy's two equines running together to follow. Leroy poised his revolver and Leaning Bear shoved Alli behind him, tossing the tomahawk and knocking the weapon from the man's hand. He took the knife from Alli and turned back toward the men.

Leroy grabbed his hand but bent to retrieve his weapon. "You'll pay for that, injun, pardon or not."

Leaning Bear quickly grabbed a piece of the burning wood from the fire. He swung the firestick toward the one remaining horse. The animal took off and the brothers both took a step back from him.

Pete poised his weapon, the brothers eyeing each other and them. "We don't find them horses, we'll gut you, injun, and then we'll take your pretty until she's all used up. And the day you ain't hiding that horse, it'll be all mine, Medicine Man."

Both men eyed each other and with a nod from Leroy they turned to go, making him think that had been too easy. But now, these men would be seeing their revenge for wrong-doing. He turned back to face Alli once they were gone and to his surprise she held a pistol, just at her skirts, though she was frozen in her fear.

He took her hands in his and eased the weapon from her.

"No, I'm all right…I am." She shook her head. "I suppose I scared them from us, though it's not even loaded I'm afraid."

Leaning Bear checked and the weapon indeed held no bullets. "This weapon you know how to use?"

"Well, I've never used it, Maud sold it to me and…no, I have no idea." She shook her head, the entire of her body still shivering. "I tried to shoot a rabbit I saw in the garden, but then…I couldn't shoot it. Well, I did shoot but missed and some part of me was glad of it." She reached into her skirt pocket and retrieved two bullets holding them out to him.

"Is not wise to draw weapon unless you plan to use." He spoke in a whisper. He was not sure how it would have gone if they had seen her weapon. But the alternative could have been a quick shot from Pete or his brother.

"I've been taking it to the stream with me and to town in case of the men, so when I was standing there, I realized it was in my bag within reach, but the bullets here." She shook her head, touching the pocket of her skirt. "What are we gonna do? I will not pay them, though I lied about the money."

"Good lie. Men will be angry. Have been angry

before." He tended the fire once more, adding back the lit log he'd grabbed. "Best not to be alone very often. And best not to argue or fight with Bakers. Not deserve words from you. Only to make trouble. Don't talk they will go."

"I am not afraid of them." Her voice broke, as brave as she'd tried to be, but then she leaned into him, tears coming along with her sniffles.

He was not sure about touching her, but allowed her to hold him. "Some fear is good thing. No fear is dangerous. I would not let men harm Paint The Sky, no matter."

She held onto him. "I know, but you have no gun and what if they do take Paytah or hurt Fern and you or me?"

"Bakers not very smart. Will come to end soon enough, this I know." He spoke the words he should not have. He had plans for the Bakers and in time they would find their fate, but he had to be sure of the timing.

Harder for him was not wrapping his arms about her for comfort, though all of his being wished for that permission.

Chapter Fourteen

The cool night brought a breeze that tickled Alli's skin to goose flesh. And once again the cries of Two Doves found her. Her friend's voice had echoed across the reservation for several hours now, causing her concern. School was long over by hours, and she'd lingered, waiting for news of her new friend giving birth. She glanced into the sky. It was dusk and yet she wasn't going to leave until she could believe all was well. If need be, she'd use the cot in the closet room for the night as the recent skirmish with the Baker brothers had kept her on edge anyway. Fern had settled into her school basket and fallen asleep over an hour before. The puppy had accompanied her each day she went to teach for weeks now.

But waiting at the school was torture. No one had thought to give her any word on Two Doves and by goodness she was going to go and ask. She grabbed her shawl and wrapped it around her shoulders, the evening wind cooler than usual. It had turned downright cold now with the sun sinking below the coming night.

She glanced at the line of soldiers' quarters where men sat outside at a table playing cards. There seemed to be fewer men of late. With Captain Bartley on a trip back East to visit his wife's family it seemed the soldiers that were in camp paid little attention to her or anyone else for that matter.

Childbirth claimed many mothers and babies and Two Doves had been in labor since early morning. Her own mother had been a midwife and she'd often heard her say first births could take a long time.

She walked toward the row of teepees which Leaning Bear called a lodge. The darkness was broken by the glow of small campfires or lanterns inside each, white smoke sifting from the top of some. Several of the Cheyenne lived in the rows of houses behind the tents and many of those were shared by multiple families. And she'd come to learn that some of the inhabitants of the reservation lived on small nearby farms, not guarded by the soldiers at the gates but with some sort of checks in process. Those were expected to farm and share with the reservation.

Two Doves had pointed out her teepee when the two had once walked along with the children as they searched for bugs and ants to study. The lodges were much taller than she'd envisioned when back home in Chicago, their bases a wide berth of living space.

Alli approached, not surprised to find Leaning Bear outside the opening, ushering in women who carried small baskets and steaming water. He let the tent flap fall and faced her.

"I was beginning to worry." She whispered, tugging her shawl around her in the evening chill. She hadn't seen him in a few days, though she had a feeling he watched her and her home in his passings. Sometimes when she had the feeling someone was watching…she convinced herself it was him.

His tunic sleeves were rolled high, and he stepped past her to wash his hands and arms in a basin on a table built with pine. "She has brought the child and is well."

“And the child?” Alli’s pulse raced as she watched him wash.

“A girl. Also well.” He grabbed a cloth to dry his hands and arms and tugged back down the sleeves of his tunic.

“Did you…help her deliver?” It was an awkward question, she supposed, but had he helped with the birth? Would a medicine man do such a thing? The men back East would never, unless a physician, even contemplate the idea.

He peered up at her with a nod and turned to hang the cloth for drying. “It is as you say.”

“I suppose I hadn't thought a Medicine Man would do such a thing.” Her mother had been a midwife and there were times even male doctors called her in to help with deliveries. “Might I go inside for a moment?” she asked unsure of breaking tradition and given the women had gone in with food and warm water she was uncertain.

He glanced up as the lodge flap was opened. One of the ladies she'd only heard as called Broken Hand, due to a crippled hand, motioned with her good hand. “Come. Come teacher. Please.”

Alli let her lips curve and she gave the slightest nod and she stepped to the lodge, ducking to enter the warmth inside. A small fire played close to the center and beyond Two Doves leaned against pillows, the length of her hair braided and a bundle in her arms.

The women, Broken Hand, Archisha, and Halona worked around her. Broken Hand sat beside the other two ladies and though Alli had spoken a few hellos to each of them, she was a bit nervous. She eased closer and was motioned to sit beside Halona.

“Alli. Come. She is a girl.” Two Doves patted the

blankets beside her and she sat closer admiring the baby.

The new mother angled the baby for her view.

“Oh, Two Doves, she’s so beautiful.” Alli admired the sleeping baby, so tiny.

One of the women handed her a bowl of steaming soup. Was this the tradition, to eat? She was famished.

“Thank you.” She waited but the women dove into their meals, chatting in their language amongst each other, as the new mother dozed.

Alli followed the other ladies and dipped the flat bread into the soup. The clear broth was tasty of spice she wasn’t sure about.

Two Doves opened her eyes again. “I have named her Chanti. She is of my heart and her father is very pleased.”

“So precious,” she whispered, fighting back her emotion. It never failed around newborns or pregnant mothers for her own regrets to surface. She pushed her thoughts aside out of sheer need to do so. She was happy for Two Doves, even in her own sorrows.

She tried hard to focus on what the other women were saying but they spoke so fast.

Two Doves must have recognized as much. “Halona says her son, Black Moon, was born in horrible rainstorm so no one hears her cries in her birthing. She said she was brave and did this on her own.”

Alli glanced at the woman. “I'm sure that was very difficult.”

Two Doves interpreted for her again. “Halona asks about your own children. I tell her about your operation.”

Alli took another bite of her soup and set the bowl down. It wasn't that she couldn't answer but it always seemed awkward. “Yes, I'm afraid as a young woman I had illness which required an operation and as a result I've not the ability to have children."

The chattering stopped as Two Doves explained to them further and their sympathetic eyes fell onto her. "Archisha worries of this disappointing your husband. I explain of your husband's illness and…death as you shared with me. They are sad for you, but this makes you a strong woman says Halona."

"My husband was much older than I. He would have loved children, but he became ill after a few years," she explained and received various nods from the other ladies, as if they did understand her English.

Two Doves sat up, adjusting her position and placed Chanti into her arms.

She shook her head but took the bundle. "It has been so long since I've held a little one, my nieces and nephews are almost grown. It was always a joy." The baby stretched and rolled back into the bunting; her eyes closed in sleep. "She's very beautiful, Two Doves."

"She will call you Auntie as you have told me your sister's children call you as well." Two Doves placed a hand to her arm that held the baby.

Alli fought emotions and touched the baby's tiny hand. "That would be an honor to me. Thank you."

The chatter of the women continued as Alli studied the baby, but Two Doves closed her eyes. It was best she made her way to go and let her friend rest. She'd bring soup in a few days to add something more for Two Doves.

"I should go now and allow Two Doves rest." Alli handed off the baby to Broken Hand. "I thank you for this time of sharing the meal."

"We will see teacher at quest for rain, for dance?"

The woman cuddled the infant and nodded.

Alli beamed, that they all seemed happy about it. “Yes, the children have asked me over and over. I would be very happy to attend.”

Archisha nodded and the others looked at her as she made her way out of the lodge where she bumped right into a wall. She bobbled back and glanced up, face to face with Dancing Fox.

“Oh, I…pardon me. I didn’t see you.” She gained her balance, meeting his gaze though he said nothing still. “The baby is beautiful. Congratulations.” She offered, uncertain of the appropriate remarks to make. He was as large a man as Leaning Bear, but seemed always to wear a scowl.

He held her gaze a short moment and stormed past her, entering through the flap and letting it flop back down behind him without so much as a nod.

She let her jaw fall open but then closed her mouth. She hadn’t seen him at all since he’d come by the school with Hawk and scolded her about the uniforms. She tugged her shawl tighter with the chill and turned to find Leaning Bear standing close by.

“I didn’t mean to…offend him of course.” She let out a flustered breath. Why did the chief seem to dislike her so much?

“He is distracted, is no harm done.” He held several lengths of thin roping in his hands.

Had he waited on her? She wasn’t at all to be able to guess. “I suppose not, but it did me good to see Two Doves and the baby. And the ladies reminded me of the coming dance…for rain. They would like for me to attend just as the children have asked me to.”

“This you will do?” He began twisting the twine

together.

“I think it would be impolite to miss the event, given their asking.” She brushed a strand of stray hair away from her face.

“You will ride buggy home this night?” He changed the subject.

Had he waited on her to see Two Doves and was now inquiring of her well-being? “No, I planned to stay tonight given it’s late. I’ll sleep on the cot in the closet at the school. There is no school tomorrow, and I can go home early morning. I bid you good-night.”

She couldn’t be sure, but it seemed as if relief relaxed his features. She turned to walk back toward the school and was certain he watched her the entire way.

Millie had been cared for by the soldiers and would be fine for the night. She glanced at Fern, who slept in her basket as she arrived back inside the small school. She picked up the basket with the dog inside and placed her on the floor inside the closet. She returned for the lamp and bolted the door from the inside of the small closet as the school door didn’t lock. While she’d much prefer a wash up, she could take care of that tomorrow when she got home.

She took a moment to take off each of her boots and giving her feet a good rubbing. It had been a long day but now all was well. She was relieved for Two Doves and the child. She lay back on the cot and pulled the blanket over her and dimmed the lantern to a soft glow. Her thoughts went back to Leaning Bear and his care of her friend. He was many things to this tribe and their dependence on him was for good reason. He studied herbs and plants and he’d delivered babies and cared for the sick. And all of it he did with no complaint.

There were many things about the tribe she didn't understand, but she was honored to have been somewhat included in Two Dove's celebration of birth. She closed her eyes, content that her new friend had done well. But holding the baby. Her emotions threatened again. Not because of her own loss of having no children, but maybe more out of being accepted even if a little by the tribe.

Fern whimpered and jumped up onto the cot beside her and settled at her side. And she allowed it, somehow not wanting to be alone this night. She let her mind wander to the upcoming rain dance. She'd heard of such things but had no idea what she would wear or what was expected as a part of the custom, but she hadn't known the women of the tribe were happy to welcome her as well.

But now all she could think about was that Two Doves had told her that Leaning Bear would be at the dance and that he was a good dancer. Well, she could hardly imagine. The only dancing, she was sure of, was the kind done in ballrooms back in Chicago. But a dance in the open where rain was somehow summoned, she had no idea what to expect or how to prepare.

Well, she'd look forward to it anyway and ask the children more questions so she could decide just what to wear and how to figure her hair. She thought about Leaning Bear having asked her about her attendance at the dance. Would he really be there? He hadn't said as much, but she had to think his questioning her reason enough to think so. And somehow the thought of that warmed her deep inside her chest.

Chapter Fifteen

Dusk had settled in over the reservation and drums echoed in the distance of the far side past the school. Leaning Bear pulled the deerskin tunic over his head. The small fire at his feet held the last of its embers. He glanced at the full feathers he would wear moments from now as he and the men danced to welcome rains for an early harvest. He raised his gaze to the darkened sky. Low-lying clouds had moved in earlier in the afternoon and this night would show the tribe rain before it was done. That was good. The people needed the dance and the respect of rain for mother earth. It would be as it should be, all except for the confining fences, which made the mountain lion pace restless inside him as always.

He had gone with Dancing Fox for speaking to Captain Bartley about the yearly dance with its large fire and feast. The captain had allowed for extended hunting of many of the men who had returned this morning with game. The women had spent the day preparing the meat and sweet potatoes with roasted vegetables. There would also be sweet cakes with sprinkles of sugar and honey and hard cookies with sugar sauce covering them. The smell of roasted venison filled the air. His stomach growled. Hunger was good. It reminded a man that all things were not given.

The women were dancing with the children and

laughter found him well enough to take his negative thoughts at the confinement of the reservation. The Cheyenne and even the Sioux needed the time to be one, to call for the rain and to eat well and dance no matter his thoughts. He pulled on the headdress and let the trail of feathers fall down his back. He would wear the feathers of his grandfather, Stalking Eagle, with pride as he had not the dress of his father.

He lifted his gaze again when the warmth of Alli's laughter found him. She had come with her invite from Two Doves, who he was certain had to seek approval from Dancing Fox, who would deny his wife little. He stepped closer to focus on the bonfire and the teacher.

She danced at the fire holding the hands of two of the children. They laughed with her as she tried to follow their direction. She swayed and moved her feet in step picking up the dance that had belong to his people for centuries. The wind kissed tendrils of her light hair, the embers of the fire shading them like the sun. He leaned against the table outside his lodge, consumed by her and moments passed without his knowing. He bent to tie his moccasins. How he longed to touch her, touch her hair and the paleness of her flawless skin. The moccasins were the good pair he saved for dances or the times he met the white government officials with Dawson. His tunic and pants the same, those dyed with hints of blue like the sky…like her eyes.

Her giggles penetrated the night again and he couldn't keep his gaze from her. She had her hair pulled atop her head and it was then he noticed she wore moccasins like all the others. She was slender and her tall frame moved in unison with the children, her height above the other women dancing along with them. And she was beautiful. So much so it stalled his breath.

Damn it! He scolded himself with the white man's curse that Dawson almost always used. *Damn it*, her laughter found him. *Damn it,* she rode his thoughts most all the time. *Damn it,* the time spent at the stream made him long for more days with her. But what his heart wanted, his mind was well aware would never be, not in this world or the next.

He folded his arms. He had no right to the thoughts she provoked inside him. Those thoughts of her naked beneath him, of touching her were forbidden. He glanced away from her. The dance he would yield to for the rain, for his people but his dance would belong to her.

He lifted his gaze again and in spite of the beauty she displayed, he was more attracted to her mind and thoughts. While she had been ill prepared for her arrival to Lame Deer, she was wise to many things. His exposure to white women had been most often limited to Dawson's mother, a woman called Dodge, whom he had found enlightening in her words and thoughts. He had also learned many things about herbs from Dawson's wife, Haven, though she was young and for the most part very quiet of speaking. But he had learned the most from Dawson's brother's wife called Tess. She was a doctor and shared many things about wounds and injuries and how to help with healing. All were very strong women and wise in their thoughts.

Alli was much the same, though her lack of fear when challenging the Bakers was not as it should be. He didn't agree they should back down from the men, but her challenge would increase their anger and responses. This she should fear, though he had not yet failed to watch her home for a few hours each night without her knowing. And the day would come on his plans for taking care of the Bakers once and for all. This he knew.

Yes. Alli was much like each of the McCade women he had spent time with. She spoke without reservation. She accepted each person as they were, allowing the good and not good of each. He had found it pleasing to discuss issues with her while she painted. She had strong opinions though as it was neither white man nor his brother Dancing Fox were accepting of a woman who would challenge them. But a good discussion, even with a woman of differing opinions was sometimes a good thing. Her constant chatter and sharing her thoughts had become his comfort. A place his mind was given rest from the things that plagued him.

He shook his head as he continued looking on as she danced with the children. She was much a challenge and it might be that was why he was attracted to her. She danced as if it had not occurred to her, she was different from all around her. Yet she did so, and he was indeed a fool.

Dancing Fox rounded his lodge. “It is with you, Brother. Have the spirits called for the dance to bring rain?”

He grabbed his bow, the fancy one with feathers and beads. “The spirits have spoken this.”

Dancing Fox wore his own full beaded head dress adorned with feathers and fake golden coins with wooden beads painted in red and gold to match. The chief scoffed. “Your gaze gives you away, my brother.”

His thoughts about Alli were his alone. “The spirits will bring crops and heavy rains in the coming days.” He answered, dusting his buckskin trousers and adding the feather ties to his thighs and calves. He had bathed that morning in the stream near his camp in the trees and allowed the sun of the day to dry his hair. It was now in one long braid down his back to his shoulders with blue beads woven into it by the ladies readying the men.

"Always with Grandfather's words. Never to the argument at hand." Dancing Fox narrowed a hard look at him. "Careful where you gaze, my brother. Let us dance anyway."

The chief wasn't sincere and turned to walk toward the fire as the echo of the drums filled the darkening night. He would be expected to lead the men in dancing for the rain and crops and for the health and freedom of the tribes. He was chief, it was his to do. As for himself, he did carry his grandfather's final wish for peace for all the tribes. The ongoing devastation and fights would mean more loss of life and had there not been enough of that? But he no longer wished to live inside the fences and there were no answers for making things different.

He scanned for Alli again, but did not find her as the men moved in to dance around the fire. He allowed the beat of the drums from centuries before to consume his thoughts, set the pace of his movements and allowed his prayers to *Maheo* to be heard. He walked toward the fire, tying the feather straps to his wrists one at a time Aligning his naked arms with a length of feathers in white, brown and blue to match his blue stained buckskins.

He closed his eyes and allowed the spirit of his totem bear to encompass him, his feet skipping into the dust in unison with the other braves. He chanted along with the other men and raised his arms inviting the clouds that would carry the rains to come. And his prayers to the spirits filled his vision with the coming rain…and her, the teacher.

His skin prickled in the heat as he made his dance before her just as a bird insistent to capture his mate's attention. He postured to the beat of the drums and chanted, pushing thoughts of her aside. Though he could not resist her. He closed his eyes and swirled using the wings in flight once more. Sweat ran down his neck, chest, and back as he continued. He caught a glimpse of her sitting with three other ladies, a pencil in her hand sketching in the midst of the dance and song. And somehow his dance was for her, for her alone. His mind understood this. His body understood this. His heart understood this.

He worked harder to dance as did the men around him, thunder calling in the distance with the spirits answers. The great cat hissed, yet the bear stood reaching to the sky and Leaning Bear soared as the eagle, using his grandfather's visions to allow peace and one tribe.

Then he soared across the stream, and red paint splattered across the canvas. Sweat dripped from his body and the screech of an eagle found him as the drums stopped and thunder boomed and lightning streaked the sky. He stopped his dance holding her gaze and a light rain began to fall. She smiled, a gesture he was not permitted to return with all in view. He lowered his arms and stepped away from the fire, because keeping her in his sights was too intense. The rain had come and the crops would yield. And somehow so would the deepest part of his heart in wanting to claim Alli Crockett as his own.

****

Alli sat back down beside Two Doves, who cradled her bundled newborn across her lap. She'd held hands with some of the children, learning the steps to the drums and even some of the chanting she understood. She'd learned some of the dancing steps and chanted where she could. The older girls had taken a great deal of time to teach her but the younger students, even the boys, wanted their turn holding her hands, showing her their own dances. She had been welcomed by them all, even the elder women, Broken Hand, Archisha and Halona sat nearby handing her a plate of roasted meat and vegetables. And she now wore a buckskin skirt and blouse that Elina had sewn for her, the gift having brought tears to her eyes with her hug of thanks. It was beautiful and a perfect fit. But more than her own surprise in receiving such a gift was to see the girl's pride at having made it.

"You are a very good dancer." Two Doves placed the baby in a basket beside her and took up her plate.

"I'm afraid I have more to learn to dance as well as the children." She tasted the roasted venison which was tender and flavorful. "This is delicious."

"Esevone." Two Doves nodded to her plate. "Tatonka."

"Buffalo. I had thought it was elk or deer." Alli nodded as she'd understood from the women that the men had gone to hunt for bison but found none. She had seen numbers on the prairies when she was on the train and had been surprised at their size, but they remained scattered and few.

Two Dove's infant squirmed in her swaddles, then screwed up her tiny face in a swift squall. "She will be hungry as she smells the meat too."

"The sweetest little face." Alli admired the baby as she continued eating. Two Doves had adjusted overnight to her motherhood role. She put her bowl aside and placed the baby to her breast, covering the infant and her upper body.

"The men will dance as if they are most important." Halona chatted toward the small circle of the ladies with sarcasm in her voice. "The drums call them soon, so they can show us their fancy feathers and fancy feet."

Archisha laid her plate aside and chuckled as she spoke. "Big rough tatonka hunters have returned." She mocked them, leaving Alli perplexed about asking more, though Two Doves ignored them as her baby nursed. It did surprise her they spoke in English as they hadn't before.

Broken Hand rose and flitted away to stir the older boys to add more wood to the fire. Some of the younger boys attended school but the older boys had not come, the captain letting her know they had to hunt and work alongside their fathers.

When the older boys made excuses, Broken Hand grabbed a nearby switch and began flailing each with it until they went for the wood. Alli's mouth dropped open, though the other women around her laughed at the display of which harmed the boys little.

The drums stopped, making the chaos of noise around the fire cease. Then the drums picked back up again in a steady beat of depth and loudness that kept the women and children still. Even the older boys managed to find a place to sit together on the other side of the large fire pit.

The men emerged a few at a time to dance around the fire. Like the women and children, they were adorned in their best clothing with bright shards of metals and stones and so many feathers it was hard to tell who each man was. Their faces held paints of red, black and yellow. Chanting filled the air and while she still didn't know the language, Alli rocked back and forth to the beat, straining for a glimpse of Leaning Bear.

Broken Hand sat once more beside them. "It will bring rain. Much needed for more harvest."

Alli was caught up in the excitement of the dance and the possibility, not sure she believed the dancing would bring rain, though the sky had held clouds earlier and appeared to darken before them all. The women began to clap and hum along with the chanting that was unfamiliar to her, but in a tune after several rounds she began to hum.

The boys who had received the broom now adorned feathers like their fathers and danced the same steps as the braves, mingling in behind the grown men. Alli glanced all around her as every member of the tribes, both Cheyenne and Sioux were now together for something they all believed in. Something of hope more than thinking rain might come, something of oneness they all needed, she supposed. And yet they each had allowed her presence and participation in spite of the fact she was a white woman. She glanced behind them where the soldiers stood watch, three to four of them at a time, allowing the custom that Chief Dancing Fox had requested, to her understanding.

She turned back to the dance and he appeared. Leaning Bear. The full feathers of his dress flowed in blues, reds and yellows down his back. He was sure on his feet in every step the other braves took, and it seemed he did so with ease, with a grace not encompassed by the other men, smooth and agile. All at once the drums stopped and then began with intensity as Dancing Fox came to the fire, raised his hands and joined the dance as flutes were added to echo into the darkened night.

Leaning Bear rounded the fire in dance and Alli met his gaze, her heart racing. She forced herself to look away, lest the women around her follow her sights back to him. But the grace with which he danced was indeed breathtaking. He circled the fire again and she lost him as he mingled with the other men and the flames hid him.

Two Doves leaned closer. “He dances for you, Alli.”

Alli nodded as she dug in her bag, pulling free her tablet and the chalk pencil she carried. Leaning Bear was beautiful, so much so she began with the pencil across a page inside, uncaring if anyone noticed. The image of him was something she never wanted to forget, and her heart raced as she drew the feathers, the paint to his face and the fire in the background as he danced against the darkening sky with the yellow and orange flames behind him. Thunder cracked and lightning streaked in the distance, causing a commotion of movement to cover the food tables with blankets.

She needed a sketch, an outline to paint the scene when she returned home. Something inside her wanted to paint him now, in all the glory she was certain she may never capture on her canvas.

Two Doves nudged her as Leaning Bear continued to dance, watching her. She smiled at her friend; glad the other women hadn’t taken notice. She shoved the tablet and pencil back into her bag as the thunder clapped again and the drums became louder, the dance of the men more urgent. Leaning Bear eyed her again and chanted with the other men, his hard stare beckoning what held between them. And her heart now danced along with him and her breath held as large drops of water began falling from the sky. The rain came hard as if it were indeed summoned from the dance around the fire.

Two Doves stood at the same time Dancing Fox came and took her by the arm. “Must get out of rain and wind with child. Fire from the sky is now strong.”

He was right. Lightning intensified and thunder cracked again and many of the women and children began to move with the food back to their lodges. All had helped set up the feast, and each took a part in breaking it down, even the smallest children, all dancing and laughing in the heavy downpour. But the drums continued, the few playing under a lean-to in no rush to move away from the impending weather.

Alli pulled her shawl over her new buckskin clothing and glanced at the school where she planned to stay the night as late as it was. The rain began to come in hoarding sheets like a wall of water and she took off on a trot, glad she’d had the soldiers secure Millie in the stables on her arrival. Earlier she’d placed Fern inside the closet with her bed basket, something the pup had become used to on school days. She hadn’t known how long the dance would last and she hadn’t at all figured the rain to find them. She could sleep on the cot there as she had a time or two already.

She stepped inside, at the same time the thunder cracked. She jumped as lightning sent a flash across the landscape of the room, bringing her face to face with Leaning Bear, still wearing his fancy feathered dress. Startled, she let go of a scream that he covered with his mouth taking the breath she hadn’t inhaled. The door closed behind her. A soft moan escaped her as he eased her body to him, heat riding his damp skin. They were both soaked from the rain and somehow as he held her, he dropped the wet décor of his dance feathers to the floor leaving her against his bared chest. She braced her hands on the scars there, his muscles tight, his size overwhelming.

She shouldn't allow this, but she was powerless to back away from him. And some part of her wanted this and had for a long while. He kissed her with a tenderness she was sure she'd never known. And in spite of her thoughts, she allowed it, savored it, melting further into him. His arms embraced her, his hands on her hips and his breath as rapid as her own.

He tasted of mint and smelled of the smoke from the fire. Their tongues tangling in a soft dance of passion that consumed them both. Her heart pounded and the flesh of her skin prickled at his touch. Oh, how she'd wanted this, though she'd never permitted her thoughts to think further to such things. All of a sudden, she was aware of Fern barking at the closet door, but with the rain and thunder, the pup was ignored by them both.

He'd come here, knowing she would seek shelter. She should've known he might be here when he didn't escort her back to the school. He pulled from her and placed his lips to the flesh of her cheek and whispered. "Tell me I must go."

She shook her head and drew him closer. "I won't."

His mouth seized her neck and shoulders, all the while his hands massaging her hips. She shivered at the intensity of their intimacy.

She relented to his hard embrace, his mouth finding hers again. He teased her further, fresh and alive though his wet body pulsed a warmth that radiated heat to the depths of her womanhood. It had been so very long. Oh, how she wanted, clinging to him as if her life was in the balance of his touch. The touch she wanted. The touch she needed in spite of the world around them that would never accept this.

He eased from her and brushed her hair back from her face, his breath as hard as the muscles her hands found on his biceps and shoulders. He took a moment to lift a strand of her hair and rubbed it across his lips.

"Your dance belonged to me." His words were a whisper at her ear, and even with the thunder, she heard him well enough.

"Yes." Her thoughts frayed that he had come here for this purpose. "And your dance was for me."

"He held her gaze for a long moment and began lifting her doeskin tunic, easing it higher. She shuddered as his fingers traced underneath, searching and finding her breast. He fumbled with her chemise finding his way and she sucked in a fevered breath as he held the weight of one breast, then searched for the other.

"Too much clothing." His words came in a low growl. But then he murmured something in Cheyenne as he bared her chest and bent to tread his mouth across first one nipple and then the other. She lost the translation with the sear of his mouth to her puckered flesh. "Lands…Leaning Bear."

He teased and tasted the other breast and began to suck. Hard. Her knees nearly gave way at the sensation that warmed the part of her depths that wanted more, more of him. His hand traced down her belly and below the waist of her buckskin skirt, searching.

He feasted again on her nipples as his fingers eased to part her, finding the pearl of her pleasure. Every part of her being should stop him, but she was powerless as he teased her to a frenzy. Hadn't they both wanted this but never spoken of it? Hadn't they both longed for more than conversations? And her body built until she was moving her hips with him, and his Cheyenne words filled her, though she lost all the meanings save beautiful.

"So long…since…" she whispered, but then bit her bottom lip as his thick fingers filled her, stroking. His moan of satisfaction touched her neck, his breath heavy, the hardness of him against her thigh.

He spoke in Cheyenne, again words she couldn't decipher but his voice urged her, and she moved against him, his fingers working with ease. Oh, but she couldn't, not standing, not…but then the warmth of his mouth teased a nipple again and she pressed her pelvis toward him in the heated dance they now shared.

He moved to her other breast tugging and nipping harder as her body drew tighter. The bursting pleasure came with his fingers deep inside, and she drowned in the taste of the salted skin of his shoulders. And he held her to his body until her breath eased and her pulse lessened, the thunder around them shaking the school and the depths of their hearts.

She opened her eyes, her knees weak and her breath short. "Leaning Bear…"

He eased a palm to her cheek and then he was gone, leaving her leaning against the walls he'd built, the door closing as thunder rumbled. She eased her skirt back in place and let her blouse fall back across her torso as Fern sniffed and began yapping at the door of the closet. Why hadn't he stayed, why hadn't he…oh lands what had they done?

She brushed a hand across her scalded face, her breath still short. How had he teased her into such a height of bliss and not taken his own pleasure?

Why had he not allowed their joining as she was expecting? She would not have stopped him no matter the consequences. She eased the door open, and Fern scampered out of the closet and out the front door into the weather.

She lingered in the doorway watching through the storm, searching for Leaning Bear and trying to understand what had just occurred. And she had long known of her own thoughts of the medicine man, but now she understood his thoughts were the same. She held a hand to her chest. It had all happened so fast but without a doubt had been the most erotic moment of her entire life. But now, what did that mean?

No one would be accepting of her should they know. She glanced around the outside but there was no one paying any mind to her in this weather. She touched her fingers to her lips which now felt swollen and tingling. He'd been purposeful but gentle at the same time and her body had never yielded to pleasure so fast.

Fern bolted back into the school, shaking from her head to her tail and water sprinkling to the floorboards. The pup paid her no attention, grabbing her stick and going to her bed in the closet. Alli closed the school door and entered the closet and lit the small lamp she kept there.

The room came aglow, and she dimmed the flame. Morning would arrive soon, and the storm would be gone. Tomorrow wasn't a school day, and she could paint. Yes, that is exactly what she'd do. She'd paint but would Leaning Bear come to the stream? And what would he say? What would she say? She lay across the cot and tugged the blankets across her. "Well, it is no one's business save the two of us. I'm a grown woman, not some young girl who knows nothing of passion."

She closed her eyes but then opened them again. In her mind Leaning Bear danced for her again and she longed to take up her paints and begin this night. He'd been beautiful if a man could be called as such. Handsome and strong. And his dance had been for her, and she'd never forget how it was to be accepted by his people. She was falling in love with the culture and the children and…him.

Chapter Sixteen

The noon sun filtered through the trees as Alli set up her canvas, her emotions mixed over thoughts of what had happened between her and Leaning Bear the night before. It was a good thing school was out today and she could paint and try to relax at her canvas. Her nerves and emotions over the whole thing left her perplexed. Beside her Fern chewed a stick she'd carried from near the cabin, content and seemingly to have grown overnight a few inches taller.

Her first thoughts on waking had been about Leaning Bear and the tender kiss he had placed on her lips the night before, that and the intimate touch that had brought her to the pleasure so intense, she had floated to some inward place in herself crying his name against the hard muscles of his shoulder. She touched her lips, which still tingled and were a bit sore from the passionate kissing they'd shared.

But this wasn't good, was it? Or could it be? Was loving him wrong? The world would not accept what was occurring between them, in fact no one around them would. Not the people in town, her own family or even those on the reservation. Or at least what she thought was happening…and was she even to allow herself the thoughts or hints of the feelings within her body he'd stirred. He'd brought her to pleasure but not taken his own and she wasn't sure she understood why?

She opened her paint box and took out the jar she used to hold water for rinsing her brushes. She walked to the stream and bent to fill the jar a quarter full. The water was cool and clear. She stood again and glanced around her as she went back to her easel and sat the glass jar at her feet in the sand. Somehow, she had the feeling of being watched as sometimes she did prior to Leaning Bear's arrival, but as she glanced a complete circle around her, there was no one there.

No sign of Leaning Bear but after last night would he shy of seeing her here? Lands, her heart raced at the picture of him dancing around the fire. He'd been the most beautiful of men she'd ever seen if men could indeed be beautiful. He was graceful and fluid in his movements never missing a step the men all took in unison. Never missing a turn and all the while chanting the songs she little understood.

Her own dance with the children had been less than graceful but it had been so long since she'd laughed or felt so carefree. She had giggled with the girls and boys who made light of her efforts. And it had been fun. Maybe the most fun since her arrival west. But Leaning Bear…

He'd worn fancy buckskins with blue paint and shiny beads and feathers. His head dress held red, yellow, white and brown feathers. She'd sketched him and when she had time, she'd resketch him to a bigger canvas and paint him. Though today she hadn't to do that afraid he'd see what she'd was doing. What would he think of her painting him?

She sat and lifted her palate, certain as he'd danced, he had in mind what had indeed happened. And Two Doves had noticed, telling her he was dancing for her.

How had her new friend known? Thankfully the other ladies sitting near them hadn't taken notice. It seemed odd that Two Doves accepted the idea of her and Leaning Bear, but she was young, maybe younger than twenty. She wouldn't know as much about the ways of the world now, would she? And what would her new friend think of the intimacies she and Leaning Bear had shared when she herself was so unsure of what it even meant.

Why inside her heart at this very moment she was as giddy as a schoolgirl, as when she'd once fallen for Timothy. Though her infatuation with her late husband had been short lived due to his infidelity. But now she was a woman, a seasoned woman who'd been scorned and she wasn't naïve to the ways of men and love. There wasn't a man in the elite society of Chicago she'd carried any interest for and yet, of all things, she'd come to Lame Deer and fallen for a Cheyenne Medicine Man.

She had to stop her thoughts, or she'd drive herself mad. No matter how much she thought she loved him, their love could not be, could it? She added a depth of red to the brush and touched the tip to the canvas, adding dots for the red flowers on the far bank, newly bloomed. A patch of red buds tiny with wiry stems. She gripped the brush tighter as she continued, but remained conscious someone was nearby. Something was amiss and her first thoughts were possibly the Bakers, but her pistol, now loaded was in her bag on the rocks. She wasn't sure to move or not.

She scanned around her when Fern gave a growl and as she turned around, she caught the view of a mountain lion on the bank of the stream opposite her. She stifled a scream out of sheer fear to not to utter a sound. The animal watched her as it crouched and lapped in the stream.

"Do not move." Leaning Bear's voice reached as he entered her peripheral vision. He scooped up Fern and remained still, his tomahawk yielded. Fern squirmed and growled trying to free herself, but he held her at bay. "She only thirsts."

Was that supposed to mean she was safe? Her body trembled of its own will but she hesitated to breathe.

The large cat took her leisure to drink and then with one more glance at Fern, scampered away. Gone.

Alli didn't move, even when Leaning Bear pulled her to him. It was all she could do to stand, shaking so hard she burst into tears. "I'm sorry I-I was so frightened. I thought I was alone except for Fern. And what would I have done had you not come along, and my pistol still in my bag on the rocks…" She sniffled as he let her go.

"Best with cat not provoke by dog. Best if shoot gun not miss." He lifted his brows and settled Fern to the ground tying a strap of leather from his bag around her neck, not allowing her to follow the mountain lion. "No need for tears. Is fine now."

His gentleness surprised her little. "And once more I am indebted to you for your help. What would I have done had she been hungry not thirsty?"

"You would be cat supper." He tugged Fern closer with the roping, holding her gaze and then yielding a smile.

Alli let her mouth drop open as she leaned back from him, brushing a sleeve across her face. "Supper?" Her own grin came as she glanced behind her once more. "Well, leastwise she's gone."

He went on to explain pointing in the woods. "With Cat no run. Face and don't move. Bear move slow away.

No run. Look up. Climb tall tree fast. Wolf…"

"And a wolf?" Alli placed her hands to her hips. "What then?"

"Wolf not alone. Best run fast. Yell for help." His intense gaze searched hers.

"I thought perhaps after last night you might not come today," she whispered, heat flushing her cheeks.

He turned and sat on the rock where he usually did and gave a good petting to Fern, who lapped at his hand but went back to her stick, not disturbed in the least by him holding her leash. He of course changed the subject.

"Tell me of husband." He asked as she went back to her painting out of sheer need to do so. Her cheeks were flushed as she could feel the heat and he made no mention of…last night as if it had never happened. But his question was something she would have to give some thought. She gave the canvas another two strokes though her hands still shook. Where to begin and how much to share with him?

She took a deep breath and stroked the brush yet again, still leery should the cat return. "Timothy was a great deal older than I. Nearly twenty years."

He looked at her and away as if giving her time to share and have her thoughts. But she supposed he was asking to know more of what last night ha truly meant.

"My mother had us introduced at his insistence and I was already past the age to marry according to most. But we had a lot of things in common. I was smitten, given his position as a professor at the University…young and impressionable I suppose." She worked on the colors of the falls adding hints of the white water that splashed over rocks, her hands settling. "Things were very nice between us most of the time. I was a teacher in town and he at the university. It was nice evenings reading together or having a meal with my family or at his brother's home."

She listened to her own words. It all sounded good and for the most part it had been. But how much to share when her own thoughts led her to his colleagues, who dismissed her only a short time after he died. All who had shunned her much of the time due to their knowing of his infidelities.

She went on. "But Timothy became ill in the spring two years ago. Various doctors thought perhaps it was consumption, but it was then decided it was from the fancy cigars he enjoyed. Abnormal growths inside his lungs."

Strange she could talk of this now, out loud with a man she had met a short time ago. One she already loved. Somehow no tears came and her voice held steady. "So, after his death and tired of wearing black dresses in my year of mourning I made plans to come here." They exchanged glances in brevity.

"I took care of him in sickness doing all I could." She'd done that even knowing of his multiple affairs with colleagues and young students. But there was no time for her anger after discovering he was ill and it had been her duty as a wife.

"And so that was that." She was out of thoughts that mattered. "And now I am here."

"Your marriage had no children." He shrugged, but kept his sights on her.

She stopped mid stroke. She should've guessed it would be his next question. "No. I suppose my children have always been the ones I teach."

She'd been robbed at a young age of the ability to

have children. A fever and sickness enough at age seventeen and her ability to have children taken in a surgery. At times it made her sad and other times each child she taught brought her some kind of joy and sometimes that was enough. Life could be full of regrets but this one she'd had no control over. She wouldn't explain that now, as it seemed too much to share.

"My sister Jacie has four children. Two girls, two boys. They are endeared to me and I adore each and spent a great deal of time with them while they were growing up." And she had, but they were all grown up to their own lives, the two boys already married.

He turned to face her then…sitting on his rock, the sun highlighting the length of his hair that fell loose across his naked shoulders. The feather moved in the light wind. "Why did you come here? Teach in Chicago must be good."

She dipped the brush and stroked at the red flowers once more. She repeated the question inside her thoughts. Did he ask because of what was developing between them? His thoughts must be similar to her own, what wouldn't be allowed between them. "I did enjoy the children there, many from poor homes, often dirty and hungry. I felt a sense of it being worthy to teach those who have little so that some can gain more in life."

She used the tiniest brush to dot the red flowers on her canvas and went on. "It wasn't the children, why I left."

How much was too much to tell. "My husband and I had no want for money or things, due to my inheritance. And while he was very high in the University, after he died, I was quickly unimportant to the people I thought my friends. Little did they understand the money was mine." It was mostly the truth, wasn't it?

"I saw the ad for teaching on the reservation from the Office of Indian Affairs. And something felt right about going where I was needed. A calling if you will, to have meaning in my teaching and a reason to be where I am." She tried to explain how it had been.

He grunted that depth of a growl that from what she had figured was acceptance of her meaning.

"We're alike in some ways you know, you and I." She focused on the tiniest flowers again and then glanced at him.

He looked at her waiting and for a moment the depth of his eyes made her heart race. So much was hidden there. So much she might never come to understand.

She tried to explain. "As you mentioned you are caught between two worlds, having the freedom to leave the reservation, but still somehow not free. I was raised wealthy with privilege but I was much like my father, wanting to help where I could and somehow never fully accepted by those who were only interested in that money. I just never fit there with those in high society. I suppose my views and my inability to hold my tongue kept me out of their good graces. We're both caught between two worlds of which we belong to neither."

The puppy ambled toward Leaning Bear, tail wagging. But then she halted and gave a little growling bark showing him her stick and pulling against the leash. He grabbed the end of the stick to play tug-o-war with her and his smile warmed Alli's heart.

He glanced up when Fern took her stick away from him and lay down again. "Caught between two worlds, caught between two totems, two names, many things in life are not how they should be. I was free because I made myself free, until the pardon that keeps me here." He stood, digging in his canvas bag of herbs. Walking to her he set two perfect purple plums on her easel.

"Oh, what a treat. May I?" She took the fruit. "How did you free yourself then?" She wasn't sure she understood.

He walked back to sit down and gave her a nod.

The plum was succulent and sweet, reminding her of home. "I thank you. I'll save the other for my dessert after supper."

"I was free because I made myself free." He inhaled a deep breath and went on. "Sometimes white law men allow Cheyenne and other tribes for trading in towns. Reservations not always enforced. Less cavalry placed at forts and reservations. I walked to go where Dawson went for review of treaties. I walked free. I walk now free to my work. But I sleep behind fences."

"Yet you stay now?" She questioned, still chewing the sweet fruit. "On the reservation."

"Is best for tribe." He shrugged.

"You don't believe that any more than I do," she challenged. He was so fiercely independent.

"Is best for tribe if I make no trouble." He moved his hands to explain. "Best I work to bring in medicines and herbs for the tribe as medicine man. After pardon, Dawson still very sick. Need more surgery. I stay for a time. I go when he is better. He had wife and soon a child. A family. No need to stay. Belong here."

"You miss him. I've enjoyed you sharing out him and his family." She dipped her brush into the jar of creek water and wiggled it around.

"Wife named Haven. I call Frying Pan Woman." He chuckled and she turned to look at him. His laugh was deep but happy.

"What on earth? Frying Pan Woman?" She giggled.

"I don't know her and go inside Dawson's cabin. She take up frying pan and swing to my head. I fall and wear headache for a time." He kicked at Fern's stick and the pup gave a playful growl.

Alli laughed in a loud giggle. "She hit you?"

"Is not funny. Leave egg size bump on head four days. Must drink willow bark tea to ease pain." He shook his head and she used a hand to hide her grin.

"Funny now. Dawson's daughter born before snows. Asha. Name means Hope. I call her Yellow Moon for Cheyenne child name. Hair like mother's. Orange like sun." He was so handsome when he spoke in his low deep voice when talking to her and her heart wanted to warm at his candidness.

"Red hair," she corrected, shaking her head.

He shook his head. "No. Orange. Like sun."

She let it go supposing it mattered little and he was right, red hair was indeed orange. "But you stay for more than yourself?"

"It is as you say." He nodded, still teasing Fern.

"And that is why I am here. To offer myself where it might be needed. Where I can make a difference." She lifted her brush again.

"Stay for Dancing Fox."

It surprised her that he explained even more. "But you two hardly get along from what you share."

"Stay to keep respect. Peace." His dark eyes held her, watching her hand as she painted.

"He always seems angry." She commented as she turned to further face him. "Oh, but you were right. I made a gift of a nice suit for him, a fancy one with a cummerbund and tie and even a top hat. I asked permission to bring it to him with Two Doves who took me there. It was about an hour prior to the dance and I thanked him for allowing me to teach the children and for being allowed to be invited to the dance. And he offered me a beautiful blanket from his lodge in trade as you said he would."

"This I did not know." He angled a hard stare at her. Was he jealous or was he glad he was right about the gift of English clothing to the chief?

He made that guttural grunt from his throat again and didn't add anything more.

She rose from her chair and walked closer. "I'm losing the light."

"Paint The Sky gives up easily." He eyed her canvas.

"I am sorry for the things in your life that weren't right and so unfair. I haven't given up, but I will paint the sky soon on this one." Maybe she wouldn't but when she started his painting, she would paint the darkened sky with the oranges of the fire and the colors of his feathers. But they'd both done a good job of avoiding the things that had happened last night. Her face heated again in thinking of his fervent kisses and his hands and lips on her body.

"When you touched me after the dancing…did you mean it?" She held his gaze and glanced away as she sat on the rock beside him. They both watched the stream, the moving water splashing across the falls. And to her surprise his hand rested atop hers.

"Yes. This I meant."

Chapter Seventeen

Alli urged Millie onto the reservation past soldiers who waved her on through the gates. It was Saturday and she’d made plans to have a picnic with Two Doves and her baby to spend an afternoon together. Fern was on the buggy floor but propped her paws up on the sideboard, wagging her long bushy tail. She was used to the reservation and must be thinking it was another day of school.

It was nice that she and her new friend had begun sharing conversations about their lives and she enjoyed the time spent with Two Doves. The Cheyenne woman's stories were fascinating, making her own seem less worthy of being told. And because of her new friend, she now had gotten to know some of the older women in the tribe, all happy to say hello to her each time they passed.

She found Two Doves waiting with Dancing Fox. He only glared her direction, and parted from his wife, entering their lodge. Perhaps with time and her efforts with the children she'd one day win him over. If only he understood how much she'd already grown to adore the children in such a short time. She’d have to hope gifting him the clothing would be worth something in the long run.

She waited as the younger woman walked closer and sat the baby in her papoose inside the buggy beside Alli. Fern sniffed the baby and settled back to her position of standing to see outside the buggy. Two Doves lifted her skirt and climbed up to sit down beside Alli. She placed a folded blanket on her lap that wafted the aroma of foods unfamiliar to Alli.

"Good morning, Alli. It is a very nice day for our picnic of sharing our food. My husband I think must be jealous we will have this time to ourselves." She giggled, glancing back to her lodge, then settled for the ride after a quick check on the baby.

"Oh, I am sure he understands that we women need time to chat and enjoy things together." Alli clucked her tongue and urged Millie to turn the cart around. She headed back toward the gate.

"Hold up there. Where d'ya think you're heading today?" The soldier, who had just allowed her entry on the reservation aimed his question toward Two Doves.

"We are riding out to the pond to have a picnic and shall return in a few hours. It's a lovely day for it don't you think?" Alli answered before her friend could speak.

The soldier narrowed a gaze on them, glancing at the bundles of food each had brought along. Fern growled and Alli laid a hand to the ruff of her neck to quiet her. Outside the small wood-framed building that was the captain's office, men played checkers at a table made from a board placed over empty crates. It was often that way. The men playing cards or checkers and little work when the captain wasn't there.

He walked past them and glanced into the back of the buggy and returned. "I don't know. You gotta pass?"

Two Doves spoke, not making eye contact. "My husband has turned in the paper late last evening to Captain's desk."

"That right?" The soldier turned to the men at the

table behind him. “Ben, you see a note from the chief ’bout his wife traveling today?”

“Yeah, she's good.” The man yelled back, turning again to the game.

The soldier before them scoffed and spat tobacco to the ground. “It's your lucky day then. Have yourselves a nice picnic.” He moved aside. Alli gave the reins a slight hit and Millie pulled ahead. How could they treat any of the tribe members like this?

“I'm sorry.” Alli glanced at her friend.

“It is the way of things.” Two Doves smiled but it faded quickly.

“But that doesn't make it very fair.” Alli shook her head, upset at the whole thing. It wasn’t like a new mother was going to cause problems for soldiers anywhere.

“No.” Two Doves agreed. “But I will wish for better things for my baby and to learn well from teachers such as yourself so one day this is not how she must live.”

They rode for a long while in silence. It wasn’t far to the small lake, but the scenery was so beautiful. The forest of fir trees thickened and in the distance the top of mountains emerged, purple and jagged.

“When my baby is bigger, I would like very much to learn from you painting as you suggested. Your paintings are likeness of the world we see.”

“I have brought along sketch paper and pencils.” She was excited that Two Doves had the interest and it would be something more they could share. “We can sketch today, that is how I start, a quick sketch then a bigger light sketch to paint.”

“That will be a fun time. Maybe Chanti will paint one day, too.” Two Doves giggled, admiring the sleeping baby at her knees.

It was a short ride to the pond, past several of the cabin style homes inhabited by more of the tribe, those who manned large gardens for the tribes and themselves. Two Doves gave a nod to several women hoeing in a small garden.

"The crops have done well since the rain." Alli glanced back to the road. "This is the pond road ahead?" She hadn't been there but knew it was the road to the left beyond the reservation.

"Yes." Two Doves pointed the way.

The picnic had been her new friend's idea and she was almost giddy with happiness to spend the time. As Millie pulled the cart ahead, the water came into view and it was no pond. It was a very large body of water where she could hardly see the other side and seemed to be fed by the mountains in the far distance as water leaked freely from the rock walls high above.

"Here is nice place with the shade of the tree for the baby and for your pony." The young mother pointed just ahead.

Fern began yapping as a small flock of geese, flying above them in formation, honked.

"I'm afraid Fern is excited with a trip out, though I am reminded of the mountain lion I saw across the stream days back." She gave a shiver at the memory.

"We will keep a watch, but most often no big animals here when I come." Two Doves climbed down and lifted the baby's papoose to her back, taking up her bundle of food.

Alli climbed from the buggy, grabbing two stones one at a time. She placed them before the buggy wheels to keep it in place. There was plenty of long grass for

Millie to enjoy. Fern jumped from the buggy and scampered all around as they made their way closer to the water.

"It's beautiful." Alli followed Two Doves to a spot of lower grass past a few trees lined together. She'd have to sketch this and paint it later.

"Here is good." Two doves set her bundle aside and took Chanti from her back as Alli spread the canvas and then a blanket for them.

"Yes." Two Doves glanced at the sleeping baby, still in her papoose. "Come, the water will cool us. The baby will sleep longer." She bent and unlaced her moccasins, leaving them alongside the blanket.

Alli tossed caution to the wind and did the same, removing her boots and stockings. How long had it been since she'd waded in more than the stream? She followed, tiptoeing to the water and giving a yelp at how cold it was. "It's freezing as much a winter snow."

Her friend laughed and waded in up to her knees, holding her buckskin skirt from getting wet. Her deep brown skin was flawless, her legs and body thin even after recently giving birth.

"My grandmother brought me here as a child. I remember her words and laughter." Two Doves held a look of pride.

"That's a nice memory." Alli waded a bit deeper giving a shiver at the chill of the crystal blue water.

"My grandmother was a white woman. Did you know this?" Two Doves asked, walking through the water back and forth.

"No, a white woman? Really?" She hadn't known and was now curious.

"She is how I know English. She was from the South

in Georgia on the eastern coast." She explained and stopped before her. "I have seen this on the map. She told me the waters taste of salt and are very blue."

"I've seen the Atlantic Ocean on the east coast and it does taste of salt. I've never been to Georgia, though." Alli held her skirts higher and stepped a bit deeper in the frigid water. "But your grandmother was in the tribe?"

"She married one of the braves, much against her families wishes. She had ten sons and last my mother." Two Doves held her chest out with pride. "Only one girl."

"And your mother, parents now?" Alli hesitated but asked anyway.

Two Doves sighed. "My mother died of cholera. My father died before my birth on a hunt. My grandmother died five years ago, but she was my mother from a young child."

"I'm sorry. I lost my own parents to illness in their older age. My sister and I cared for them both." She waded back to shore. "That's so cold."

"It will prepare you for winter to be exposed to the cold water." Her friend laughed. "Perhaps after our picnic we shall swim. Do you swim?"

"Oh, yes, but in this…I'm not so sure." Alli let her skirts fall lower.

"It is good for the blood to swim in the cold and the heart beats stronger." Two Doves followed her out of the water and together they went back to sit on the blanket.

"I have much looked forward to this for relaxing and drawing once we eat." Two Doves began opening her pack of food.

"I've brought along Johnny cakes that I made for us since you like them and strips of pork in sauce for making sandwiches. I baked the bread last night." Alli began placing plates before them and setting open the food, only to have Fern run all over the blanket.

"Fern, no." She pointed and the pup eased off the blanket sitting in the grass to her surprise. "Now if she will stay there."

"She is well behaved. I have brought wild roots roasted with onion and turnips as well as wild berries I gathered two days ago." She placed the gourd of fruit beside the cakes. "Fruit and honey on the Johnny Cakes will be very good."

They each settled a bit of the different foods to their plates as Chanti slept.

"Is it your custom for a prayer prior to eating?" Two Doves asked. "To your Jesus?"

"Yes." Alli answered. "For making our body strong from the food and for the food to be plentiful."

"Our prayer is much the same. I will hear your prayer." The young woman bowed her head waiting.

Alli nodded and bowed her own head. "Lord, bless this bounty before us and us to thy service. Amen." She kept it short considering her company.

Two Doves began eating, freeing Chanti from her papoose and laying her on the blanket. "She will wake as soon as I am eating."

The baby stretched but still slept.

"I hadn't known that your husband is raising Hawk," Alli said, curious since Leaning Bears explanation had been rather simple.

"Yes, Hawk is his son since he is chief and Hawk's mother and father are in the camp of the dead from illness." The young woman chewed the Johnny cake and swallowed. "Is very good. Hawk is twelve years, very smart. He is respectful in our camp and he has come to adore Chanti as his sister. Little Wolf adores her, as well. Hawk has made a hide of an elk fur for Chanti."

Alli hesitated but asked her thoughts. "And does he think of you as his mother?"

Two Doves shook her head. "He calls all the women mother. All mothers take care of his needs."

"I understand, but just hadn't known. Little Wolf is working on his speech and doing so well. Stuttering is difficult to overcome."

"Little Wolf was very young with the loss of his mother and did not speak until he was five years. Is very kind boy. Hawk's father was smart man, reads many books like Elina." Two Doves added. "I see Hawk reading *Gulliver's Travels* from your library. Little Wolf listens as he reads it to him."

Alli let her mouth fall open. "Why I hadn't known he was reading the story. That's wonderful. And his father doesn't mind?"

Two Doves shook her head. "Dancing Fox has said nothing since you have brought to him the dress clothing of the English. He has it hanging to keep it clean and will wear it when the white government men come to the reservation. He thinks it will make them offer more to the Cheyenne on the reservation."

Alli hadn't known his thoughts about it though he had given her a nice blanket in trade as was the custom. "I will hope his dress helps with his presentation to the officials then."

"My husband is a hard man as he must be as chief. He does not think the children should learn the white man language or religion, but I think he does not stop Hawk because he does think it best for the learning.

Hawk has told his father he wishes for school and will wear the clothing. It is well now."

Alli smiled with satisfaction settling through her. She tasted the roasted root vegetables with a garlic sauce. It was scrumptious. "Oh my, the vegetables are so good. You'll have to teach me how to make this."

"Of course." Two Doves nodded as the baby wiggled, opening her eyes. She lifted the child to her breast and sat back from her meal to lean against the tree.

Alli admired the tenderness. It must be a special feeling to hold and feed a child. She enjoyed the rest of her meal and set her own plate aside, allowing them the quiet.

"The Johnny cakes are very flavorful." Two Doves lifted the cake to continue eating as she fed the baby. "I see Leaning Bear often leaving the reservation each evening. I think perhaps he rides to check on your well-being." She lifted her brows and grinned. "He is much distracted since your arrival."

Alli's face heated, but Two Doves already understood her feelings for Leaning Bear. "There was a bit of trouble with men in town and I suppose he worries, but I didn't know he comes each evening."

Two Doves looked down at the nursing baby and rubbed the child's dark hair. "He is a very kind man when there is sickness and when he helped me with the birth. He is what is the word, smitten, with you."

"He is very kind." She had to agree but she was sure she blushed as heat rode her cheeks. "But as much as he is kind and we talk often, I suppose anything more would not be permitted."

Two Doves frowned. "Why do you think this?"

She shrugged. "Because he is Cheyenne and I am a

white woman. I suppose we would not be accepted and I don't know how if more should develop between us."

Two Doves shook her head. "My white grandmother was much the same, but she also told me love always wins and she was happier with the tribe than in the English cities. She was very happy with the Cheyenne."

"He calls me Paint The Sky. A name he chose as I never do well with painting the color of skies on my canvas." She didn't add the part about him saying the blue was the same as her eyes. That she kept for herself as well as the moments after the rain dance.

"He gives you Cheyenne name, must care very much." Two Doves laid the baby back down to her blankets and stood, removing her clothing. "But the baby is asleep again, perhaps we shall swim naked in the cold. It will prepare us for winter."

"It's so cold, I thought you were teasing about a swim." She stood, and in spite of herself, tossed caution to the wind and undressed. She'd never been shy but as it was, out in the open under a sunny sky, it did feel as if they were being watched. She glanced around them.

"Come, it will be cold but we will take it to our strength." Two Doves trotted for the water and made a diving splash into the crystal-clear water, springing up with a yip at the cold.

Alli walked into the water and shivered until her friend pulled her by the hand and she was covered in the water up to her neck. She gulped for air, her entire body shivering. "Lands, we might as well swim in the winter ice of Lake Michigan. Brrr."

She began to swim through the icy cold water, but when she stood again Two Doves was looking past the wagon, concern on her face.

“We are being watched.” Two Doves whispered. “It seems Leaning Bear has once again checked to your safety.”

Alli glanced the same direction and far beyond the wagon, astride Paytah, Leaning Bear turned the horse back toward the reservation. What was he doing here? And for that matter how long had he watched them? She ducked her body up to her neck at the water line.

“It is that he is smitten, I tell you.” Her friend teased and touched her arm. “Love will not be banished when it is true. You’ll see.”

Alli stayed below the water line but he was so far from them. Lands, had he seen them undress? Not at this point she should be shy about any of his seeing her. She turned to her friend and glanced back as Leaning Bear rode out of sight, though the picture of him riding free in the wind stayed deep inside her heart.

****

A light breeze flittered through the leaves, as Alli swept her brush across the lower portion of her canvas, studying the change in colors she’d added. Leaning Bear sat on the rocks in his usual spot, and neither had spoken much in the quiet, though he finally broke the silence.

"A white man measures his worth by money. By land. By things. A Cheyenne is measured against these things by white men that find him worth little."

It was Sunday and she’d opted out of joining the ladies who had invited her to their Sabbath, once again. She preferred the quiet of the stream. She preferred to paint. She preferred to spend time with the medicine man, but he’d seemed lost in his thoughts until now and she’d allowed him that space.

Nearby on his rock, he sharpened a large knife, the

one he wore in his boot. His comment was enough for her to think on in detail and he was right. Perhaps his thoughts on white men were part of the reason she now lived in Lame Deer. Wanting something more, wanting to make some kind of difference in the lives of the children she taught and be of worth herself. But not financial worth, as she had that. She glanced at him, and her pulse thumped hard inside her chest.

He was so handsome, his hair hanging free down his back and the feather tied at his hairline hanging by a strip of leather. At least he was talking but she sensed his mood was softer than usual. He was in no hurry to work as he sometimes was on Saturdays.

She glanced away from the canvas as he began peeling an apple he had retrieved from his bag. He didn't look at her as he twisted the fruit in one hand against the knife so that it almost appeared the apple wasn't even moving. Her mouth watered but she went back to her painting, not wanting to interrupt his being vocal.

"When I was boy, Grandfather would speak of war and of a day the tribes would be lost to the white men's ways. Dawson has spoken of these things and fights for the Cheyenne to keep land. Always tries. I know not why he does this for many years. Government does not listen. He always seeks to find the good. Reason for friendship. But like Grandfather, he sees to be accepted must become like the white people." He stood but continued with the apple, keeping his gaze on her. His deep brown eyes were intense and focused on her just as they had been on the night of the dance when he'd…she didn't allow that thought.

"But this is no good life. Fencing. Houses not as we make. Food not as we eat. White man's church is not our religion. White man's government is not ours to follow. Rules and marking the land into territories on a paper map. Fences so even the animals may not pass of free will." He spoke but his tone wasn't in anger. His expression remained still as he focused on the apple.

And it might have been the most he'd ever spoken to her at one time. The meaning of his thoughts so different from the world she had imagined until she had arrived. She turned back to her canvas painting the browns of cattails on the far edge of the stream. How could she understand the plight of the Cheyenne or any tribe as did he? But she had compassion to understand, didn't she?

"My grandfather, Stalking Eagle, told me as young man. Fight is not good. Run is not good. Hide is not good. But you are smart with the herbs and medicines he tell me. Learn the white man's language from Dawson and it will serve our people. Learn the Medicine from the white lady doctor and it will serve our people. This is yours to do. And so, I do this." He inhaled a deep breath and continued the task with the knife.

"Tess?" she asked remembering the physician was married to one of Dawson's brothers.

"Learn from doctor and Dawson many things, but learn language from many travels." He nodded and used the large knife again to shred peeling from an apple in the tiniest thin sliver that now touched the ground without breaking. "Learn from Paint The Sky."

She laid her brush aside and turned to face him with her body. Had he learned things from her? "What have you learned from me with all you've been through in your life, all the hardships of the Cheyenne?"

He stopped with the apple and studied her again. "My words are upsetting."

She shook her head, supposing her quick turn had been interpreted as being upset. "Your words only hurt that you have lived the realities of what you speak. So many things have not been as they should be for your people, my people being responsible. And here we are meeting somewhere in the middle of it all."

He glanced at Fern, who lay sleeping in the high grass and back to her. He could be so hard to read but then he stepped closer. “You think of the time after the dance.”

“Often.” Her cheeks heated, but she held his gaze. She had thought of that night every hour of every day.

“I think of this too.” He held out the apple letting the peeling drop in one coiled piece to the ground, where in an instant Fern grabbed it in her mouth running to play with it as if a string and then sitting to eat it.

He laughed but then turned back to her, serious, holding the apple out to her.

She reached for it as she rose and at the same time his hand cupped beneath her own. She didn't move as the fruit sat on her palm and his large hands held hers. She shivered ever so slightly, yet her heart raced at the idea he was leaning ever closer.

She glanced back at the fruit. He'd carved away the peeling to leave it round with no hint of divots or uneven cuts. It was a perfect sphere of yellow fruit, yet she studied the contrast between her pale skin with his much darker hand. It was beautiful in a way others would never understand. And if she could paint a quick memory of their hands together, the moment would never become lost.

Alli lifted her gaze as his face drew nearer to hers with no hesitation. His breath touched her before the impact of his lips. She closed her eyes as he held himself there unmoving. Unhurried. Purposeful.

Strange the birds chirped, and the squirrels rustled nearby in the leaves with Fern giving chase. The water trickled a current that filled the gaps of time that held them together as one. Nothing changed by his touch other than the melding of her heart with his.

He eased away and nodded for her to take the fruit. Her heart raced and her body trembled. So, he did think about their intimacy. And now he had kissed her again.

"I will offer no apology for that night." He touched a wisp of her light hair.

“And I will ask for none." She fought her emotions, her voice but a whisper.

He leaned closer again but this time, he brought his mouth to her ear. “I will come to you this night with the storm.”

Alli’s heart raced, did he mean…“Yes.”

He backed away and lifted his bag over his shoulder, and in seconds disappeared back into the depths of the forest.

She sat and studied the apple as tears spilled down her cheeks. His tender kiss had sealed them to their fate. He was Cheyenne and she was a white woman and the world would never see it as they did. Yet, she accepted what hadn't been spoken, but was forbidden. Love.

Chapter Eighteen

Alli paced back to the window as rain began to patter across the roof. Fern whined outside the cabin door, scratching, and she let the pup back inside. She glanced into the distant sky as thunder rumbled louder and heavy drops of rain began. Her pulse raced at the thought Leaning Bear would come to her tonight. The words he'd whispered to her were enough to shorten her breath and make her heart speed up. He'd said he'd come but it was already very late.

She scolded herself out loud and Fern's ears perked. "Oh, I should be nervous, shouldn't I? But maybe the rain delayed him. Or had he changed his mind?"

And while her heart did race at the idea of his visit, some part of her worried at what was occurring between them. When she looked at him, she saw strength and compassion in a very handsome, smart man. Yet, their time together wouldn't be accepted now or in the future. She might little know the way of the West, but she was well aware of what people would think of her feelings toward the medicine man.

"Oh, Fern, what am I doing anyway?" She spoke to the puppy these days as if she were human, as she did to Millie and even Andy the owl. Any sane woman would have turned Leaning Bear down due to etiquette and the appropriateness of not being married, no matter the difference in the color of their skin. And what would happen should they be discovered? Well, she wouldn't think about that. She was a grown woman and could do as she pleased.

Their love couldn't be and somewhere deep inside they each understood that. If she were admitting any truths to herself, she and Timothy had consummated their marriage long before the wedding, so why wasn't her love for Leaning Bear the same? Wasn't love a rare pearl that should be right?

She'd arrived back at home to bathe and redo her hair, pulling it atop her head and pinning it in place. She'd dressed in one of her fancier gowns, one that had satin sleeves and ribbons of gold with a taffeta blue that matched her eyes. Underneath, she had crinoline layers and pantaloons and her corset holding her breasts high. Perhaps she should wear nothing beneath the dress. No that would be much too forward, wouldn't it?

He hadn't said a time and she had supposed he'd wait until it was well past dark, but then the rain might have changed his mind as now it was pouring heavily. But it had been him that mentioned the impending storm. Maybe he wouldn't come. Maybe it was best if he didn't. No, she'd long decided even if it was a sin that she loved him and that was that. Was that wrong? This was the one time in her life it had ever felt so right. She hadn't meant to fall in love with him, but time and circumstance had brought them together anyway. It was as they had discussed, two people who belong nowhere in their own worlds and not in each other's, but together they were…they just were.

Fern ran to the door, pawing and whining as thunder cracked louder, making Alli jump. She followed, listening, but heard nothing though the pup gave a bark, the same kind she gave when she saw Leaning Bear approaching at the stream, her tail wagging. He was here. She could feel his presence. She eased the door open with a smile, but then it faded as Leaning Bear fell into the doorway, soaked from the rain and blood covering his deerskin tunic.

"Leaning Bear!" Alli grabbed him to keep him standing and he caught himself. "What on earth happened?"

He stumbled but kept his footing.

She reached around him for support. "Come, you must lie down…"

He shook his head. "I am well. Just need rest."

Alli helped him toward the bed where he sat, holding his side. "You are not well, what on earth happened?"

He shivered hard and swayed.

Alli grabbed him steadying him. "Lie down. Please, lie down, are you shot?"

"Knife, not gun." He groaned in pain, shivering hard, watering dripping off him. "Come make sure Paint The Sky is safe. Must go."

"Oh, Leaning Bear." She drew up the quilt to wrap around his shoulders. "I'll get some tea and bandages. You can't go back out in this storm."

Outside thunder clapped loud and the cabin shook. She cringed again and Fern ran to her basket in alarm.

"Must get Paytah." He touched his swollen lip as Alli ran to the stove and poured a cup of hot tea, stirring in sugar.

"The Bakers did this to you…because of me…because you've protected me. And they took Paytah?" It wasn't a question as she already understood the truth of what she'd said.

"Bakers wanted horse for long time. Not your fault." He bent, resting his elbows on his knees as she brought a cloth and warm water. She set the small bowl on the bedside table. He glanced up and his gaze searched the full of her body, his noticing her dress.

"Paint The Sky…so lovely." He swayed again and his eyes rolled back and he fell forward. Alli caught him, laying him back to the pillows and fighting with his weight to put his legs onto the bed. He was such a large man, over six foot and bulky in muscles. She began with the ties of the tunic to open the front without any hesitation. Never mind the tea to warm him, he'd passed out.

Blood seeped down his side, mixing with the moisture from the rain. She pressed the cloth hard across the open cut. He didn't move and his skin felt cool and clammy to her touch. He was so cold. For a moment she wanted to panic. She was not a doctor and he might need one. But at the same time, she held the cloth in place. He'd been before her many times with no shirt, but as she pushed the cloth across his dark skin, her breath caught. His chest was smooth, save the scars from his sun dance, hairless and the muscles of his chest thick and his abdomen knotted in the squares of rippled muscles.

"Leaning Bear," She lifted the cloth to view the wound, but he didn't move. The cut was a deep slice but did not look as though he'd been stabbed. It would have to be stitched. Howling wind outside rushed through the hearth, stoking the fire. Rain pelted harder across the roof and Fern whimpered again as thunder echoed. She glanced at the door to make sure she'd barred the door. If the Bakers had done this, they might still be around.

She laid the cloth back over his side and went to add another log to the fire. It wasn't cold but she needed to keep him warm. In her basket Fern fretted with the storm, turning circles and finally hopping onto the bed to lie beside Leaning Bear. Alli shooed her away, but he needed warmth and she could use the help, or at least the encouragement.

He needed a doctor. But there was no doctor in Lame Deer. There was no doctor with the soldiers on the reservation either. She had to do what needed doing.

She went to the stove and poured hot water into a basin and in it she mixed a bit of lye soap. From there she poured from the kettle of boiling water she'd been heating for tea. It might not help much but she had to clean the wound and stop the bleeding. She had no whiskey or the like to help his pain. She dropped several cloths into the bowl and returned to set the steaming bowl on the bedside table. It would need to cool a little.

With a bit of hesitation, she began to remove Leaning Bear's moccasins one and then the other, surprised he had no stockings or socks on his feet inside them. Her hands trembled at her efforts. She washed her hands in the soapy basin and dried them on a clean cloth.

She opened the night stand drawer and in a small tin retrieved a length of thread adding a needle. She had never been the best seamstress compared to her sister, Jacie, but she could stitch this wound. What choice did she have? She'd seen her mother do the same before.

She balled the end of the thread, estimating the length she might need. Leaning Bear had yet to move. What if there were more cuts…more wounds? She pulled back the cloth. For the most part the cut didn't bleed further. Those Bakers were horrible men and someone needed to stop this. What if Leaning Bear was worse off than the picture before her? She wanted to panic. Town was too far and the reservation also in a storm like this, not to mention she wouldn't be able to get him into her buggy in this condition.

"All right." She spoke to herself though Fern tilted her head, always attentive.

She glanced at her dress, once her best. It was wet with a bit of blood on the bodice. Oh, she could clean it later. She pulled up the chair and lifted a warm cloth from the soapy water and wrung it. No telling how dirty the Bakers knives might be and infection could kill Leaning Bear even if she did stitch it well. She laid the warm cloth over the wound and a slight moan left him.

"Leaning Bear?" She whispered but he didn't respond. She used the cloth to begin cleaning around the cut which she estimated to be at least ten inches in length but not as deep as a stab wound might have been. It was more of a slice and she cringed as she widened the wound to check.

She cleaned the cut with care. Leaning Bear moaned though he didn't open his eyes. Satisfied, she took up the needle and thread and ran it through the soapy water.

She dried the thread with one of the clean cloths as thunder cracked enough to shake the cabin. Fern whimpered and put her head down on Leaning Bear's arm.

"It's all right, Fern." She pulled together one end of the wound but Leaning Bear grabbed her wrist his body shivering hard.

"Only need rest." His voice was but a whisper.

She held the needle. "Leaning Bear, it's deep enough to need stitching. But…are there more wounds?"

“No.” He closed his eyes again letting go of her. “Begin.”

“I'm afraid I have never been the best seamstress but…I’m all you’ve got.” She dipped the needle through the edge of the wound and did the same on the other side and swirled it through its own knot and pulled it tight. A small part of the slash drew together. She glanced at him but his eyes remained closed. She tied off the stitch and knotted the string once more and began with the second. He flinched assuring her he was awake. “I'm sorry. I know it hurts.”

“Have hurt many times.” His breath came in rapid spurts.

Alli continued closing the wound. “What will you do about Paytah? You can’t do anything if you go out in this. You must stay here for now.”

“Horse rides no one. Will throw rider. Does not like saddle.” He chuckled and then his face wrinkled in pain as she stuck the needle again. “Will find him or he will find me.”

“The Bakers cause so much trouble. How did this happen?” She pulled the thread through again.

It was a long moment and another stitch before he answered. “Tied Paytah to swim across pool at base of stream to bathe before storm. Dried when I hear thunder and put on buckskins and moccasins. Dark and rain began…caught off guard. My fault.” He touched her hair up in its chignon. “Thoughts distracted.” He gave her a faint smile.

“Perhaps another time then.” She pushed his hand back down aware she was blushing. “You are in no condition.”

“Don't worry, Paint The Sky. Will deal with Bakers

soon." He closed his eyes again and he gave another hard shiver.

"But back and forth fighting with them, it will never end." She fought her emotions and to steady her hand.

"I will end this." He spoke sure, though he grimaced.

"But you are hurt, you can't…what if they kill you…they aren't beyond trying?" Her voice cracked.

"Paint The Sky, not to worry. This not fight for you." His voice faded and he closed his eyes again.

Alli urged him to drink the tea, which he gulped and fell back to the bedding. She'd finished closing the wound and added ointment and a dressing. How could the town of Lame Deer take so much abuse and no one do anything about it? And darn it, she'd been the reason this happened to Leaning Bear. Well, she wasn't gonna sit down about it any longer. She would send a telegram to the Federal Marshall's office since there was no real sheriff. Enough was enough. What if they did kill Leaning Bear, or even her? Something had to stop these men from continuing.

"It's done." She let out an exasperated breath.

But then Leaning Bear tried to sit up. She pushed him back to the bedding. "You cannot go out into this storm in your condition. I won't let you."

"Is not good to be here." He groaned, holding his side.

Alli placed her hands to his upper chest and pushed him back until he gave in. "I'm not afraid of the Bakers or what people think. I'm not afraid of who knows about us. But I am afraid of your being hurt or perhaps…killed."

He held her gaze taking her hand in his. "Paint The

Sky is white woman. I am Cheyenne. Best that not to be known. Will go by morning."

Alli nodded but didn't let go of his hand as he closed his eyes once more. From the look of the bruises to his face, he'd been hit hard besides the cut she had stitched. And to her best guess, the Bakers would have their revenge once this storm ended, but until then it was going to be a long night of worry with little sleep. But come the storms end, she'd go to town and see what could be done about those men the legal way.

****

The noon sky still held clouds making Alli 's skin prickle with the matching light wind which was cool. She'd woken, still in the chair, to find Leaning Bear gone in spite of his injuries. How she'd slept that hard sitting up she didn't know, but he had. But the storm had dissipated leaving the streets of town nothing but black mud.

She urged Millie with her buggy to a stop outside the Trading Post. She hadn't come to town since the skirmish with the Bakers at her home and her pulse raced at the idea, she would send her telegram to the Federal Marshall's office today. And after Leaning Bear's incident, someone had to stop the Bakers once and for all.

Millie's hooves squashed into the puddles of soaked earth, mud clinging to her lower legs. Alli had worn a plain skirt and blouse and her broad brimmed hat in case more rain began, but it did appear the sun was going to show its colors today. She glanced down at her high heeled boots, well they'd have to do, all she had that was leather and wouldn't allow her to gain trench foot from the dampness.

She needed supplies along with this visit to town, though she worried about Leaning Bear. He'd been so fatigued and if the wound she'd stitched festered he could become very ill or even…no she wouldn't think of that. But how could she continue to live in the town of Lame Deer if she had to fear the repercussions of the Bakers each day? And how could Leaning Bear continue his work for Maud if he was at risk? Would the town citizens join her in wanting the law to intercede or had they not tried that before?

She jumped down from the buggy outside the Trading Post and tossed her bag over her shoulder, stepping gingerly. She needed to mail a letter to Jacie and see if any had arrived and send that telegram. She was out of flour and wanted to purchase more meat from the butcher as she'd yet to have the nerve to try to shoot the rabbits or squirrels that played around her home. Maybe it was that she didn't have the heart for such. And while she kept the pistol in her bag, she had a mind to use it if the Bakers or some animals were to attempt to harm her once more. She turned to look about her hoping she avoided the Bakers for today.

She eased her way through the mud on tip toes, stepping up to the wooden sidewalk of the Trading Post right as Mrs. Landers and Mrs. Rogers came toward her. The women whispered back and forth. She'd not attended the local church yet. It might be she'd attend at some point but it wouldn't be these ladies who lured her there.

"Good morning, ladies, I do hope the week has treated you kindly." She stopped before them.

Mrs. Landers scoffed and walked on past her, though Mrs. Rogers held her gaze for a long moment and then walked on passed her too.

What had happened? Why had they ignored her and not even spoken a simple hello? “I’m sorry, what…” She didn’t finish as the ladies crossed the street as if scandalized by her presence.

“Afternoon, Mrs. Crockett.” Maud still never called her Alli.

“Good afternoon, Maud.” She still watched the ladies walk away from her. “It must be I have the plague or either it’s because I’ve not attended church since my arrival.”

Maud shoved her hands into her pockets and spat tobacco to the muddy street but walked closer to her. “No, ain’t that.”

Alli turned to face her, Maud’s tone assuming. “What has happened that no one wishes to speak to me?”

Maud glanced around as if she too were worried of speaking to her. “Well, Mrs. Crockett, Alli, most in town know the Bakers fought with Leaning Bear, cause old man Baker took a knife to the belly, though he’s gonna be all right, much to the chagrin of most. But…” The woman hesitated but shook her head. “The brothers, they been about spreading word of…well, that…” She leaned closer and whispered. “That Leaning Bear has been a stayin’ nights at your place.”

“What?” Alli’s mouth dropped open. “I beg your pardon, but yes, Leaning Bear was in my home last night because he was badly hurt and needed stitching is all. They have no right to…”

“Don’t matter much around here, Ma’am…news travels fast in Lame Deer.” Maud still whispered glancing around them. “Best you stay clear of town for a while, Ma’am. You ain’t no problem with dealing with me here at the post, but it might be you have trouble elsewhere."

Alli shook her head. How had this happened? The one night in the school no one knew of and last night had been innocent enough in caring for Leaning Bear's injuries. But then, she'd known this might happen but…now what to do. Maybe Maud was right.

"Maud that is not how things happened. Leaning Bear was cut in the same fight I assume as Mr. Baker. He needed help, what would anyone have had me do, leave him to die? He was there until the storm was over. Nothing more." Alli held her voice steady, not allowing emotions to overtake her thoughts.

"Well, those Baker boys spreading rumors ain't nothing new, but you'll have a hard enough time of it if'n you ain't careful." The rotund woman spat a slurry of words in a whisper.

"You know he was repairing my porch but…so those brothers have lied spreading rumors of that. If the Bakers know this then there is proof, they are watching my home and that in itself is frightening. They came by a few weeks back as I was doing the wash and I have no ideas of their real purpose in doing so other than to take what they wanted, trying to sell me a horse I'm sure was stolen." Alli gripped her hands to fists.

"Shhhh." Maud waved her hands to shush her, glancing round them and pulling her farther away from those browsing outside the Trading Post. "Best not to say the like, those Bakers will do more than what's already happened, Ma'am. Come, I've a letter for you inside, anyways."

Alli followed her inside the store, still unable to fathom the thoughts of the women and the gossip the

Bakers had spread. And now what she and Leaning Bear had spoken about their differences had surfaced for all to know. Even a town like Lame Deer would never be accepting of them together. And maybe the rain had interrupted for reasons last night that she didn't understand until now.

Maud leaned closer. "Those Bakers rode into town with their Pa bent over his horse, bloody as a stuck pig and the boys themselves with bruises too. Best Leaning Bear keeps in hiding, though there ain't no sheriff to do much about it."

Alli's pulse raced at the thought. It was by far not over as Leaning Bear had said. The Bakers would be riled further and then what? She stopped at the counter as Maud went behind and held out a letter to her.

She took it and put it inside her bag. "Maud, why have the citizens here in Lame Deer allowed the continued abuse from the Bakers, you yourself paying to keep them from harassing you? They take what they want, require payments from shopkeepers, why can't they be stopped? Why can't all band together in this effort to be rid of them? I am bound to telegram the Federal Marshalls at this point." Alli talked in a strained whisper.

Maud's eyes widened and her voice hushed further. "Don't speak of it, Mrs. Crockett. That would be worse for everyone here and bad for yourself. That's right you don't know do ya?"

Alli shook her head. "Know what?"

"Ya know that burnt tree at the fork where you make your way to your cabin?" Maud leaned in. "We had a tinker in town a few years back, he wouldn't pay the Bakers, found himself tied to the tree and burned till there weren't nothing left all on account he threatened to contact the law. He was made the example for all."

Alli let her mouth drop open for a moment. "Lands, I had no idea, but still, how can we all live afraid and allow them to take and take and take. I stitched a ten-inch cut in Leaning Bear's side. It's not right and if we all band together, get the Marshals here, why couldn't we stop the Bakers?"

"Don't say it, Mrs. Crockett, they'd kill the lot of us, it's just the way it is here. This is Lame Deer, no good luck found in this town. Nothing good much here except passing through." The older woman straightened items on the shelf beside them and glanced at her again.

"So, if'n you're a planning on staying for any time as teacher, best you keep quiet and let things go. All of us would be wise to do the same. You bring the Federals here and those Bakers might'n kill us all." Maud's chubby face went scalded red as she forced the bit of an angered whisper.

"But why? They cannot kill the entire town." Alli argued, stepping closer. "Someone has to stop this."

Maud scratched her cheek and blinked hard. "Then Mrs. Crockett, you'd be ready to be first on their list?"

"We cannot live in fear like this. We could all stand together, do this as a town." She leaned in closer to lower her voice yet again.

But Maud changed the subject. "Meanwhile, what are you needing? Best we stop a sayin' things. You should get your shopping done. Keep to yourself at home while things calm a bit." Maud warned, glancing around the store.

Alli wanted to say more but it was apparent Maud had already figured everything for her. And while she'd wanted to telegram for the federal marshals, it seemed if the Bakers told the story, Leaning Bear would be the one to pay the price.

"I have need of flour and I'd like a large bag of gumdrops to share with the children as well as a pound of sugar. Do you think I can go by the meat market without reprehend?" she asked Maud as she needed meat for her meals and for Fern.

"I'll add it all to your tab for now, you go get the meat a 'fore it gets later in the day and be quick about it. And you see Leaning Bear let him know I'll get his pay to the captain; he can be trusted. Though it might be best you didn't see him for a while. He needs to stay out of town, though I reckon he'll be a knowin' that." Maud picked up the sack of sugar.

Alli held the woman's gaze and nodded. What more could she say? No one in Lame Deer would believe Leaning Bear…or her. And if all thought Leaning Bear had stayed in her home, she had to wonder about her survival here in Lame Deer. If everyone in town shunned her, what would that really mean? Dread flowed through her.

"I see that concern on your face, but the Bakers, they are figuring you have money, Mrs. Crockett. You hide yer money multiple places and don't show around here for a while. And don't face off with those Bakers about horses and say anything. Maybe you might think about leaving a'fore it gets worse." The older woman nodded and led the way to the counter with a few of her items.

"Maud this is my home now. And I adore the children and they are learning so much. I can't leave now and let go of the promises I made to them. I won't do that to them, like all the previous teachers." She shook her head at the idea.

Maud glanced at her. “You only come to town on Sunday mornings from now on. Those women will be in church and the Baker boys are usually passed out from Saturday nights in the saloon. Stay out of sight for a while, ’cept you’re teaching on the reservation.”

Alli nodded. It was best she kept to herself for now. Leastwise, until she could know Leaning Bear’s thoughts on it all. But now as she turned to the rest of her shopping in town, she hoped the gossip didn’t find her again. Her thoughts drifted to Leaning Bear and how he was faring. He’d been so weak. But as it was, she needn’t warn him about things he already understood far better than she.

Chapter Nineteen

Alli sipped her tea and moved the beef stew around on her plate. It had been a week since she'd been to town. She'd thankfully seen anything of the Bakers but she also hadn't seen Leaning Bear since she'd stitched his side. She could only think that he was hiding out to let things simmer down.

The week with the children had been a good distraction as had the return of Two Doves to school, wearing her baby on the papoose on her back most of the time. Chanti was a good baby and the children, even the boys seemed to adore her. But this afternoon, Two Doves had spoken of Leaning Bear traveling elsewhere to sell herbs and she hadn't known when his return would be. Her friend had known her melancholy over the fact he wasn't in camp.

She put her plate on the floor where Fern sat waiting, her tail thumping the wooden flooring. The dog didn't move until she gave her permission. "All right."

The pup dove into the stew as if it were the last food on earth and licked the plate clean. It was late anyway and Alli rose to add another log to the fire, but turned with the screech of Andy the owl from outside. It wasn't unusual but it didn't sound like the exact sound the owl made most of the time. But then…what if it was…the Bakers?

She moved to her bag and took out the pistol she'd

cleaned and reloaded earlier. She dimmed the lantern to darken her cabin and the call came once more. No, it wasn't the Bakers, and she waited for it to come again. How could she tell him, she was aware and it was safe for now? Leaning Bear must be outside as the call was from him and not Andy. But he shouldn't come here, should he?

Fern scampered to the door ahead of her, tail wagging. Alli pulled up the bar and stood in the opened doorway. And he was there, Leaning Bear, dressed in his buckskins, her heart relieved of the worry in the single moment he took her into his arms, closing the door behind them.

"I knew it was you, I've been so worried…" Her words were interrupted by the warmth of his lips, taking her mouth. She moaned and wrapped her arms about him, holding him to her and he paused his kiss.

"You are well." He whispered, though he didn't let her go. "I worry about Paint The Sky and I watch but cannot say I am here."

"I'm fine." She clung to him, so very relieved. "I've a stew. Are you hungry?"

He let a slight smile curl his lips. "Am hungry but not for food." With that he took her mouth again as Fern scampered over to her basket with a small bone he handed to the pup.

Alli touched his side where the stitches were gone and scabbing had formed.

"You took out the stitches." She whispered, surprised how fast he had healed.

"It is as you say." He gave a hint of a grin and held her tighter. "Easy, good sewing."

Alli moaned again at the capture of her lips and the

taste of mint. His kiss was firm and warm and he took his time, exploring her body with his hands.

His gaze held hers but he tilted his head closer. It was strange how his dark eyes could hold her captive with little effort. “You would have this? My touch of you?”

She was being shunned in town, and he had been on the run, but here they were once again. “Yes…”

And as the word left her throat his lips traced across hers. She shivered and parted her lips allowing his tender access. He traced a palm along her neck and the side of her face as he teased with his tongue. The complete of her body flushed. He pulled from the kiss and of all things raised his hand to touch her hair, tugging away each pin one by one as she stood breathless. Her hair began falling over her shoulders and down her back. It had been so long for her, so long since his previous touch but even longer since…Timothy. He captured a section of the length of her hair and brought it to his face inhaling and closing his eyes for a long moment as he touched it to his face.

He opened his eyes again. “And if I touch you, the sun will still rise come morning, no matter the consequences or thoughts of others.”

She nodded assuming he was telling her nothing would change for either of them. He could promise her no more than this night. And if that was all they had, then…“Yes.”

His hands eased around her hips and as he held her in his sights, he tugged her blouse free of her skirt and began with the buttons one by one. Alli’s breath caught at the tenderness with which he touched each button, taking his time. Her blouse fell off her shoulders and down her arms as he brought his lips to her neck kissing multiple places, a soft moan escaping him.

"Ne'me'hota'tse." He whispered as his palms rose to her stays. He let his hands slide around the back to the ties but she pulled the length of the bow to release it for him.

"I love you, Leaning Bear." Her pulse raced at his words as his hands moved to her chemise that he eased up and over her head, leaving her chest bared before him. She shivered as his hands traced the skin of her breasts, though he never took his eyes from hers. She tugged on the ties at the front of his buckskins and he stepped, back allowing her to untie them.

Her own boldness shocked her but she had no idea how a Cheyenne man would go about the act. But somehow there were no expectations or need for her to find herself bashful. She wanted this, the hard press of his body to hers, no matter they were from two different worlds. She kicked from her boots and they clunked to the floor one at a time as he pulled her to his smooth chest, crushing her breasts between them. He held her that way for a long moment.

She placed her palms flat to his chest. He was solid, so hard with the muscles she'd long admired. She stroked over the rounded scars from his sun dance and he watched her fingers trace each, saying nothing. She let her fingers touch his hair as he had hers. It was loose, hanging about his shoulders and to her surprise soft and untangled. He smelled of earth and leather and she lifted his hands to her breasts. "Touch me, Leaning Bear."

He rubbed both palms over her nipples but then he slid his large hands down her sides and over her hips pushing down her skirts, which didn't give. She did that for him as well, it evident when she let her eyes stray that he was more than ready for her. She let the skirts fall, leaving her in her pantaloons.

"Too many clothing." He whispered and touched her hair, sliding a hand to her neck and drawing her forward, taking her lips and kissing down her neck to her breasts. As he bent further, he drew down her pantaloons and touched her there, a soft growl leaving him. "This like the sun too."

She placed her hand with his, a slight giggle escaping her at his surprise she was blonde where he touched. That had amused Timothy once as well. "Blonde…not sun."

He groaned and lifted her into his arms and carried her to the bedding, plopping her down on the top covers. She scooted to allow room for him but he didn't lie down.

He stood at her knees and removed the medicine bag and bear claw from around his neck, setting them on her table, all the while keeping his dark eyes on hers. Alli's breath hitched to a complete stop as he bent and removed his moccasins followed by his buckskin trousers. She took the depth of breath she'd missed as he stood before her naked. He was beautiful, solid and his skin a perfect bronze.

Her pulse raced and would she know how to please him? It had been years now. He pushed her back into the bedding, covering her with his body, his mouth finding hers in a teasing dance as a hand found her breast. He squeezed with a palm, and she moaned as the warmth of his mouth found a nipple. He hovered above her as he found the second, sucking it to a taut peek and her chest lifted from the bed as he feasted back and forth.

Oh, Lands, she wanted so…right or wrong, it was a real love that built their passion.

He traced one hand down her torso and to her blonde curls again, his knee between her thighs parting her legs further. She kissed his shoulders as he pushed her thighs wide and found the pert nub of her pleasure with his fingers. She panted as he teased with purpose.

She placed her hand to his cheek, wanting him to stop, wanting the hard crush of his body into her making them one. He lay between her thighs but waited, holding her gaze as if for permission. She placed her lips to his, granting him what they both wanted.

The breech of him came swift and deep. She kissed his shoulders and neck, tasting him and pressing herself to meet him with each stroke. And as awkward as it could have been, no words were needed as they became one, touching and tasting and urging each other to the pulse of pleasure. She ran her hand down his hard back urging him, her body growing in heated bliss.

She tensed as the pleasure came, her body splintering into the heights of heaven. She bowed at the intensity and cried his name. And as she landed back in his arms he groaned, withdrawing and shuddering through a growl as she held him. He hadn't finished inside her, but she held him anyway as his body shook with him atop her.

Leaning Bear rolled from her, still holding her, his breath heavy.

"You did that to protect me." She spoke though she didn't move from him.

He inhaled the sweet flowery smell of her hair, understanding her meaning. "Will not bring shame to you with a child."

She rolled to her back and took his hand to the scar along her belly he had touched but had not asked about. It was long, from her naval down. He leaned up on an elbow and touched the texture, it's line faint in the light but palpable.

"I was very ill as a young woman and I had a surgery. I…there can be no children." She whispered, their fingers tangling.

He angled his head again and traced the scar once more. "This is hard for you not to be a mother?"

She touched the scar herself and sadness was easy to see across her features. "At times I am sad for not having children, but that feeling comes and goes as I have learned to live with it. Perhaps why I do so love the children I teach so very much."

It had to be difficult for any woman who could not become a mother. He had not known this about her. "For this I am sorry for Paint The Sky."

"It's as things are, like you tell me." Her voice held sadness that he could not take away, yet she pulled him to her. "Never mind that, but there is no worry of children when we make love."

Some part of his heart warmed with her brave smile. "Then I will make this love again this night."

She reached for his medicine bag and the claw from the table beside her bed. "Tell me about these first." She placed them both over his head to hang around his neck.

He rolled to his back and lifted the claw. "Trade this claw with Dawson on first meeting. Next, I see him he will give me a small knife to carry and I will give this claw to him."

"And the pouch?" She handled the bag and laid it back to his chest.

“Medicine bag, holds my strength. Is to keep health. Sacred.” He whispered as he touched her hair playing it through his fingers. He’d easily become fascinated in how it pulled straight but bounced back into curls.

“Am I allowed to ask what it contains?” She lifted her head, looking at him and then the small pouch.

He grinned, in spite of all that had happened and wanting to tease. “Can tell you but would have to kill you after.”

Her mouth popped open. “What? You are making light of me and I am trying to be respectful.”

He let his hands run down her back and across her bottom, easing her to sit atop him, ready to have her once more.

She moaned closing her eyes and moving as he led her. This she had done before. And now he would not leave her body when he reached the height of his passion. He lifted his hand to her face and he would hold her as he brought the same to her again. “Will show you contents of pouch at stream, not now.”

And with that he urged her to glide along him in a slow dance, touching her and watching her dance upon him. How free she moved and allowed her body to be pleasured. When she went rigid and cried into the night, he joined her, pulling her down and holding the only song his heart would ever hold.

Chapter Twenty

Leaning Bear stood against the night air at his camp in the trees. The moon was full, giving the trees around him a silver color as they lifted in the light winds. He'd been here after his time spent with Alli, time he should not have taken. His love for her put them both at risk, something he didn't want to bring to her. But he'd been powerless not to hold her as he'd longed. The hints of the small fire behind him added smoke that drifted in soft waves before him. And the bear inside him remained quiet, yet the mountain lion paced uneasy.

He tugged in several deep breaths. He had left the reservation with ease after dark and in spite of his recent fight with the Bakers, gone to her again. Their time together had been with a comfort of which he had not known in a very long time. But he could not shake the idea all he had done was bring danger from the Bakers closer to her again.

He had not seen the men since the night of his attack, but he understood from Alli that their rumors had caused some of the white women in town to shun her. That was not good. None of the white people in town would approve of his spending time with her at the stream, much less the time spent in her bed. But this was done. She was his heartsong and he could not deny her or himself.

But he did not think issues with the Bakers to pass

them by and if he endangered her further with his love, then he had to do what was best. Decisions were sometimes hard, but he would not allow those men to harm her. That meant the Bakers would have to be stopped—but how to do that without losing his own life was one thing. But if he took theirs, he was a dead man.

He was not afraid of death, except for the part that would keep him from her. Never had his heart been as full and never had he desired the body and mind of any woman as much. As he kept saying, he was indeed a fool. And it was clear that Dancing Fox as well as several other Cheyenne had figured some of his dilemma. The men made light of his problems when he stayed on the reservation and tonight, he would not deal with them, by staying in his camp in the trees.

He was missing out on making money from not being able work at the Trading Post, due to keeping himself from encountering the men again, but that would come. With no law in the town of Lame Deer, it was not as if he would be hunted down for their recent fight, but if he was present in town enough, there was always the chance he would be hanged with little thought from the Bakers and a few others only due to the color of his skin.

But Alli had become the song of his heart he'd never found until now. And whatever it took to free her and himself from these men he would do. He wanted to sit close by her as she painted, he wanted to talk with her of things in their lives and he wanted to hold her in passion again and again. But he had broken all the rules that had been placed between them and all the reasons he should not love her.

"Ppfftt." He scolded himself. He wanted so many things from her besides that which beckoned his body.

He wanted to watch the wind touch her light hair and see her smile when her painting pleased her. And he had grown used to her endless chatter. White women did that. Talk fast and about so many things and never stop talking.

He bent to his knees for prayers to those in the camp of the dead and for answers from his totem and the spirits. When morning came, he'd see her again at the stream. Perhaps she would arrive early, perhaps she would paint the sky as he called her. Never had he thought he would find his heartsong in a white woman. Never had he seen any woman more beautiful.

The fire crackled behind him, and he stood and turned back to his camp. The semblance of a home, high above the stream that played off the river—the Bakers nor any of his Cheyenne brothers were aware of this place. He lay across the large buffalo hide, glancing into the stars scattered across the clear sky. He closed his eyes and her face appeared before him as if in a vision. She always held a smile…the edge of her lip curling, her eyes turning as if a light kept them aglow. He allowed himself the sleep his body desired with her still floating along in his thoughts, giving himself to sleep.

****

Alli stood outside the school and rang the morning bell. She welcomed the children to class as she did each day, and on the blackboard had chalked out their morning work and routine had set in. The children laughed and went about their individual tasks without delay. She glanced toward the captain. Two wagons of soldiers and men dressed in full fancy military dress stood before the captain.

Leaning Bear had told her that government and

military officials were visiting the reservation to review living conditions for the soldiers and the Indians. She watched for a long moment as the soldiers lined up and saluted those addressed to them. It was rare for any of them to be in some kind of formation, and certainly never dressed as orderly as they were today.

She glanced back at her classroom full of children in their uniforms. It had not taken them long to appreciate being prepared, and dressed well each day for class. She smiled but movement toward the lodges caught her attention. Leaning Bear and several other men followed Dancing Fox who, of all things, wore his full English clothing with his hair braided and hanging down his back. He was wearing her gift and she found herself in awe at the spectacle.

As the chief and braves passed the school, she caught Dancing Fox's gaze. He was aware she had not seen him dressed in his finest. And while he said nothing, he held her sights long enough that he understood she was applauding him wearing the clothing she had gifted to him. At least it seemed so.

She looked at Leaning Bear who didn't acknowledge her either but then it was best he didn't. And if Dancing Fox was handsome, then Leaning Bear, in his full buckskin dress with blue dye was every bit as distinguished in leading the men to the meeting. He was so tall and held himself with pride and he was the man she loved. Her heart raced inside her chest in just looking on.

He'd said little about what the meeting would encompass, other than it was a necessary yearly meeting. It was set to benefit the tribes by way of food or medicine or now might ultimately decide the fate of the reservation’s continued existence. No matter, she was well aware he thought most of the promises were lies.

He and his people had lost much to the history of broken promises from the government. He had lived firsthand the written treaties that promised the slaughter of women and children. Things he most often didn't wish to talk about and her own stomach had turned at the horrors he had shared.

She moved back into the school. Each student was at their work, even the boys, who had learned if their morning work wasn't complete, they didn't get recess at lunch but had to eat at their desk. Oh, she wanted the children to have fun and have a recess but setting the rules made things better for all.

And as she assisted those who had questions, she was conscious of looking at each child's face. To study them and understand the lives before them. Hawk even worked hard at his studies; another book chosen for him to take to his lodge for reading. And the best she could hope was that these children before her lived lives that were better because of her work here. That each found more than this reservation in their futures.

Somehow, she had come here for this very reason. To make sure these children, who might matter little to her white world and government, acclimated over time and were accepted as smart and eager workers. She glanced at Elina.

Weeks ago, she had mailed Jacie the girl’s transcript and written of her abilities in reading and arithmetic. She'd asked Jacie to act on her behalf of going to the university to ask of Elena's acceptance there in a year when she was done with her studies. The girl’s mother was pleased with the idea but her father, a man called

Bent Tree, had scoffed at the details. Time would tell on that but should she not be accepted, there were many women's colleges and she herself wouldn't stop until Elina had found placement.

She stepped to the door again and the men were standing in their opposing groups, with soldiers on one side of the table and the Cheyenne on the other. Dancing Fox and Leaning Bear in the front.

The scene made her heart race as she hoped the braves could hunt and the reservation would be official land for the Cheynne in the coming years. Leaning Bear's stories were often about how many times his people had been moved with no choice in the matter. She studied his face.

He showed no emotion. He spoke and pointed to the table tracing a finger. She assumed a map before him. Dancing Fox stood stoic with his arms folded though he nodded at times.

She turned back to the children as Hawk walked to look out the door alongside her. "The white soldiers promise to give us this land, but my father says they will lie once more. He says men in fancy hats never tell the truth."

Alli wasn't sure how to respond. "Perhaps this time will be different. Just as you children are learning here in this classroom maybe the soldiers will learn more of the Cheyenne ways."

Hawk walked closer to peer out. "One day I will fight for keeping our land and hunting as my ancestors hunted. I will be brave like Dancing Fox and my first father."

Little Wolf ran to the door to peek out as well. "I will be Medicine Man like Leaning Bear 'cause I am smart already about the leav…leav…leaves and herbs."

"Indeed, you are and it takes smart men to do both those things." She touched his shoulder and turned back to the classroom of children. Perhaps he would one day be a medicine man. "All right, it's time for arithmetic, take up your slates. The problems are on the board for each grade. Complete your assignments and we'll see how you all do."

The children grumbled, at least the boys did. She went to her desk as they worked. She worried most about Hawk and his wish to fight. He wasn't much different from the boys in school back home who were ready to go to war when the war between the states had begun.

She lifted her chalk and went to the board to go over the arithmetic as the students began finishing. How she wanted to watch from the door to see Leaning Bear's exchange with all the men. And somehow, she wanted to sketch the scene of the men at the table. That's what she'd do later when she got home.

"How would you all like to draw today?" Cheers erupted and she began handing each child a piece of paper from a tablet. She was unable to focus and supposed it was much the same for the children. "You may all draw freely of your choosing but it needs to be about something that makes you very happy."

Eagerly the children lifted pencils, all but Hawk who glanced behind him out the door once more. She understood his feelings well enough and when his gaze met hers, she gave him a nod. He disappeared out the door quiet enough the other students paid him no attention.

She eased to the door and looked on as he ran toward the other teen boys waiting near where Dancing Fox and

Leaning Bear met with the officials. How could she keep him from observing history being made, even if it might not go as planned? But her focus remained on Leaning Bear. So tall and handsome. And how the topics at the meeting went would now affect her too, because she'd grown to love these people and the children. And mostly because she had grown to love the medicine man and all he stood for. Fern whimpered at her feet and she lifted the pup and walked her back to her basket and gave her a biscuit to stay there. Her mind held the picture of the scene on the reservation so she went to her desk and joined the children as she lifted a chalk to her own piece of paper.

Chapter Twenty-One

A heavy rain had continued all morning as Alli made her way back to the porch from inside her cabin. She held a bowl of chicken with dumplings and a cornbread muffin for Leaning Bear. His arrival had surprised her given it was daylight. But when he hadn't found her at the stream, he explained his purpose was to check on her well-being. The thought might have been nice had she not worried about the Bakers. He'd been the one surprised to find her painting on her porch, where she could keep an eye on Fern. The rain and frustration with the blue sky of her painting made it easier for her to step away to allow him the meal.

As he didn't have his nearby rock to sit on, he sat on the edge of the porch whittling at some thin slivers of wood. She gathered not what for and hesitated much to talk about their night spent together and he had not mentioned it either, though he had pulled her against him embracing her on his arrival.

"I have a bowl of dumplings and cornbread for you." She set it beside him on the porch and returned to her chair to paint. The rain had lessened to a sprinkle, but the light was not like it had first been on the canvas, and as usual she'd yet to add anything for the skies in this newest painting. She was Paint The Sky, so why couldn't she do that?

"Appreciate bowl and bread." He set the knife and

wood aside and smelled the steaming bowl with a nod of satisfaction.

"The children loved it when I served it in class for the break a few days ago. While we enjoyed our lunch, Elina read us a story she wrote about the flight of an eagle. It was exceptional."

He nodded. "Elina much like mother who reads and writes in English."

"She has been reading since she was small so I'm afraid I cannot take much credit for her learning. She has consumed every book I brought from back home." She lifted a brush and touched the canvas with yellow. "I've asked my sister to mail more books as she has the opportunity."

"Mother assume credit for Elina's education." He turned up the bowl instead of using the spoon she'd added.

"I met her mother, Sprouting Swan." She remembered the shy woman. "She was very proud of her daughter but when I mentioned Elina would be an excellent student at University if she applied, she was uncertain it was a good idea as her husband wasn't very fond of the plans."

He gave a grunt and continued chewing. "What good University for Cheyenne girl, can't leave reservation to teach."

She shook her head. "She would make an excellent student and if not permitted to teach outside the reservation she would be very good at teaching as I do here. The Universities often allow those who test well free tuition, well, at least at the women's colleges."

He set his bowl aside. "What good even free?"

"She would like to be a teacher but she'd also make

a fine doctor or lawyer or other choice. The possibilities are many." How could he ask such a question and not see how things would change for the girl if she had an education from a university?

"Cheyenne woman with much school would not change many things. I have been to cities. I see University. Many women. White women such as Paint The Sky." He lifted his knife again and whittled at the thin length of wood, his dumpling bowl empty.

"But you read and understand English very well. Why not allow this for her or others who have the ability." Her voice rose an octave.

He didn't say anything for a long time. "Cheyenne teacher will teach Indian nation. Not welcome to teach in white schools. Why this needed then?"

"I would think passing up the opportunity is a shame for such a smart girl." She glanced at her painting where the yellow had dried darker than her liking.

"Then must convince mother." He glanced at her when she tsked her painting.

"Well, it's her father who isn't happy with the idea. But you were saying it wasn't a good idea and you think so now?" She questioned him further, dipping the brush again.

"I ask what good. Show mother that good. Show father that good." He took a bite of the cornbread he'd set on the porch.

"So, you agree?"

"Not my child to agree. Mother to decide." He sat for a moment without saying more. "Must understand purpose and reasons."

"Well, for education of course." She set the brush aside in her continued frustration of him and the paint.

"Parents must understand education at university. Must understand daughter to leave for city alone. Must understand time. Must understand money. Must understand what will come after study. This you know? Explain to mother and father." He used his hands as he talked. He did that from time to time and she was caught up for a moment in the motions he made.

"Well, what is wrong with education for the sake of education? She could broaden her ideas and knowledge tenfold." She folded her arms, shaking her head at his not understanding.

He placed the cornbread into the bowl. "You have plan for after? Otherwise, she comes here again for nothing."

"No but I could…"

"You have plan. Tell mother then." He interrupted.

How could she plan for sure? There were many Africans and a few Indians who had been at the university where she had attended. "Yes, maybe I will then. Oh, I forgot, you left your bear claw here." She ran inside to grab it from the table by her bed, where he'd left it.

She turned and he stood at the porch looking past her. Alli glanced across the room to where the painting of him at the dance was finished. She hadn't meant for him to see it yet but now he had.

He stepped a bit closer. "Paint The Sky puts me on canvas?"

She offered the hint of a smile. "Come closer. I sketched you that night at the rain dance and have been working on this each evening. I'm very happy how it turned out. I hope you like it."

He studied her work for a long moment. "Not see

myself dance until now."

"Well, it was very nice or beautiful as you men danced together. I found myself wanting to paint many things but mostly you." She glanced from the painting back to him.

He turned to her. "Like it very much. Colors true."

"Yes." She shrugged, "And I painted your sky."

He nodded at the painting but leaned closer and pulled her into his embrace. "My sky holds the colors of your eyes. This I tell you."

Alli relished in leaning into him, but he eased her back and placed the bear claw necklace over his head to hang at his neck.

"We haven't talked about our time here together since it happened." Her heart raced as she mentioned it, the timing seemingly right.

"What to say of it?" He angled a curious glance at her.

"Well, what it means between us?" She then whispered. "The words of…love."

He allowed a slight grin. "I tell you in my words each time I lie with you."

"Yes." She answered. "But I wonder what this means for us. I loved your words, but you still have not found Paytah and the Bakers are always a waiting threat of worry. And I've not been back to town as Maud suggested. I suppose it's hard for me to feel like I am living in some kind of fear all the time. Maybe hearing your words again will be something I wait to hear once more."

"Paint The Sky not to worry." He spoke in a depth of voice that sounded convincing and embraced her again. "I am watching. Will find Paytah. Suspect he is in

Baker's barn. Suspect they wait for me to come and when time is right, I will go."

"But they'll hurt you or even kill you, aren't you afraid?" She fought impending tears at the idea.

"Have no fear of Bakers. Do not fear death except where it takes me from Paint The Sky. This is my fear." He placed a palm to her cheek and brushed away the tears there. "Not to worry. No tears."

She nodded.

"Will see about Millie in barn, clean stall." He nodded to where she'd set up her ironing. "You iron things. Will wait on porch. Best I am here to work should anyone know."

She brushed both her cheeks dry and stepped to complete her ironing. Her thoughts raced over all the details but as it was, he was right. She could live in constant fear or try to get back to normal. The ironing was complete in no time it seemed and she set the iron aside.

She walked back to the front door and swung it open and stepped out onto the porch. The rain continued to clatter and before her Leaning Bear sat at her painting. She stopped in her tracks. The painting was finished, the teal sky merging to a hue of lighter blue until white clouds floated in the distance. Beautiful.

"Leaning Bear." She walked closer. "You painted the sky."

He nodded. "This not good idea?"

"Oh, it's fine. Beautiful in fact, the colors as I remember." She touched the edge of the canvas.

He studied her for the longest time. "When young man. Meet Dawson. He sent my drawings on paper to University in the East. Art college."

"Really?"

He shook his head. "University interested until white men there find drawing by Cheyenne. Sent me not to come letter."

Alli fought not to show the depth of her emotion. "How could they…" But then she was aware it was once again the way of things neither of them could control. "It saddens me how white men, women have treated your people and how they have treated the Africans, any of those not white. Maybe that is more reason for someone like Elina to go to university. The more education the more change can begin to take place."

He took a deep breath and let it out. "My grandfather think this too, but this idea will be long time coming."

His words defined once again the fact he was Cheyenne and she was a white woman and no matter their love, they would remain unaccepted by those in each of their worlds. She watched as he touched the brush to the canvas to add a bit more paint to the sky. Maybe it was that she had come here to make a difference even if it was for one of the student at a time, but without a doubt she had come here to love this man, no matter what anyone else thought.

****

Leaning Bear stroked a hand through Alli's light hair and drew her mouth to his. Coming to her again was dangerous even at the hours long past darkness. He had not been to her for several days and his body yearned for this moment though his mind would tell him better of it. Touching her…a white woman, was forbidden yet his want of her was stronger than any he had ever known.

He had been careful. And now with a single flame atop the table in the center of her home this night with her would bring no harm. He tasted the mint of the tea she had consumed and lifted from the kiss. Never had a woman perplexed him to the delirious need of her mind and her body. Never had a woman given of herself to talk to him and find him human in spite of the color of his skin. The color of her skin and his thoughts of her often led him to look long past this time now, to a time when they could spend each day together. Though inside his head, he was well aware this would not be accepted by anyone but themselves.

But Alli was different…open and bold in her thoughts and conversations. Caring about his ideas and things he told her. Interested. Interesting. He had not slept the nights in between without thinking of the cries she had made with her pleasures, so open to touch and loving him the same. He had come to her once more, for all that she was and for all he was when he was with her. Her sky-colored eyes were wide with desire for him. And maybe they were both made of foolish hopes.

She eased from her clothing as he watched and then sat on the bed, naked. He pulled his tunic over his head; no words being needed. She had expected his visit but as he laid his buckskin shirt aside, he eyed the bed which presented a problem. He didn't like the off the floor bed.

He took her hand and urged her to stand. Her brows narrowed as he let go and stepped to the bed. It would be easier if he laid the mattress to the flooring. Yes, that is what he would do. He leaned and in a single effort picked up the mattress and bedding and dropped it onto the floor by the hearth, making Fern scatter from her basket with a whimper.

"What are you doing?" Alli tugged one of the loose blankets about her.

"This better, on floor. Bed not familiar to my liking." He nodded and took her hand again. "Best lay down, tonight will take my time."

"Oh, I see." She knelt and lay across the bedding.

"Warmer here, first talk." He spoke it as he did not plan on rushing the night and because while he loved touching her as he planned, he loved more listening to her talk. Sharing his own conversations to be near her.

He lay beside her, both on their sides looking at each other. She was so peaceful for him to view, to watch, to touch. He took her hand into his again.

She reciprocated with angling a glance at their connected fingers. "So, what shall we talk about?"

He shrugged. "Talk of things of Paint The Sky."

"I know, I received a letter from my sister Jacie." Her face beamed. "She and her husband are well, as are the children, her oldest boys are married and the eldest's wife is expecting. She'll be a grandmother. Of course, she misses me and is still begging me to return home as always. Oh, and she even asked of Dancing Fox's English clothing, imagine when I tell her I've seen him wear the clothing more than once."

He laughed at her amusement. "I tell you he would accept gift. Fickle."

"Fickle? That's not a word I've heard you use, but you're right." She giggled and his heart warmed.

"Fickle mean likely to change mind or thought." He nodded, rolling to his back. "Definition in book Dawson gave to me."

Alli leaned up on an elbow letting go of his hand. "A dictionary, you have one?"

He nodded. "It is as you say. Read words sometimes. Find out meaning and remember."

"I had no idea you still studied English." She touched the scars from his dance with the sun as she had that night he was last here. "I know you told me of the Sundance meaning, but did this hurt to leave such scars?"

"Hurt badly but for short time." He allowed her finger to wander his skin.

She traced a gentle finger across his now healed scar of his side, the one she'd stitched. "This?"

"Not bad. This bad." He ran a hand across the one rib that protruded a bit higher than the others on his left chest, below his breast. "Broken by soldier before trial. And this." He sat up and pulled up his trouser pant leg, showing her his shin. "Fall far as young boy, down cliff, land on leg and bone comes through."

Alli cringed and took his trousers setting them aside with a lift of her brows. "Oh my, I'm surprised it healed well enough that you don't walk with a limp."

He nodded. "Grandfather tend my leg, stay still for many weeks, learn to walk again."

"I can see." She lay back beside him again scooting closer. "You've so many scars you have shown to me. I've only the one scar, but it comes as hard earned. I don't recall pain but for the first few weeks and I healed quickly."

He turned to his side again and touched her sun-colored hair. "Sometimes pain of scar is carried long after."

"Yes."

He placed his lips to her cheek and let his hand slide down to her belly where her scar began at her navel. "If this pain I could remove I would."

She rested a hand to his cheek. "I believe you."

He raised himself up and eased between her thighs

to join them. Her mouth opened and she watched him as he began the soft pace, suckling from one breast to the other. She was silky, warm and let her hands roam his torso and maybe he liked that best. He held her gaze as her body tensed each time he sank to her depths. And his own body rose in passion he fought to hold back.

She began moving with him and sweat rolled off his body and small bits of water covered her light skin. He tasted the salt of her as he continued, wanting to feel her find her pleasure. Oh, she so wanted the pleasure he'd bring yet he took his time. Each press of his body faster and faster against her, touching that part of her…

"Oh…" She grew rigid as if wanting to push him away but he held her tighter giving her more of himself. And she cried into his ear, and he fought to keep loving her until his own body gave way and words left him as he met his passion within her. They were one vision. One soul. One…love. He didn't move, keeping himself inside her as he shuddered again and again.

"Leaning Bear." She brushed his hair back and kissed his face. "What did you say…"

He focused on her as he moved to her side. "Best left unsaid."

She let her jaw drop though she smiled. "I do believe you cursed with a bad word."

"Cheyenne know no words of curse." He closed his eyes as he held her closer to him, not wanting to part from the heated warmth of her.

Her warm lips found his in an open-mouthed kiss and then she giggled. "You cursed. I heard you."

"Paint The Sky find this funny." He tilted his head back.

"You rarely ever joke of anything. And yes…it's

funny." She leaned across his chest looking at him. "You're handsome when you smile."

"Then I shall use swear words more often." He narrowed his gaze. "And smile more times."

She lifted her light brows. "And of us…together like this…and neither of us have said the word…I mean not really saying it."

Why did women always push for the words to comfort their heart? Why did they wish for a man to say love, when he was showing that? He had told her many times now.

"I have show you how I feel." He took a long depth of breath. "Some do not ask about love because they are afraid of the answer."

"And you. Even though we have said it before. Is it still love now, each time?" She tangled her fingers through his hair brushing it from his face as she lay across his chest. "Are you afraid of the answer?"

That was what attracted him to her. Unabashed. Open. Questioning all things but he answered her. "Yes, it is as you say."

"Really." She shook her head, her lips curling into a grin. "You are not."

"Yes, much afraid of women." He kept his smile at bay on purpose. "Afraid of Cheyenne women more. Stern. Run the family. Tell the man to work. Kick him out of tent when he is drunk or not working. Don't let him back in. Why I never marry."

"I've figured some of that but you are not afraid of me or you wouldn't be here. Tell me the truth." She angled a hard glance at him.

He touched her hair, tangling his fingers in the blonde curls. "Only afraid of the weight of us."

Her brows narrowed. “The weight of us?”

How did he explain the reasons he did not leave all around him and take her somewhere they would remain untouched by the scorn of others. “Together we are heavy for those who would look and find Paint The Sky and medicine man different. Find us wrong.”

“I suppose I've thought of this too. They'll never accept us in town, no matter.”

“It is as you say.”

“Well, I don't care then. I'll love you no matter how difficult.” She brushed a kiss across his lips and chin.

“Is easy to say now but time may come when is not so easy.” He didn't want this conversation. He did not want any of it. She deserved far more than he could ever give her. Far more than the people of town or his tribe would allow her. And still she loved. And because of this he answered her original question. “Yes, I love Paint The Sky and no, I am not afraid of that love. But have something to tell you.”

“Really.” She lifted of her light brows.

“Paytah has returned, unharmed. Came to reservation, no saddle, no Bakers.” He studied the blue of her eyes.

“Oh, Leaning Bear, but…where is he now?” She shook her head. “And for that matter where are the Bakers…won’t they come looking again?”

He touched her lips to stop her words. “Horse is hidden. Bakers will come to their day soon. Paint The Sky should carry no more worries.”

In time he would deal with the Bakers once and for all.

Chapter Twenty-Two

Alli urged Millie from the reservation, the darkness long closing in for the night. She hadn't meant to leave later than usual, but she'd waited on a light storm to pass, which now left the trail muddy, the buggy sliding a bit behind the old horse. Fern sat beside her in seat, her tongue hanging out and panting, the heat a bit much after the storm.

"Steady does the job, Millie." She spoke to the horse glancing around her, uncertain she should have made the trek home when the skies still held black clouds. She'd hoped Leaning Bear might follow her home, but he'd been elusive for a few days, she suspected due to checking wherever he'd hidden Paytah. But now that he had the horse back, she worried more about his words of seeing the Bakers taken down. She feared for him a lot of the time.

Andy the owl, gave an annoyed hoop at their arrival but instead of staying in his barn he swooped toward the cabin and turned again in his flight to reach the barn. That was odd as most times he stayed and called out in his hooted annoyance.

She pulled the buggy right into the barn and stepped down, fumbling to light the lamp that hung by the door. She struck the match and added the flame to the wick and the barn came aglow as she closed the glass. Fern growled causing her to glance around the inside of the barn.

The owl swooped again, and she ducked. “What on earth has gotten into that fowl tonight? Come Millie, it’s all right. Fern it’s all right, only the echo of thunder from the storm.”

She went to the old horse and began with her harnesses to free her of them. Millie scampered right to her stall and waited on her oats. This had become her quick routine each evening as she returned from the reservation. “Millie, I do think the haircut I gave you is very becoming. You look ten years younger.”

She scooped from the bucket of oats and fed the horse giving her a good pat to the head. “Oh, and tomorrow you’ll get your rest, hobble out to have some of the nice grass near the stream.” She’d planned on taking the horse with her since it did seem the grass would be to her liking. She’d made a satchel to carry all her paints, canvas, and chair across Millie’s back while she led the horse. But that adventure waited for morning and tonight she was tired and famished. Fern gave a heavy growl again, though she stayed in the buggy.

The owl hooted, flying off once more. “What is it tonight with you, Fern, you and Andy?” The owl flapped his feathers but never glanced at her or Millie. Unsettled, she supposed due to their return after dark but then the hair on the back of her neck stood. Something was amiss.

She reached for the rake on the side of the barn wall at the same time someone grabbed her. Fern jumped from the buggy running toward her. She screamed and the owl took off in a flurry of squawking feathers once more. Alli fought to free herself, but then caught sight of Leroy and Pete Baker at the barn door. And as it was it seemed the owl had tried to warn her. But her bag, the pistol was in her bag inside the wagon. Pete snatched up Fern by the gruff of her neck, the pup growling and yelping as he held her out away from himself.

Alli screamed again trying to pull away with all her might. The one holding her was Don.

“If you don't scream, I'll be a little gentler about things.” His breath held the flavor of whiskey and his words slurred.

“Leave her be, she’s just a puppy.” Alli stopped resisting. “What are you doing here? What do you want?”

“Well now,” Leroy started as he moved closer. “First things first. We understand we owe you some apology for your first day here on the road outside town. We was only funnin' you a bit.”

“Yep, just playing.” Pete chimed in angling a glance and looking her up and down as he tossed Fern back and forth by the neck. The pup had given up fighting though she gave a constant growl.

Alli’s heart raced. “You overturned my buggy and could have hurt me and my horse. And then you all made your threats when I did not prefer to purchase a horse from you. Now let me go and please don’t hurt her.” She tried to jerk free to no avail with Don's hold and she bent in pain when he gripped her shoulders hard.

“Now it wasn't that bad, but we do understand no one much comes west without money so we're here to make a deal about how much we'll be expecting each week.” Leroy leaned against Millie’s stall. “Or, we can trade a few things instead of money if it comes down to it.” He eyed her up and down.

“We’ll be a step up in the world, you ruttin’ with the injun and all.” Don chuckled and held her tighter against him.

“You are out of line, sir.” Alli had met their kind in Chicago…those who harassed others and coerced them for money. “I’ve only the money to buy sugar and flour when I have it. I won’t be paying you anything.”

“Well, now that’s not what we’ve been a seein’, Leaning Bear over here working for you, quite a bit, the cabin looking all new.” Don laughed. “How ya payin’ him, woman?”

“And we see those children at the rez wearing new clothes and shoes. That didn't come cheap now did it?” Leroy spat tobacco juice to the dirt of the small barn. “Shoot the pup!”

“No, please.” Alli waited, stopping her fight. “Please, I’ll cooperate.”

Pete laughed and held Fern high in the air. “Good thing for you I’d say.” He grabbed a rope and tied it to Fern’s neck and the end to the stall post.

Alli’s heart pounded inside her chest. At least if Fern was tied, she’d be safe. She wanted to allow tears and scream again, but it would be futile. And she had hidden what money she had we'll enough but what were they planning for now? They’d never find it and she'd never tell. Nope she wouldn't. But Fern…

“The clothing was paid for by the government.” She gritted her teeth in pain from Don’s grip.

“You'll be needing to tell me where you keep your money because it seems someone from back East is taking right good care of you.” Leroy stepped closer, placing his hands on his hips.

How could he know that? And then it dawned on her that she'd sent telegrams to Jacie when a letter would take too long. A sweet woman from behind the counter at the telegraph office named Lucretia must have told of her requests or even been forced to do so.

“So, start talking, sweetie, or it’s gonna get really interesting as we search here and your cabin.” Pete stepped closer, and walked around the barn knocking things over, searching. The owl flew out of the barn and then back in a huff of feathers.

Don pulled her closer, his breath wreaking of whiskey. “I’ll bypass the money for now.”

Alli held Leroy’s stern glare.

“All right, Pete and I’ll search the cabin then.” Leroy shook his head and both turned to leave the barn. “You and Don could use a little privacy anyway, looks it.”

Don turned her and planted his mouth to hers. Alli slammed a knee toward his groin freeing herself to run but he caught her and pinned her against the stall. Her breath left her in a huff, her ribs aching at the impact. She was sure she might pass out but instead gulped for air as Don raised her skirt from behind.

Fern yelped, fighting against the roping.

“No, Fern…no…” Alli fought harder as Don kicked the pup away. She scampered behind the stall near Millie, still tied.

Alli twisted away, but then Don hit her with a fist, knocking her senseless. She stumbled against the stall catching herself as another fist found her side twice more. She crumpled against the wood trying to keep herself upright sucking in a strangled breath.

“You are a pretty one. Won't take me long at all you be still.” His hands rode to her skirts pulling them up as he fumbled behind her.

“No, no, you cannot…I won’t allow you to…” She tried to fight but Don hit her twice more in her side and she let go, unable to fight or make sense out of what was happening. She tried to dodge his next hit but it found her. She tasted blood, confused and unable to keep her stance.

She had to fight…stop him but her breath wouldn't come…she coughed and tried to gain air but he shoved her harder and her mind faded. He hit her once more in her side and she collapsed to her knees and fell into the straw, coughing and inhaling a raspy breath that cause her pain. Her eyes watered and she gagged trying to breathe, her mind blurring as she attempted to crawl but instead fell to the dirt of the barn floor.

She opened her eyes and Don was gone though she caught a glimpse of Leaning Bear…she tried to call to him, but his name wasn't even a whisper on her lips as her world faded from view.

****

Leaning Bear tied Don's hands and feet, the young man unconscious. He glanced at Alli, who lay slumped in the hay outside Millie's stall. He needed to get to her, but he could do anything for her until he had all the men subdued. Above him the old owl hooted his warning.

He twisted a length of rope through the man's tied wrists and eased into the darkness, holstering his tomahawk at his hip once more. He had not hurt the one called Don but he would have much pain in his head come morning. And should he think about this twice, he would kill the man for placing his hands on Paint The Sky. Yes, he would think no more about that or Don would be a dead man.

Inside Alli's cabin the other two brothers made no reason for being quiet going through her things. And as it was the odds were now better. He dragged the young man by the rope across the dirt and to Paytah. He'd brought the horse out of hiding and planned to stall him inside the reservation where he could be watched by the soldiers once more. He bent and pulled off the man's boots tossing them aside and then pulled off one sock which he stuffed into the unconscious man's mouth. He tied off the rope to Paytah and added a second that he stretched along the path toward the porch.

It was good the man was quiet for now and his next grab should be the eldest brother. If what he planned worked, he'd only need to handle Pete and that wouldn't be hard at all.

Worry over Alli weighed heavy but he could not help her until the men were first out of the way. And now trouble would begin but the sons of Roy Baker had done plenty and his time of patience was growing thin. The mountain lion grew more restless by the turns of the moon and as it was, all he was doing would bring Alli more if this wasn't ended soon.

Inside the men searched knocking over furniture and bickering over finding not what they were looking for…money. He squatted in the dark beside the door. He would have but a second to take them men by surprise. His breath held though he had to get this done to get back to Paint The Sky.

The men had brightened the lamp to full and the house was as if the sun lit it from the inside. The spirits had been restless and he had known this night with the full of the moon to be unsettled. Now he understood why.

Leroy stepped through the door first. "Let's go, aint nothing inside, we'll shoot the pup and the horse if she doesn't talk."

Leaning Bear grabbed the man's weapon from his

side and slid the noose to his wrist and whistled before Leroy could yell for Pete. The eldest brother bobbled down the porch stairs into the dirt as Paytah took off dragging the two men into the night. The horse had done this enough in the past. He would not stop until the reservation where the men could then be detained for their harassment, at least for a time.

Pete ran out of the cabin with his pistol poised. Leaning Bear caught him in the throat with the wooden handle of his tomahawk and the man dropped to his knees gagging and sputtering. Easy enough. Leaning Bear grabbed the pistol and tossed it into the yard.

Blood dripped from Pete's nose and he gurgled as Leaning Bear pulled him to his feet.

“You won't get away with this, injun.” The man protested in a grated whisper, as Leaning Bear jumped from the porch and pulled him down. He stumbled and followed. “My father will have you shot for this.”

He pulled him along to the road and pushed him to his knees at the first reservation fence post and tied him there where he would never free himself. The cavalry would find him soon enough, like his brothers.

Leaning Bear ran for the barn and bent before Alli, who still lay unmoving. The man who hit her should be dead. He placed a hand to her swollen cheek and spoke her name.

“Paint The Sky?”

She didn’t respond but her breathing was even and unlabored. She was bruised but would be all right as best he could tell.

He walked through the stall to untie Fern who whimpered and ran to her, licking her face. He returned and lifted Alli into his arms, and surveying the Owl above, thanked the spirits for the warning.

He stood and rested Alli against his chest. He would take her to his camp in the trees where no one would ever harm her again. Yes, that is what he would do.

Chapter Twenty-Three

Leaning Bear pulled a heavy fur blanket onto Alli, who slept at his camp in the trees. Darkness filled the sky and while she had woken once for a brief moment where he had reassured her, she had slept since. Beside her on the blanket, Fern slept as well. He had washed Alli's face of blood and placed salve to her wounds and the bruises to her side. Though nothing was broken, she would require rest and willow bark tea for pain, at least for a few days.

He sat at the fire, his knees up and his hand laying across hers, just to touch her. Her injuries were his fault as he should not have left to retrieve Paytah so soon. The horse would have long arrived to deliver two of the Baker brothers to the captivity of the reservation.

He tucked her hand underneath the heavy fur once more. She lay naked there as her clothing had been torn in the skirmish. He studied her bruised face. Never had he seen such beauty of heart and mind. And she was his and he could not allow the Bakers to have freedom from this, though he suspected with no law and only the captain's discretion, that not much would be done.

If trouble had not found him before this, it had found him now. This was not good. This would not be good for Paint The Sky. The night would not last and the morning sun would bring the truth. He suspected much trouble one way or another. Paytah would have dragged Leroy and Don right onto the reservation and Pete would be found as soon as soldiers made their way to or from town.

Roy Baker would not like that his sons had been ill-treated no matter their arrest by the soldiers or not. The man held a power over most in town, cheating many though he was not fond of being cheated himself. He would have words and more than that, be vengeful.

No matter, the captain would have words with him either way as was usual. But the men would have harmed Paint The Sky far more had he not been there. He should have killed Don Baker for touching her as he had. No matter what he faced he could not allow that again. The Bakers' days were almost done. Yes, that day would come soon enough.

He suspected on her waking she would prefer to be back at her home. One stubborn white woman who had not the sense to be afraid of the men who had harmed her. He might return her but he would have to remain elusive for a while, but watch out for her just the same. Roy Baker would be on the lookout for him and that might find him at the end of a rope or gun.

He added another piece of wood to the fire. It would do well for him to rest before dawn as no one would find them here. He lay on his side close to her and tugged the fur to cover him as well. Sleep would come, but not the kind that gave rest. This he knew.

****

The crackle and pop of a fire brought Alli's mind to the surface of her existence. She blinked and licked her lips, the coppery taste of blood lingering in her mouth. Where was she? She had the faint memory of Leaning Bear's soothing words from the night before but not much more than Don Baker hitting her.

She touched her side and decided moving wasn't what she could do right now. And while she wasn’t sure of her where abouts she was certain of not trying to move again.

“Paint The Sky, lie still.” Leaning Bear hovered next to her on his knees. He dipped a finger into a jar of salve and touched it to her swollen lip. She winced when he tugged her hand away from her side.

“I don't remember…” She'd gotten home after dark and the Baker brothers had been there and she'd fought with Don who had hit her numerous times. He’d also tried to harm Fern. “Fern?”

“It is best not to remember. Fern sleeps beside you.” His voice was soft and his eyes held worry.

She glanced around again. Her side ached and her head wasn't clear. “Where are we?”

“You are safe.” He used a tiny wooden spoon to stir the contents of a small tin bowl.

“Yes, but where…” She hadn’t walked here. Had he carried her? “How did I get here?”

“My camp in the trees. I brought you.” He pulled the blanket back and his warm hand spread the medicine to her painful ribs. “Will help pain.”

Her breasts were open to air and underneath the heavy fur she was indeed naked. He had undressed her? But with a great bit of tenderness, he covered her again. As bad as she felt, he had seen her naked before now anyway, and she’d not worry about it with how poorly she felt.

“Drink.” He held a gourd of liquid to her lips, and she sipped.

She coughed at the bitter taste but took more.

"Willow bark will help you rest."

"Leaning Bear what happened?" She couldn't imagine what he'd done to the Bakers or what they may have done to her cabin.

He held his worried gaze to her. "Rest."

"No, I remember you fought them…I saw you." Her voice broke. "Tell me." What if he had hurt or killed the men, any one of them? He'd be hanged all in protecting her.

"Tie two brothers to rope. Paytah drag them to reservation. Tie Pete to first post of fencing for cavalry to find." He explained as he stoked the small fire.

What did that mean? "They'll be arrested?"

He shrugged. "Not know."

"But they'll kill you…oh, Leaning Bear…we must wire Federal Marshals or…" she fretted but her head was foggy and her eyes heavy. Sleep was trying to take her back due to the medicine.

Leaning Bear placed a thumb to her cheek. "This not happen. Sleep now." He let his thumb trace her bottom lip so tenderly. "Paint The Sky rest. No talk. All will be well."

Alli nodded. "What if they come back because they aren't detained? What if Roy Baker comes…"

"They will not come here."

She nodded and placed her hand along Fern's soft side. "I've never been hit before like that. With a man's fist."

He stoked the fire using a charred stick. "No woman or child should ever know fist."

"I think I am more in shock than hurt…I woke in the night and you were beside me and…" she held his gaze. "I wanted you there so I didn't need to be frightened."

She tried to smile but then touched her painful lip and tears cluttered her vision.

Leaning Bear eased down beside her once more. He spoke to her in Cheyenne, words she was beginning to understand. Something about his love for her along with her bravery and for her not to worry. She curled into him, hanging onto him as if he were the breath within her.

"Please." She took his hand into hers and sniffled. "Please. Promise you will not get yourself hurt by those men in trying to take revenge. You already have not been able to work in town, and you have to do so for the tribe."

He turned to his side. "Hard to make promise unsure I will keep."

"They are so evil, and they could hurt you badly or even…kill you, please don't let that happen. I will be all right." She pleaded further. "I'll heal but I'd never heal from losing you."

"Rest, Paint The Sky, nothing will happen this day."

****

A light wind trickled through the leaves of the nearby trees. Alli shivered, and it took her seconds to remember where she slept. She was still within the furs of Leaning Bear's camp in the trees as he called it. How many days had it been and where was he? Where was Fern?

She eased to her feet, pulling the top fur around her to walk to the edge of the small camp. He would be back and wouldn't leave her for long. She hadn't known this small place was here though she would never have thought to climb to such a height. How on earth had Leaning Bear carried her up the steep incline of rocks and tall thick pines?

She scanned the tree line and below, spotting

Leaning Bear and the pup along the creek bed. She walked to the far edge of the camp in order to see them better. Leaning Bear stood naked at the stream's edge pouring water over his body. He was almost ceremonial about it, and then she understood when his chanting in Cheyenne reached her. Fern played at the water's edge tossing a stick about.

Alli pulled the fur around her tighter. Perhaps her watching was an intrusion, but she continued to do so. He raised his arms to the skies, his eyes closed. His bronze skin fit into the scenery as if he belonged there. As if he were made for the surroundings. And wasn't he?

Her heart raced. He was beautiful. Tall and thick muscled and so graceful in even his prayers. Maybe she was intruding. She turned back to the camp, hunger making her stomach rumble. She was still bruised and sore, but she was better than she had been. She should think about returning home to her cabin, but would it be safe? It was probably in shambles after the Bakers went through it but at least Leaning Bear had checked daily on Millie who was fine inside the barn.

It was likely all of town knew of her and Leaning Bear and she would no longer be welcomed there, would she? And if she couldn't go to town for supplies, what existence could she make in Lame Deer? As she'd lain here for several days she guessed, all she could think about was the fact it felt like the life she'd created here had come to a halt. What would become of her now? And what of Leaning Bear?

It was hopeless to stay and that would mean leaving Two Doves, Millie, Fern, the children and…Leaning Bear. Her heart sank to its depths. How could she leave them all, breaking her word and her heart? And where would she go? Back home to move in with Jacie and her family and pretend none of this had ever happened? Pretend she hadn't fallen in love? Walk away from the beautiful man who had rescued her over and over and who loved her in spite of all those around them.

No, she wouldn't run back home with her tail between her legs fragile and broken. She would stay here and rebuild her home and love Leaning Bear anyway. And one day they'd build a life together. There had to be somewhere they could do that. Live in peace together. And how could she walk away from a love so very perfect?

She sat on the log by the embers left in the fire and tugged the fur tighter. Maybe the cold wasn't from the air around her as much as what was happening inside her. But instead of allowing tears, she stifled them with a sniffle. She wouldn't do that ever again over the Bakers or the people in town who wished her ill. And she would face them all again and stand as tall and as proud as she ever had. Who were they to judge her anyway?

Chapter Twenty-Four

Leaning Bear slipped under the fencing at the far end of the reservation and made his way toward his lodge. He had taken Alli back to her home and saw to it she would rest for a few days more. She had been upset to miss time with the children, but he'd insisted he would talk with Two Doves about teaching until her return.

He had been reluctant to leave her, but Dancing Fox had found him and told him the captain requested his presence. He suspected the captain was not happy that Paytah had dragged the two Baker sons right to his office. The chief had let him know that the captain hadn't been in the least bit happy at the occurrence. The horse had done as much before to one of the soldiers a while back when the man was caught stealing from his cart of wood that belonged to Maud. That soldier had been returned back East in a jail wagon with bars. At this point he didn't suspect that would be the same thing done to the Bakers.

He glanced at the school where the children were collecting and headed that way to dismiss them to Two Doves who stood ringing the bell. He turned toward the school and stopped before his sister-in-law as the children gathered around.

"A-ho…" The group of children stopped chatting as he explained about Alli's absence. "Teacher will not come for two days. Two Doves will hold classroom for students."

Two Doves gave a respectful nod, ushering the children ahead of her inside. "Alli is not well."

He waited on the children to all go inside. "Was attacked by Bakers, but will be good in a few days."

She frowned. "I will go to care for her, hold school until another time."

"No, not safe for you or child." He shook his head. "She is healing. I will be watching her."

She gave another nod and entered the school, saying no more.

He turned for the captain's quarters. Best not to delay further. He found the captain a man who was most often kind but also efficient about things. The captain had been integral in helping free himself and Dawson from the firing squad planned for them. And he was the only man to be trusted of all the soldiers, according to his own thoughts.

He stepped up to the porch where several soldiers parted for him to enter. It was unfamiliar that they all remained silent and didn't stop him. He walked past them and inside closing the door behind him with Captain Bartley's nod. It was common practice that formalities were often dismissed between them most any time he arrived for discussion.

The captain sat at his desk fussing over papers but then folded closed the large ledger he was scribing into. He stuffed his quill back into the ink signed one last form and glanced up.

"You can sit, Leaning Bear." The captain nodded to the chair and leaned back into his own.

"No need to sit." He wasn't going to be here for very long.

"Leaning Bear, to start I had a visit from Roy Baker yesterday morning. Let's just say it wasn't a social call after his sons were dragged in here by your horse, skinned from head to toe. And Pete got brought in, ant bites all over him." Bartley shuffled in his chair. "You can't take the law into your own hands and tie men up. Baker wasn't happy I detained his sons for a time making excuses as to why they'd been kept, but I have no jurisdiction here to hold them beyond a citation of harassment. Is Mrs. Crockett all right?"

"Caught men tearing apart her cabin and she was beaten but will mend. She is resting. You are captain, you have teacher in your care, this should not happen." He folded his arms, holding the man's gaze.

"I can have a soldier escort her home before and after school." The captain took a deep breath and let it out.

"This should be done before now, not after teacher has been harmed." He couldn't risk the captain knowing about him and Paint The Sky, but as it was, the rumors had probably reached the soldiers too.

Captain Bartley pulled off his hat and laid it on the desk. "Yes, perhaps I should have but I'm hearing from the soldiers about the…connection you have with Mrs. Crockett. Need I remind you that there are men in this town who would kill you on the spot, Leaning Bear, for the time you've spent with any white woman. You should know the repercussions of such. It might be wise that you take one of those extended hunting trips and spend some time away from the reservation. I'll write the dated pass for you. I think that would be best for now. Roy Baker will be out for blood as you well know."

"Roy Baker will find much trouble where he looks

for it." He wasn't going to incriminate himself or Paint The Sky on any note of being together, not to the captain. Not to anyone. "Will not allow further harm to teacher."

"I'll have her an escort but Leaning Bear…" The captain shot to his feet. "If you go after the Bakers, if they don't kill you, the law will."

"No jurisdiction for Baker's sons to take as they please from many and sell elsewhere. Horses taken over and over. What jurisdiction needed for a time when they take from your horses or your wife or children?" The soldiers had often been harassed and there had been horses taken from time to time.

The captain took a deep breath and shook his head. "It doesn't work for you to take the law into your own hands."

"There is no law here. There is no metal chest to see to the right things for protection of citizens." He understood how things worked without any doubt, but it was time for questions and answers though it appeared there were none. If he killed the Bakers, he'd be hung or worse. If it were proven he'd been with Paint The Sky, much the same could happen.

"Look, you know as do I, the territories have few lawmen, mostly just those in the bigger towns. It's all I can do to keep my men out of trouble in the Baker's saloon. I know he and his sons are a problem, but I had nothing to hold them on. No way to arrest them." He shook his head. "Leaning Bear, it's you I worry about. They wouldn't stop at having you hang for no reason at all and you and I both know Dawson McCade would approve ill of your ideas."

"These Bakers fight with soldiers. Your hands tied. You scold soldiers. These men harm teacher that white man government sends for you to protect. You scold me and my horse. Your hands are tied, but hers are not. She is bruised because she fights back. I will not allow this to happen again." He set the bag on the desk and pulled out several revolvers he'd taken from the Bakers. "My hands will not be tied."

"Wait." The captain came around his desk. "They won't hesitate to hang you or shoot you for no reason. Leaning Bear, you're a walking target. You have to get out of here."

"This I do not fear." With that he left the captain and walked past his men back toward his lodge. If the soldiers could not handle the Bakers, then it was time for him to do what he'd been planning.

Chapter Twenty-Five

Alli sat at her desk enjoying Elina reading a story to the younger children. The older students listened as they did their work, the smaller ones in a circle near the older girl who read each day now and was very animated at it. Two Doves had left for the afternoon to see to one of the elder women who had taken ill.

Returning to school had been good for her and the children, though she fathomed she might be looking over her shoulder for a long time. Little had been heard from the Bakers and while she felt safe on the reservation, she worried at night, though she was sure Leaning Bear was nearby.

At least on the reservation she had been somewhat protected, and Captain Bartley had sent a soldier to escort her home each morning and evening. But she had not seen Leaning Bear much where she could speak with him.

Elina laughed with the children and continued reading the story, making funny faces that went along with the character actions. Alli smiled in spite of herself. Her worries were for Leaning Bear and the fact there was no doubt the Bakers would seek their revenge. Look what they had already done.

The children giggled again but then Little Wolf pointed to the window behind her. "Teacher, fire!"

The children ran to the window, along with a

barking Fern and Alli followed, smoke billowing from the distant trees up into the sky.

"It is the place of your home, teacher." Hawk spoke pushing closer to the window to see outside.

Alli turned to run from the school, though she was aware Hawk followed her and Fern barked wildly running ahead of her.

"Teacher, the horse there." He pointed to one of the horses with only a rope around his neck, with no saddle. She grabbed the rope and pulled herself up with Hawk's assistance. "Hawk, please take Fern so she won't follow…"

The boy lifted Fern into his arms.

Alli shouted and the horse took off. She yelled to the soldiers as she rode toward the gate. "My home is on fire, please, I'll need help."

She rounded the horse, her body bobbling as she tried to stay atop the animal. She bent closer trying her best to tighten the neck roping where she could hang on, though her mind wandered to what might have caused a fire. She had not left any lamp burning or flames in her hearth. What on earth could have happened?

She fought to hang onto the horse as it galloped along the gravel and then the dirt road to her cabin. The travel was shorter with the horse than it was with Millie and the buggy and as the cabin came into view, a scream left her.

Before her the cabin was engulfed in flames on one side, the area where her bedding and clothing stayed. She glanced at the barn and the owl swooped away into the trees as she dismounted. She shook her head in a moment of panic but ran to the stairs and inside. Flames and smoke pooled around her as she grabbed her kerchief to hold over her nose and mouth, coughing through the blackened smoke.

What should she do? Her clothing chest was full of flames and her bedding on fire. Half the cabin was burning in flames so hot she worried of her hair. She ran toward her desk to lift up her journal shoving it into her blouse. Then she trotted toward the drawer on her small night table and yelped when she burned her fingers, but she used her skirts to open the drawer and drew out her mother's pearls and the small box of pictures of her family and the ones of her as a child. She grabbed her extra boots from under the bed, the flooring there already burning through, charred and black. She coughed, gagging as the smoke burned her nostrils, trying her best to think what else she should save.

She stood again and glanced around the cabin, more of the flames taking over her cabin. She inhaled the black soot and gagged as she ran to Leaning Bear's portrait, the one of him dancing that night. She fell before getting there, out of breath, but she forced herself to crawl that direction, the heat of the boards underneath her scalding her hands and knees.

She lifted the portrait at the same time someone pulled her toward the front door. She coughed as her view cleared and as she fell to the ground past the stairs. Leaning Bear ran past her. He returned with Fern's basket filled with some of her clothing she had assumed burned. She wiped her eyes as he trotted back from her home and the roof caved on one side.

How had he known? Had he been watching her still? She forced herself to sit up, still holding his portrait as her home burned further.

He fell beside her, coughing and retching up black

spittle.

"Leaning Bear." She coughed again, as she reached for him, but he pulled away.

She didn't understand until she turned and several patrons of town ran onto the scene. Men with buckets and even some women. They began gathering water from the stream and passing he buckets. In a matter of moments, a line of fifteen people were handing buckets of water to toss onto the fires in the cabin.

Leaning Bear joined them. She forced herself to her feet but coughed so hard she fell again to the ground.

"Mrs. Crockett, just stay a restin', not much can be done about this now." Maud held her back, the rotund woman breathless from running to arrive.

"But my cabin, I don't know how this happened." She coughed hard and vomited black soot as Maud beat her on the back.

Her cabin wouldn't be saved. And now the town would think Leaning Bear had been here, wouldn't they?

"Maud, Leaning Bear saved me from the fire, didn't you see him?" she asked. Hadn't they all seen him help?

"Mrs. Crockett, ain't nobody seen nothing 'ceptin a fire to help." The heavy woman sat beside her breathing hard and coughing along with her.

"Maud, I left nothing lit in my cabin this morning prior to school." She coughed again, watching the townsfolk and Leaning Bear continue with bucket after bucket of water from the stream.

"I don't want to make no accusations, but those Baker boys rode back into town right a'fore we all saw the smoke." Maud shook her head. "Some says they's talking again about you having Leaning Bear here…and honestly, Ma'am, you need to tell him to go. The Bakers been talking about stringing him up if he returns to town. Going to figure he's the best worker I have and they gonna run him off."

"They cannot know how things are and I won't let them kill him." Alli stood with great effort, coughing but still running to Leaning Bear. "You've to go now, or the Bakers, they'll kill you. They are who set this, Maud saw them. They'll come here…you must go."

He tossed the bucket of water and tugged away from her, handing the bucket to the man who took them to be refilled. He glanced toward Maud and then back to her and took the next bucket pushing her back.

"They will not come now." He nodded for her to look behind her.

Alli's mouth fell open. Ahead of her coming down the trail from the reservation was a line of soldiers, Cheyenne and Sioux from the reservations all with buckets. They all joined the line of those passing buckets and even a second line was made. And as they all worked to stop the fire in her cabin, it was town folk, soldiers and the tribes working as one. Unable to stand from her exhaustion, tears fell freely down her cheeks as she leaned into Maud once more.

****

"We could go somewhere else…anywhere but here." Alli waited as Leaning Bear's searched her eyes, shaking his head. Her cabin still smoldered with only a small portion of it remaining, though standing behind it unharmed, the outhouse where she'd hidden her money. All the effort had been important at not letting the fire spread but it has been futile in saving her cabin.

"I am Cheyenne. What we have cannot become more even if we leave. The weight of us will be found once again no matter where we are." His voice was softer than she'd ever known.

She blinked, the soft rumble of his deep voice calming as they sat in the grass before the cabin. "I have little concern what others may think of…us. No one, save Maud, has more than tolerated me anyway. I'm uncertain that will improve given how everyone has helped today. Even if some will think what they will."

He inhaled a deep breath and let it out slowly. "Paint The Sky, any reason make it wrong that I should love you…but I I love still."

Her heart crushed further with the impending dread of saying goodbye. "Maud says the stage will come tomorrow and I should go back home to Chicago as you have said…but how can I leave you and the children?" Tears rolled down her cheeks as if they had a will of their own and her heart crushed inside her chest. "And Fern and Millie. No one will love them as I do…no one will love you as do I."

She glanced at her burnt cabin and Fern whimpered and rolled into the high grass at their feet. "Fern would never like the city and she'd miss you too, take her with you, please."

He placed a tentative palm to her cheek, the warmth of him so familiar.

"Anger at myself for ever bringing this pain to Paint The Sky."

Alli placed her hand over his, sniffling. "You always call me brave, but I don't have any strength left in leaving you behind." Even if she didn't agree, it was best that she did go, or he wouldn't leave Lame Deer or the reservation to maintain his own safety. If she didn't go, he would still be here for the Bakers to find, and she had to let him go. There seemed to be not other choice.

"I am not so good at breaking promises. And the children, I told them I was not going anywhere…they'll not understand all the reasons why I must go." She brushed a hand across her cheeks.

He studied her with intensity and then glanced at his soot covered hands. "Children resilient, will understand home was lost and choices not many. Best I go. Dusk soon enough. You must go to town and step onto stage tomorrow and never to look back, Paint The Sky."

"I know…" She tried to be brave for him knowing she had no more choices but she leaned into him and his arms embraced her as she wept, his tears mingling with her own.

****

The sky gave the last of its light as Leaning Bear held Alli, inhaling the sweetness of her hair. His people spoke of each having one true heartsong and she was his. No other love would ever come to him again with such force, with such strength.

He closed his eyes and waited, not wanting to let her go. But the spirits had spoken. Theirs was not to be more than this last moment.

She let go of him as she took her mother's beads from her neck. The ones that were white and round. She took his wrist and with tenderness double wrapped the strand of beads around it, hooking the tiny metal clasp with care.

He shook his head. "This belonged to Paint The Sky's mother…cannot take…"

She touched his lip with her finger. "I want you to have them."

"If the love inside me is such that it brings harm to

you. This I cannot do. Not now. Not later. Will wear these to remember all things of Paint The Sky." He leaned his forehead against hers, wanting to take away the pain for her. It was his to let her go, not give her further reason to stay. He stood drawing her up next to him.

"My heart will always belong to you." He touched her hair. "And when you are an old woman holding your last breath…I'll be there waiting to catch you as you fall away from the earth to your heaven."

She brushed tears from her face. "And I'll be there waiting for you."

"Will not watch the stage carry you away, will take Fern to stream and sit there once more on rocks until night fall. When Paint The Sky arrives home to sister, the stars I see each night will be the same you see." He picked up the puppy.

"Always." She sniffled and let go, giving Fern a good rubbing. "I wish so many things…"

He pulled the knife from his moccasin and as she watched he lifted the leather strap holding the feather to the braid in his hair. He cut the leather and lifted her hand placing it and the feather into her hand. "Keep." He kissed her hand and then her lips, tasting the salt of her tears.

"Always. If I don't go now, maybe I never will…" She wept freely but turned and began walking toward town, not looking back. He stood for a long moment, until she was gone and then sat Fern to the ground.

"Stay." He spoke the word not expecting Fern to obey though she did.

And now he would turn and walk back into the forest and find the man he was before he had loved

Allison Crockett, though that man would no longer exist. And given his plans, he would be leaving the Bakers to what they deserved no matter how it ended for him. And he would do this tonight.

Chapter Twenty-six

The sky offered no moon, and darkness laced his camp in the trees. Leaning Bear sat at the fire and dipped his fingers into the mix of animal fat and Devil's Club Bark. The greased mix formed a paste that would paint his face and body for the fight before him. Tonight, he would take down the Bakers. He did not do this for the town. He did not do this for himself or his people. He did this for Alli, and only for her.

He traced two covered fingers across his right cheek leaving war paint there. It had been many years since he had placed such paint to his skin. It had been many more since he had chanted the words to match. He traced the fingers to his other cheek the same.

Beside him Fern sat, watching his movements and seeming to understand they were fighting for her. For Paint The Sky, no matter the outcome. He placed his palm into the mixture to cover it and then laid it to the pup's side, painting her in the colors of war. He chanted, raising his hands over the fire and the pup howled along to his song.

He stood and used the mixture to paint his chest in four palm prints along his torso on one side. He placed yet another to his naked back and then used a cloth to clean his hand, tossing it into the flames which sparked blue, a hiss of the death to come.

He inhaled a deep breath and kicked sand to snuff

the small fire in the pit. Fern sat beside his feet, watching. She was at unrest from not being with Alli. He was at unrest without her the same and would be for his lifetime. Darkness surrounded him and the weight of her memory fell through him, his chest tight. His tomahawk rested at his hip and a knife weighted each moccasin. He lifted his canvas bag though it was not full of herbs. But it did hold a small pipe and in a tin of peyote powder sealed tight.

Little by little he climbed down the rocks to Paytah, who wore drawings of red paint to his length. A circle around his eye in red. More handprints to his withers and feathers attached to the reins of his halter roping. He lifted Fern, who had followed, and tucked her into the leather bag that hung over Paytah's rump. He needed to keep her out of trouble, as he went to what lay ahead.

Tonight, he would ride and take the Baker men one at a time, no matter what might become of himself.

Alli would be gone by stage tomorrow afternoon and his heart would bear the weight of her loss for his lifetime. This was not her decision or his. It belonged to the white men called the Bakers who had reigned for too long, the citizens who had shunned her and his own people who would never understand their love. So, he would do what was needed. Take down the Bakers and leave the reservation never to return.

It was now he wished for time to summon his brother Dawson, who would at best support his efforts with another pair of hands. Dawson would also lecture on the reasons this was not best. But his friend was not here.

He lifted the bear claw necklace from his chest holding the claw in his fist and whispering the words to the ancestors. Those who waited in the camp of the dead who had once made their same cries of war with the White man would now reach his brother with hints of trouble. But this was his war. For her. For Paint The Sky. He added his medicine pouch back over his neck and let it hang beside the claw, and far into the night the squall of the mountain lion found him, urging him to his path.

He tugged the roping and the horse headed down the trail until the edge of town where he went south for about a mile toward the Baker's homestead. The trail was dark, but not unfamiliar as he allowed the horse his pace of the darkness.

The house held light in two windows and chatter among the men occurred from inside. It was one of the fancier homes in the area with two levels, but like everything the Bakers owned, this home had been taken, not purchased.

It was not yet the mid of night as he dismounted Paytah and dropped the animal's rope. The horse would stay unless there was gunfire, but he carried no gun. He used a rope to tie Fern to a small tree, giving her an elk bone. She lay in the dirt and went right to work on the morsel.

He moved closer to the barn, the entrance doors propped wide. Easing inside he moved quietly behind the stalls and waited. The Bakers would find their fate with him one at a time and it would not be luck assisting him. He reached into his bag and took peyote from the tin and packed the powder into a small pipe, which he held in his fist.

Laughter came from inside the home. A door on one side opened and Leroy paused to light a cigar before sitting on the stoop. He would be easy to take down as he sat smoking alone. Leaning Bear slipped from the rear of the barn reaching the fence line grateful the dog they kept must have been inside. He circled the home to fall on the other side of Leroy who blew out a puff of smoke that held white against the darkness of the night.

He crouched and moved closer and, in an instant, grabbed him by the neck, forcing him to the ground without a sound. He gripped the man's throat tight enough to keep him from yelling, placed the pipe into his nose and blew on the other end. He then stamped out the lit cigar.

Leroy tried to yell, his eyes wide as he fought snorting and sputtering at the peyote. Then the man relaxed, stunned and staring. Leaning Bear grabbed his arms and dragged him to the side of the house, leaving him in the shadows. The powder would subdue the men for now and later they would suffer hallucinations, visons and dreams.

The door opened again, and Pete exited the house carrying a lantern and heading toward the outbuilding. Leaning Bear leaned against the side of the house and then followed. He eased closer to the outbuilding and waited for Pete to do his business.

When shuffling inside alerted him the man's britches were up, he swung open the door and jerked him to the ground, blowing the peyote into his nose before he understood anything was going on.

Pete blinked and sputtered snorting trying to climb to his knees. He lifted the slender man across his shoulders and carried him to lay beside his drooling father, neither of them moving, though Pete snorted and coughed.

He leaned against the side wall of the house once

more and listened. It was quiet inside, except for the sound of boots on the hard flooring. It was some time before the dog's echoes of barking from the woods came, bringing Roy to the door with his shotgun. The hound ran free coming his direction, barking wildly. He tugged another elk bone from the bag at his side and handed it off to the dog who ran off with the morsel. That had been easy enough. He waited a moment longer and as the man stepped onto the porch, he grabbed the barrel of the gun and tugged the man to the ground onto his knees.

Roy Baker growled, fighting to stand as the gun fell from his hands. "What the hell?"

But before he could say any more Leaning Bear smoked him with the peyote and shoved him back. Baker coughed and gagged, fighting to keep his stance. Leaning Bear backed up and let the peyote do its work. The old man staggered to his feet only to fall again. He looked up reaching to grab him but missing. "I'll get you."

The old man gagged again and fell forward onto his face and moved no more. Leaning Bear stepped past him drawing his tomahawk and stepped inside the house waiting. The fire in the corner crackled as he stepped toward the stairs, loud snoring letting him know where Don could be found. He crept up the stairs not allowing his moccasins a sound as he followed the snores.

He glanced inside the room with a bed where Don lay sprawled on his back, mouth open, loud snores coming from his throat. This had been much easier than he thought. He moved closer and blew peyote into his nose and stepped back. Don sat up and coughed. His eyes widened when he saw him and he lunged for the gun that lay on the night table. Leaning Bear grabbed it, tossing it across the room into a pile of clothing.

"You can't…but…" Don never got up from the bed, holding his head and trying to blow his nose. Leaning Bear gave it a moment more and lifted the man to his feet by pulling his shirt and britches.

"Damn injun…" Don sputtered, though his words slurred and he coughed and then gagged.

Leaning Bear patted his face and the man fell backwards. He pulled him back upright and tossed him over his shoulder making it back down the stairs and outside. He dumped Don beside his father and went to the barn for horses which he did not saddle. He found leads hanging across the stalls and placed one on each horse and returned to the men, who lay unmoving. He first pulled up Roy Baker and with great effort got the large man over one of the horses, tying his hands. He grabbed Pete who was lighter and mumbled on and off things that made no sense. With Pete secured on the back of the horse, he added Don and then Leroy to the next horse securing them as well. He grabbed the roping for both horses and led them toward the woods in order to retrieve Paytah and Fern.

This part of his battle was complete. But now it was time to see it done. As he arrived to where he'd left the animals, Fern barked but went back to her elk bone, her tail wagging.

He untied her and lifted her back to her pouch on Paytah, her bone still in her mouth. And surveying the men were still secure he mounted up on Paytah heading toward the town of Lame Deer.

Riding along with a bit of the moon, the trail to town was easy. The horses carrying the men followed along with ease. The men remained quiet in their stupor except for a now and then cry from Pete, lost in his confusion.

It was a ways to go on the morning sunlight and what he had planned could mostly be done quick and efficient. He made no commotion with his string of horses as he entered town.

The streets were quiet with no one about, which would make things easier. He stopped Paytah in the center of town and dismounted, tying the horse off with the others right outside the Trading Post. There was no light coming from inside, but in a short time with the rising sun, this entire town would awaken to what he was about to do. He glanced at one of the top windows at the Trading Post. Alli would be there in her slumber, but all he could feel were her tears. He would never willingly have brought those tears to her and he was certain her sadness would be his death. Her stage would arrive by noon and this task before him would be done. The Bakers would meet their end right here in front of all in Lame Deer.

He left the men and animals and went about pulling together wood from Maud's burn pile behind the Trading Post. He did so as quietly as could be managed, not wanting a spectacle of things before dawn. Now if he could complete this part of his revenge on the Bakers without Maud or anyone else waking, he would rid the town of the Bakers for good.

****

Darkness held though the stars in the sky moved toward dawn. Leaning Bear rose from his chanting, and surveyed the scene he had created. He had placed four posts around the men he had captured, these to be lit so the whole town would watch the spectacle when he took care of the Bakers for good. He lit one at a time and the town of Lame Deer began to glow. On the stand and tied to the posts were the Bakers staked out for the big fire he had planned.

Pete sobbed, mumbling in hallucinating riddles of confusion. Don and Leroy had come around swearing at him but not over the peyote enough to be themselves or fight. Before him Roy Baker only stared at him slumping forward against the ropes and slobbering down the front of his naked chest. He had stripped all four of them down to their long underwear and bared feet.

“You can't do this injun. They'll burn you alongside us.” Leroy spat, his words slurred and slow.

Leaning Bear bent closer to them and traced the line he would light to begin the fire that would consume them in glorious colors of flames. The length of the line was the same as used for dynamite and would spark to ignite things to progress the war he was ending tonight.

“You can’t burn us alive you bastard. You can't get away with this,” Don swore struggling at the ropes in confusion.

“We're gonna die brothers,” Pete cried. “We’re gonna die while we burn. We’re gonna die, we’re gonna die.”

Town folk had begun gathering around the scene but with no sheriff, it wasn’t like anyone was going to stop him. He did not acknowledge any of them. He also expected a bullet to find him should any one of them prove loyal to the Bakers. And that he would take should it come, but the number of people began to increase with lots of chatter and commotion. Lame Deer was waking to his plan before them.

“What's he doing? Tarnation. What's he gonna do, kill ’em?”

“It's that Leaning Bear the one that was pardoned.

They'll string him up for this."

"Should we stop him?"

"Hell, not me, I heard he took down more cavalry than the lot of a whole tribe once."

"Those Bakers need a good lesson, let 'em burn."

"Help us," Don called to people collecting. "Someone shoot him. You can't let him set us on fire."

He paid them all no mind and began dancing and singing the song of death. His horse was painted, his dog was painted, his chest and face were painted and before him this war was about to end and for good.

Chapter Twenty-Seven

"Wake up, Mrs. Crockett, Alli, wake up!" Maud slammed open the door to the room where Alli had been sleeping.

She jumped up and out of bed startled. "What's wrong?" It took her a moment to even remember where she was and what day it was. "Did I miss the stage? I slept so hard."

"No, Leaning Bear has those Baker boys and their Pa at the stake about to burn them alive a'fore the whole town." Maud clomped back down the stairs in a speeding huff.

Alli tossed off her nightgown and pulled her dress over her head, stepping into her pantaloons and boots as fast as she could. She ran her hand through her hair as she left the room, pulling the strands to her head and into a lace tie.

What on earth? Why would Leaning Bear do this? They would kill him for even the thought. She ran down the stairs and through the Trading Post, her heart pounding so hard in her chest she could feel it in her temples. She had to stop him.

Town was light even at this hour. The old clock in the Trading Post had said five o'clock. She followed Maud onto the porch, and her mouth dropped open.

Crowds of people had gathered. Men and women alike, some cheering and others scrutinizing the scene before them all. But before her the Bakers were tied to posts with wood all around their feet to be burned. Leaning Bear chanted and danced in a circle around the men, a torch in his raised hand. His skin was painted with red and black handprints and stripes of black across his face. War paint. A quiver full of arrows and his bow were across his painted shoulder. Lands!

No. He couldn't do this. Not for her. Not for himself. She yelled but he didn't turn. “Leaning Bear…no!” She ran but Maud caught her holding her back.

“Don't go out there. They'll probably fire guns any moment, and you’ll get shot.” Maud held her back.

“They can’t do that either, I won’t let them.” She tried to pull away again but Maud was much stronger. “Ain’t a lettin’ ya go Alli.”

Leaning Bear ignored all around him as he danced in the gray light of morning, the flames on the posts giving yellows and oranges to brighten the town of Lame Deer. Yet no one went to him to stop him, and no guns were displayed.

Alli had to get to him, he could not murder these men by burning them, no matter the havoc they had caused to all. But the crowd was thick as she pulled away from Maud at last and worked her way to him. He couldn’t kill these men, or he would die too.

She stumbled over her skirt and caught herself on the railing of the porch at the same time the cheering for Leaning Bear to do what he was planning increased.

He’d be hanged or shot. No. She fought to get through the crowd but people were so thick she couldn’t find a way. The Baker boys pleaded as Leaning Bear circled them time and time again with his torch. She little understood his song but his tone was clear. Staunch and unrelenting as if he fought.

"Someone shoot him, assholes," Don screamed again, cursing those around him.

"I don't wanna burn, brother," Leroy cried, fighting against his ties.

"Pa do something!" Leroy pleaded, but Roy Baker slumped as if he were unconscious.

She had to stop Leaning Bear, but she couldn't get through the crowd try as she might, though she caught a view of the men at the stake. They were naked except for their long johns britches, and couldn't escape this fate but she wouldn't allow this. He held up the torch and stopped his dance, the town going quiet.

Leaning Bear met each man's gaze and with no emotion placed the torch to the base of the wood. The fire zipped round and round the base of the wood climbing higher as the sparks rounded. The crowd cheered but her screams went unheard as she was pushed back farther. She bent to peek through the thickness of people as Leaning Bear walked away from the Bakers and the crowd, his head held high. And no one tried to stop or detain him, regardless this wasn't right, and he'd be held accountable for all of it even if the town wanted this.

Alli fought to see through the crowd at the same time an explosion took everyone by surprise. Her ears popped and people screamed. Some fell to the ground and others ran while many held their stance to watch the men burn. Alli was knocked aside and instead of falling, she sat on the porch, holding the rail and blinking at yet another explosion. She screamed, but where was Leaning Bear going? What was happening? He could not have done what he intended.

But then the sky erupted in colors of popping explosions.

“Fireworks?” She whispered to herself, unbelieving.

“It’s fireworks. He ain’t gonna burn ’em.” Maud sat beside her with some effort as if enjoying the show in the sky that went on and on. Bright colors burst in whites and oranges and reds. Pop after pop continued creating a vibrant canvas in the dawning skies.

“I don't understand.” Tears streaked her face. Leaning Bear hadn’t killed the men but what would become of him now? Of her? It was an elaborate display of fireworks. He had done this not to kill them but to embarrass them in front of all the town.

Laughter erupted as the Bakers screamed and cried at the fireworks popping at their feet. Blast after blast of colors lit the sky, to a flaming bright variance of colors. Alli had seen fireworks numbers of times over the years but never like this where not one second went without a new spout of raining colors.

It lasted a solid twenty minutes until the last pop sounded. Quiet held and the Bakers, still alive wept and slumped against their ties, defeated.

Once the smoke cleared, the men in Lame Deer took the Bakers down one by one as everyone cheered. Most all in town had been cheated or suffered theft at their hands and it seemed no one was upset at all by what had just happened. People even began to throw rotten fruit and vegetables toward the men who were still in their underwear and bare feet.

The Bakers continued to plead their case, but to no avail as they were marched toward the unmanned jail.

“And ain’t never seen a thing like it.” Maud beamed as she stood and helped her up.

Alli wiped her eyes and searched for Leaning Bear, but he was out of sight. Didn't this change things for them? But her fate was already settled to the arriving noon stage. A single tear fell down her cheek. What would happen now other than what was already planned?

With the Bakers gone, the smoke settled and people began to disperse in groups with cheers and conversations of what would happen now with the Bakers gone. Alli glanced at the stakes where Leaning Bear had threatened to burn the men to make them a spectacle for all to see. It occurred to her to now wipe away the tears and giggle. Only Leaning Bear would have thought of this. Thought of a way to rid the town of the Bakers without killing them or dying himself in the process.

She turned to glance the direction Leaning Bear had taken and caught a glimpse of him riding Paytah out of town with Fern in a sack on the side of the horse from what she could tell. He must have hidden Fern and the horse nearby. She supposed he'd left to protect her from what town folk might still think of them both. Tears threatened but she didn't allow them to fall. She sat on the bench, her heart heavy as the town settled into its normal day and she supposed more than a few hours passed as she waited.

"About time, the stage runs anytime from now till noon. Be here afore ya know it." Maud glanced at the pocket watch from her vest and then returned it.

Alli didn't respond. Wasn't she now at liberty to change her plans? The entire weight of her travels and the children…how could she leave them? Millie and Fern and even that blasted owl, would never forgive her for going away. So, she was going nowhere.

“I sure hate to see ya go, Ma’am, but I could bring down your things when you’re ready.” Maud sniffled, taking a wrinkled handkerchief and blowing her nose like a honking goose.

“Maud, if you cancel my board for the stage. I'll return for Millie in a few days. I’m not returning home.” Alli shook her head and stepped into the street.

Maud scratched her head and nodded. “Where're ya going?”

Alli took a deep breath. “Home. I am going home. Home here.”

And with that she put one foot in front of the other and headed back toward the burnt tree, her burnt cabin and the reservation, not looking back at the town of Lame Deer. This was her home now, no matter what the town folk thought about her love for Leaning Bear. She belonged here for herself and the children and a way of life she understood little but adored. And she belonged here where her heart was full. With Leaning Bear now and always.

She smiled to herself, never surer of anything in her life. She would not leave the children, the animals or the one man she truly loved. Her life was here. And now she would never leave it ever again. And with any luck she would find Leaning Bear, where she suspected he might be. She stopped for a moment to view her burnt cabin. It could be rebuilt, together they could do anything. With a nod to herself she angled off the road heading toward the stream.

And as it would happen, she stopped at the clearing to find him on the rocks in the shade of the trees. A broken man sitting where his heart had once been full. Tears filled her eyes but she brushed them away. She'd never have brought him to any sadness. She said nothing as she sat quietly on the rock beside him.

He didn't look at her. But after a time, she placed her hand onto his. Wanting…needing to touch him. Fern raced to her and fell at her feet rolling to her back and nipping at her boots.

"Paint The Sky will miss the stage to home." His voice was a whisper.

"My home is where you are." She would not accept another decision that would send her away. She was not going back to Chicago.

"Not good idea." His answer was swift.

"Yes, well, the towns folk have gotten rid of their vermin thanks to you, and they'll just have to accept me as I am. Paint The Sky." Fern nuzzled her, the pup's tail wagging. She lifted her to her chest hugging her close.

Leaning Bear studied at her as she held the wiggling pup.

"I decided I am not leaving. The children need me. I promised them I wasn't going to leave like all the rest of the teachers. Besides, Millie would never forgive me and I already missed Fern so much…but I had my bags packed for the stage…I couldn't do it. I won't leave you ever again no matter the weight of us."

He inhaled a deep breath, it odd he'd cleaned the paint from his face but not his body. "Children will be happy. Fern and horse will be same. Owl same. Happy."

"And you?" She asked though worry scored through her center.

He lifted her hand into his and inspected her fingers. "No paint on skin. Not good that you are not painting enough to keep paint on skin."

"I'll have to send for paint and canvas when I can. I

lost my basket of paints in the fire." She glanced at her clean hands and back to him.

He studied her and let out a deep breath. "Cheyenne people are nomads. Never to stay in one place unless there is reason enough. Will not stay behind fences any longer in this life."

She could understand what had caused him to live as he had. "My cabin could be rebuilt, I've money."

He shook his head and studied the stream. "The people in town helped with fire but still will not want you and I…"

"No, but I suppose in time, the news of us will be old news and we can stay in the cabin. I'm sure the captain would see to it you would be allowed," she explained.

He looked at her again. "Your religion allows for marriage to Cheyenne man?"

Alli's mouth opened and it was a moment before her words came. "I may marry whom I choose, and are you asking for some purpose?" She teased but her heart fluttered hard inside her chest.

"This white teacher comes and she lives unafraid, but knows little, must be I should protect her, but won't sleep on tall bed." He lifted his brows.

"I see, well then when the cabin is rebuilt, we'll just toss a new mattress at the hearth." Her lips curled into a smile. "And will the Cheyenne accept us together, should you find the way to marry this teacher?"

"It is as you say."

She dug in her bag and lifted her journal. "The fire took most everything but I saved this."

He watched her fan the pages.

"What you did to the Bakers made it all so clear for

me. It was certain to me for the first time in a long time where I belong…here with you. I suppose I have never known that feeling until now. When I first thought of taking the teaching job, I never thought I…I never thought I would find…love. I find it ironic the only things saved from the fire were this book and your painting and the pearls." She handed him her journal. "The things I most treasure."

He took the book from her and let go of her hand and thumbed through it. "It is the weight of us in words."

"Yes." Alli angled a glance from the journal to him.

He balanced the book on one hand his palm up. "The weight of us will be comfort. The weight of us will be heavy again. This you want?"

"Yes, I'm rather fond of trouble it seems." Maybe there was more truth to that statement than any they were exchanging.

"This book very heavy then." He held the book toward her.

"I write the truth of us. I am Paint The Sky, no matter what anyone else thinks." She took the journal and set it aside.

"I take breath away. It is as you write it." He postured tossing out his chest as he read. "He is so handsome and when I catch his eye on the reservation it sometimes takes my breath away."

She giggled. "Yes. You take my breath away."

"Would like to do that again. Many times." He took her hand and pressed a kiss to her palm. "But there is more to this book you will write."

"Yes. There is so much more to this story." Alli's skin prickled the length of her body as he pulled her to him wrapping both arms around her. She relished the warmth of his embrace, as familiar as a spring sun. She clung to him. Nothing more in the world mattered than the moments, they were in…together.

"Then you will paint the sky with medicine man for your lifetime, for my lifetime?" He whispered, tangling his hand into her hair.

"Is that a proposal?" She whispered.

He placed his lips to hers and kissed her, then held her close once more. "I should do this different?"

"No, it's beautiful actually." She leaned into him, almost afraid to believe how things had occurred. She wouldn't be going back East, and she wouldn't be leaving the children or Fern or Millie or even the owl. "I love you, Leaning Bear."

"This I know." He lifted her hand and placed a kiss now to the back of her hand.

"And you said when I was an old woman on my last breath, you'd be there to catch me. I'd like that very much." She leaned into his embrace as if all life held was the comfortable ease at which they existed together for the first time without the judgement of the world around them.

"This I will do."

Chapter Twenty-Eight

Alli peeked out the one window in the school room. “My, so many did come, I hadn’t thought to be nervous until now.”

Jacie, her sister, flitted closer taking her own look at the crowd who were gathering where the fire for the rain dance was held each season. “Why, there are dozens of people from the reservation and town. Maud told me this morning, many from town would come.” Her sister hugged her in a brief embrace, “I still can’t believe I am here with you. I’m so happy about your marriage.”

Alli returned the embrace. Her sister was really sincere in her happiness, and it was so nice to be together again to share this occasion. It wouldn’t have been the same without Jacie. Months in the planning and the arrival of her sister and her husband Easton, had been such a welcome surprise.

“I’ve finished the beads to add to the front of your dress.” Two Doves adjusted the shoulder of her traditional Cheyenne wedding dress, sewing in place a few last beads to the beautiful garment of deer hide. “You will be the most beautiful of brides as this matches the sun and your hair.”

Jacie nodded, watching as Two Doves quickly finished the last-minute touches.

“If I know anything at all, I know Leaning Bear will

find you the most beautiful thing he's ever seen." Haven McCade stepped closer, holding William, her month-old son, who was sleeping in her arms.

"You are both very kind but I'm no young girl about to be wed, rather the opposite. Though I do think I may truly be a blushing bride with the crowd we've drawn." She turned to study herself in the long mirror that had been brought to the school along with all the things needed for her wedding day. She was beautiful with her hair pulled up and tiny yellow flowers layered in.

"I've known Leaning Bear for a very long time and he deserves this happiness along with you." Dodge McCade moved in behind her.

She turned to face Dawson McCade's mother, having enjoyed this week of getting to know Dawson, her and Haven and the children. "Thank you, Mrs. McCade, you've been so gracious in coming all this way for us."

"I wouldn't have missed an occasion so important to Leaning Bear. When he wrote of the plans for the wedding, I told Dawson right away I wanted to attend." Dodge held her gaze in the mirror. She was a tall slender woman, maybe in her sixties, but so pretty with her light gray hair and high cheek bones and the same piercing blue eyes as her son Dawson.

"Me marry Leaning Bear too," Dawson's toddler daughter, Hope, danced around in her fancy pink dress admiring herself in the mirror before Alli. She was such a precious little girl, with long flowing red hair like her mother and she'd been more than smitten with Leaning Bear, following him to everything he did all week they had visited.

Everyone laughed as the little girl twirled and then

kissed her own reflection. Haven bent to her daughter. "You'll find another husband when you're all grown up, but right now you just need to be a little girl."

She shook her head in defiance. "Then I marry Papa." She folded her little arms still keeping an eye on her own reflection in the mirror. "Can we have cakes?"

"Oh, we'll have cake after the wedding but you have the most important job of all, carrying the flowers for Auntie Alli." Haven reminded her and stood again as baby, William, began to fuss.

Chanti toddled along to follow Hope to the flowers that lay in two bouquets on the school benches at the front of the school room. Just barely walking, the small Cheyenne girl took every step along with her new friend.

Alli glanced out the window again. She was beautiful and more than ready to wed Leaning Bear. She hadn't seen him today as it wasn't proper that they should see each other until the wedding. She'd spent time last night with many of the tribe and Dawson's family, sharing a meal as a small group, but outside the school room, where the bonfire was held each year, Two Doves and the ladies of the tribe had decorated a large gazebo with flowers and feathers. And it had been Two Doves who had hand sewn the blanket she and Leaning Bear would share during the ceremony where Dancing Fox would speak the words to wed them.

"Oh, I so adore all of you for being here for me. It is a special day, as I never thought I'd find love again and while marrying Leaning Bear is never what I expected, my heart is so full." She turned to face them all, shrugging but so full of hope.

Jacie sniffled, and brought a tissue to her eyes and then her nose.

She smiled at her sister and glanced toward Haven and Dodge. “I suspect not much for us will be easy, but together I believe we can overcome anything. He’s so happy that Dawson and his family are here to share the day and I owe each of you so much for making this special. My life is now here on the reservation with all the children and with Leaning Bear. I could never think of anything other than this life I’ve found here.”

Hawk appeared at the door, wearing full fringed buckskins beaded with golden metal coins, his hair braided in one long braid. “Father says its time, teacher.”

“Oh my, Hawk, aren’t you so handsome?” Alli took his arm and stepped outside the front door of the school to face all the people who had and would support her life with Leaning Bear.

Hawk beamed with pride.

Two Doves hugged her and quickly led the two little girls ahead of her, both carrying their bouquets of flowers. Hope took Chanti by her hand they toddled right up the aisle ahead of her.

Alli stepped ahead, Hawk holding his elbow out to her and she steadied her focus on Leaning Bear who stepped up beside Dawson, both waiting before Dancing Fox.

Her breath held at Leaning Bear in his fancy buckskins that she’d understood had been made by Broken Hand for this day. She met his gaze and a part of her wanted to run to him, embrace him and never would she regret this day for the entire of her life. There were people from town and Dawson’s family as well as Maud who actually had on a smock style dress though she wore her straw hat. And the children had come along with their families to celebrate. Jacie sat with Easton near Dodge and Haven, who gathered the little girls along with Two Doves once they laid their flowers on the small table near the front.

The gazebo was an arched piece of wood with feathers placed in bundles and along the ground.

The men played a steady beat of drums in the distance, not loud as when they danced for rain each season, but a soft beating that sounded as if two hearts would indeed become one.

And it was today, she would seal her love with Leaning Bear for all to see, forever hold their peace.

The people in attendance stood, waiting on her arrival as she came before Leaning Bear. Hawk placed her hand into Leaning Bears and stepped away to sit with Two Doves and his younger brother, Little Wolf.

Somehow, she fought tears, the ones that meant she was happy and she glanced up to meet Leaning Bear's gaze for a long moment before Dancing Fox stepped closer. He too was dressed in his fine suit she'd purchased for him a while back when she'd been new to teaching on the reservation. And so not only would two hearts be entwined today forever, two cultures had merged in acceptance at least for this day and to her surprise, Captain Bartley and his wife and two daughters sat nearby with a group of soldiers that were also her friends.

"You are very beautiful." Leaning Bear spoke to her in Cheyenne in a soft whisper.

Her voice almost wouldn't come. "And you are handsome as ever."

Dancing Fox began speaking in Cheyenne and as planned Dawson stood beside him and translated each of his words at every pause.

"This day brings with it the sun and the moon and the joining of hearts of Leaning Bear and this woman Allison Crockett." Dawson wore the same style buckskins, a feather in his hair as he always wore and moccasins the same as Leaning Bear. They called each other brother and his arrival had been special for them both.

Dancing Fox went on. "At this time Leaning Bear will speak his heart for Allison Crockett." Dawson followed with the English words.

Alli took a deep breath, her heart pounding as Leaning Bear took her other hand, turning her to face him.

"You, Paint The Sky, have found the softness in my heart. A part of myself that I had hidden. The place where two become one. I will always offer you my embrace and protection in this life, even as the weight of us becomes difficult, I will be there for you in all things. The spirits and your God have brought us together for this moment of marriage and I will never need more than your love in this lifetime. I promise you all of my heart and all of myself from this day forward and to our eternities. Paint The Sky is my heartsong for this lifetime and my love will always belong to you."

A single tear escaped down her cheek at his words of love and devotion. They'd both prepared their own vows of love and now it was her turn to speak to him for all who were present to hear. She swallowed hard and cleared her voice glancing down at his hands and back up to his gaze.

"Leaning Bear, you are my home now as I share all of my heart. I am only whole when I am with you, near you. When a man takes a woman's heart, he defines the rest of her days, and these are mine. I am Paint The Sky, Alli. I was given no choice in becoming your heartsong and for all of my life, I shall paint the color of my own heart to match your own. We together are love, whole in itself and no matter the weight of us when it's light or heavy, I shall always paint the sky for you." How many times had she rehearsed to memorize those words and she meant each one.

Dancing Fox began again. "Rings will be exchanged for Allison Crockets wishes."

Dawson held out his fist to Leaning Bear who took the two gold bands. He placed one on her ring finger and kissed her palm. She then took the other from him and placed it on his finger. The rings had been her idea to add to the ceremony, and Jacie had brought them both from back East.

The chief spoke the marriage blessing with Dawson translating in English. "Now you will feel no rain, for each of you will be a shelter for the other. Now you will feel no cold, for each of you will be warmth to the other. Now there is no more loneliness. Now you are two persons but there is only one life before you. Go now to your dwelling, to enter into the days of your life together. And may your days be good and long upon the earth."

Ali held Leaning Bear's gaze as he leaned to kiss her, holding his lips to hers for a long moment and then pulling her into his embrace as Dawson and Two Doves placed their marriage quilt around them. The warmth encompassed her and holding him was all her heart would ever need.

They turned in unison to face the crowd who erupted in cheers as the drums began again and the children and her friends encircled them all clapping and dancing.

Leaning Bear turned her to face him again and kissed her lips tenderly once more.

"We're married now." She couldn't help the depth of her smile as she leaned into him, the blanket holding them tight together.

"And this makes Paint The Sky happy." He touched her check.

"Yes, so very happy but now you'll be in so much trouble that you are stuck with me for this entire life." She lifted her brows as everyone began dancing.

A grin crossed his face. "This I know, now we shall dance together with our blanket."

He tugged her along, joining them in the dance around the small fire, keeping them together with the blanket they would share for their lifetime together.

Epilogue:

August 1883, Lame Deer, Montana...

I stare out across the pastures full of high grass, the evening sun setting a hint of yellow across the valley. A haze of bugs flitter about as if in a frenzy of flight magnified against the pale blue sky. Six head of cattle graze in the distant pasture and deer line the grasses further. A light wind wraps its arms around me and humbles my thoughts as I stroke the brush across the canvas.

I think on what it means that I sit here on the steps of this small cabin, rebuilt last fall, a semblance of peace and comfort of which maybe I have never known. Fern lies asleep at my feet, content to be close to me at all times and having grown to the height of my thigh, her coat a beautiful sheen of brown and gray.

I chuckle and she opens her eyes to make sure I am not moving off to something more. I run the toe of my boot across her back and she rolls to her belly, chewing at the ties. It's our relished existence each evening as we wait together for Leaning Bear to return from his long hunt with his friend Dawson, Proud Wolf.

"You know if you'll learn to behave, he'll take you with him when he hunts his herbs and medicines. Then I'll be waiting on the both of you." She raises her head now that I speak to her, one ear flopping over, the other a perfect point.

"Oh, and you'll grow into that ear soon enough. You know what I'm saying now, don't you?" I stroke the brush I hold into a depth of yellow paint and trace it in brisk whips across the canvas to brighten the high grasses of the prairie, the pasture such as it is.

I nod to myself in a bit of satisfaction as the colors come together of the picture before me. I adjust my position a bit angling the canvas where there is no glare. The colors are rich in tones of the earth. I continue for a time, until Fern hops to her feet with a soft whine. I stroke the canvas twice more aware that while I can't see him yet, Leaning Bear has returned. She always knows even though it's been close to a month.

I take a deep breath and let it out as I spot him farther than the deer that scatter at his presence. Leaning Bear has arrived home. I dip a new brush into a hint of brown and at the very edge of my painting I begin to add his shadowed shape walking through the high grass. His tunic made of deerskin is a light shade of flat yellow and I mix the likeness of the color to his torso. I blend in his dark hair and the feathers that hang across his shoulder. The grass masking his legs makes him appear farther yet he is almost to us before I finish the finer hints of him on the canvas.

The cows move aside as he walks past them. Perhaps they welcome him home as well. The small herd, a gift from Dawson for us to have a means of living when the herbs and hides are not enough. Imagine that, the two of us who know little of cattle have the semblance of taking care of these six head with four expecting heifers that will deliver in the spring.

We'll not set anything by the market but we'll have

beef to sell or barter for other things we may need along with milk. As Leaning Bear nears, I lay down my brush and stand, stretching my back. I smile as he meets my gaze and Fern runs to him playing at the ties of his moccasins. And somehow it occurs to me this is home, and it has been the one home I am sure of. The one place I thought I would never find belongs to me now in the fullest way.

Leaning Bear allows a smile and bends to rub Fern's belly. He stands again and offers my cheek the kiss I have come to expect. I close my eyes and revel in the gentle touch.

He is home. This place together is all we shall ever need, that and being together.

It hasn't been that long that I answered the question from Jacie of how I had ever endured all that happened. My only answer to her was I had been given no choice. When a man takes a woman's heart it defines the rest of her days and these are mine. I am Paint The Sky. I was given no choice in being his heartsong and he and I both know this.

I wrap my arms around him and inhale the scent of man and earth. His arms lift me harder against his chest and we stand like this for a long moment. It is enough for both of us, what we have as one. We together, are love, whole in itself. And no matter the weight of us when it's light or heavy, I shall always paint the sky in the many colors he sees it.

AUTHOR'S NOTE:

Throughout this story I have done my best to respect the Cheyenne and all American Indian Nations, by depicting a story as close to historically accurate as possible. My descriptions of reservation life and the town of Lame Deer are mostly fiction. I have also attempted to use Cheyenne words which are difficult to type correctly but I believe add the story. Any mistakes regarding Native American history are completely my own but made with a heart of intent on giving the utmost respect. This is indeed a work of fiction.

A word about the author…

Kim Turner writes western historical romance, and discovered her passion of writing at the age of eight by writing poems, short stories and journals. Kim graduated with a Bachelor's of Science in Nursing and holds a Master's Degree in Adult Education from Central Michigan University. Working as a registered nurse educator for over thirty-six years, she enjoys studying the medical treatments of the old west as well as keeping up with the latest western movies and television series. While she loves reading anything from highlanders to pirates, she claims to have an unquenchable thirst for the American Cowboy when choosing her reads. Kim lives south of Atlanta with her husband and calls her greatest accomplishment the birth of one daughter and the adoption of another from China-neither of which came easy. Kim is a member of Georgia Romance Writers and her motto: It's All About A Cowboy and the Woman He Loves.

Thank you for purchasing
this publication of The Wild Rose Press, Inc.

For questions or more information
contact us at
info@thewildrosepress.com.

The Wild Rose Press, Inc.
www.thewildrosepress.com

Milton Keynes UK
Ingram Content Group UK Ltd.
UKHW031004231024
450026UK00011B/602